Loving Devon Was A Risk!

When his gaze dropped to her mouth for a split second, Brittany instantly saw his hunger and need. She fantasized about the night ahead, then sighed. It would be so easy to fall in love with Devon again. Yet she knew he didn't feel the same. And she'd learned the hard way that one couldn't make another fall in love simply by loving him.

She had heard his warning: don't love me too much—I don't want to hurt you. She was definitely taking a chance. As he captured her face firmly in his hands, her uneasiness grew.

He wasn't denying that he had feelings for her; he was denying what those feelings meant. Maybe he didn't love her, couldn't ever love her, but what choice did she have?

Dear Reader:

Romance offers us all so much. It makes us "walk on sunshine." It gives us hope. It takes us out of our own lives, encouraging us to reach out to others. Janet Dailey is fond of saying that romance is a state of mind, that it could happen anywhere. Yet nowhere does romance seem to be as good as when it happens *here*.

Starting in February 1986, Silhouette Special Edition will feature the AMERICAN TRIBUTE—a tribute to America, where romance has never been so wonderful. For six consecutive months, one out of every six Special Editions will be an episode in the AMERICAN TRIBUTE, a portrait of the lives of six women, all from Oklahoma. Look for the first book, *Love's Haunting Refrain* by Ada Steward, as well as stories by other favorites—Jeanne Stephens, Gena Dalton, Elaine Camp and Renee Roszel. You'll know the AMERICAN TRIBUTE by its patriotic stripe under the Silhouette Special Edition border.

AMERICAN TRIBUTE—six women, six stories, starting in February.

AMERICAN TRIBUTE—one of the reasons Silhouette Special Edition is just that—Special.

The Editors at Silhouette Books

NATALIE BISHOP
String of Pearls

Silhouette Special Edition

Published by Silhouette Books New York

America's Publisher of Contemporary Romance

To Dona,
whose support, understanding,
information and good humor
have helped keep me sane.
Thanks.

SILHOUETTE BOOKS
300 E. 42nd St., New York, N.Y. 10017

Copyright © 1985 by Natalie Bishop

Distributed by Pocket Books

ISBN: 0-373-09280-6

First Silhouette Books printing December 1985

10 9 8 7 6 5 4 3 2 1

America's Publisher of Contemporary Romance

Printed in the U.S.A.

NATALIE BISHOP

lives within a stone's throw of her sister, Lisa Jackson, who is also a Silhouette author. Natalie and Lisa spend many afternoons together developing new plots and reading their best lines to each other.

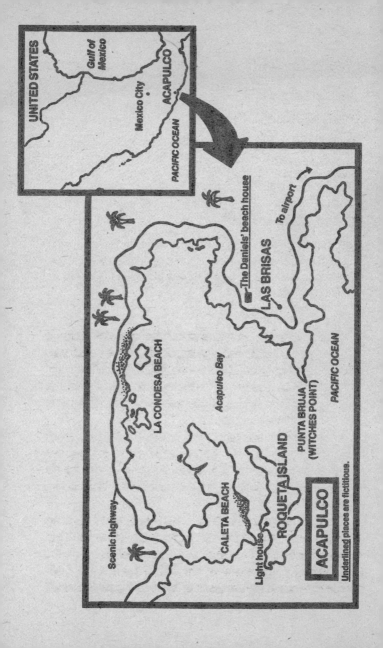

Chapter One

Brittany Daniels looked around the crowded airport waiting room with weary acceptance. Every seat was taken and luggage spilled all over the floor. With careful steps she made her way to the end of the queue at the ticket counter, thinking the four-hour layover was just par for the course on this trip.

It was her own fault. She'd missed her flight from Acapulco and had to be rerouted to Los Angeles through Mexico City. Worse yet, she was wait listed on the connecting flight; she might not make it back home until tomorrow.

Brittany dropped her blue canvas shoulder bag onto the floor and prayed the rest of her luggage would find its way back. The frenzied rush of people and parcels, the harried expressions of the ticket agents, the bad-tempered scowls on the faces of the other passengers all made Brittany dubious of her chances of getting aboard.

Still, missing her plane had been worth the few extra minutes with her father. She'd sat in the deck chair next to him, watching twilight turn Acapulco Bay from a blinding turquoise gem to a mysterious, deep purple velvet. In the silence, her father's thin hand had dropped over hers.

"It looks beautiful from here," he'd said. "More beautiful than it really is."

Brittany had smiled in agreement. Her parents' home was on the cliff overlooking the bay, and from its back deck Acapulco's glittering hotels looked more like a child's building set than the real thing. The hotels' lights were diamond pinpricks, too small to discern individually. But together they had formed a brilliant, undulating necklace of light around the throat of the bay.

The companionship between Brittany and her father had been wonderful and she'd been loath to break the spell. But eventually, although the night air was still warm, the evening breeze had made her father cold. They'd moved inside regretfully, and her father had gone to bed. By then Brittany was long past any chance of catching her flight, but she hadn't cared. Some things were more important.

"He's dying," her mother had said unnecessarily as she drove Brittany through the warm night to the airport.

Brittany had nodded. "I know. I'll be back in three weeks, before Thanksgiving."

Her mother's lips had quivered but her voice was steady as she said, "He feels badly that you have to spend so much time flying back and forth."

"I just wish I could be here more," she'd whispered.

"He probably wouldn't be able to stand it. It hurts him to have you see him so weak. It's not how he wants to be remembered."

Her mother had been right, but Brittany could barely stand the phrase "to be remembered." It reminded her of how little time her father had left. She'd thought she'd lived through major tragedies in her life but now she knew differently. Her father's illness had given her a new perspective.

At the Acapulco airport her mother had given her a quick hug and kiss, but Brittany had felt the trembling in her arms. Wishing there was something more she could offer in the way of comfort she'd hugged her back, trying not to cry.

"He wanted me to tell you something," her mother had added as Brittany stepped from the car. "Something he wanted to say but was afraid might come off too maudlin."

"Oh, God, mother...." Brittany could feel her insides shift apart.

"He said, 'Tell her to live life to the fullest. There isn't that much time in this world to let the past ruin her future.'"

It had been too much. Brittany had blindly reached for her suitcases, dragging them to the curb. Even her mother's voice had shaken as she added, "He was talking about Devon, of course."

Remembering, Brittany felt those same helpless feelings wash over her, scalding the backs of her eyes with unshed tears. Life was so unfair. Dying, her father had only one wish for his daughter: her happiness.

He wanted her to forget about Devon and start again. Fresh. New. Without the shackles of an unhappy past.

She sighed. It was a shame she wouldn't be able to grant his wish.

"Ticket?" the agent asked in Spanish.

Brittany handed him the folder. She thought about all the times she'd tried to forget Devon. All the different ways she'd tricked herself into thinking her feelings had died. She had even, for a little while, managed to make herself believe she was in love with someone else.

But nothing had worked. And even though it was a simple wish from parent to offspring, she couldn't make it happen even for her father's peace of mind.

The agent could confirm space only in first class, but Brittany assured him it was no problem. She felt tired through and through, and her mind was far, far away from the crowded airport.

She sat down next to a family with two unhappy, frazzled children but she barely noticed the noise and commotion they made.

Devon, oh, Devon, she thought, her throat hot and hurting, *I wish things had been so very different.*

Devon Michael Gallagher scowled at his front door, wondering who would be ringing his bell so insistently at this god-awful hour. He hated surprises.

In his business he confronted the unexpected from time to time; being one of Southern California's top investigative reporters made it impossible not to. But he generally had a feeling, an awareness, a sense of what was going on around him that enabled him to foresee an outcome. He was rarely taken by surprise.

His pulses quickened as he realized who it must be— Jay Lundgren, an associate and close personal friend. Jay had promised to stop by and go over the latest developments on Devon's current exposé but had called earlier and given his regrets. They'd rescheduled for the next morning, but now Devon's sixth sense told him something had happened.

He swung himself down the circular wrought-iron stairway from his library balcony, his long strides quickening as he reached the floor. Once in a while a major break unexpectedly happened that could rip a case wide open. Jay may have learned something staggering!

Devon had been after the authorities for weeks about this case, only to run up against a blank wall. No one was talking. He wasn't sure whether that was due to caution or simple ignorance, but the fact remained that his urging to look into the Broderick matter had fallen on deaf ears. So far, he was on his own. And in a lot of ways that suited him just fine.

"Just a minute," he yelled to the insistent ringing of the bell, hurriedly crossing the plush cream carpet. He didn't even glance at the breathtaking vista of night sea and sky outside his living-room window; he was too absorbed in the anticipation of Jay's news.

He moved with an easy grace, an athlete's fluidity. Devon's popularity as a television newsman and investigative reporter wasn't hurt by his appearance. Tall, lean, with a rare and very attractive smile, he was typically Black Irish. His hair was midnight dark and thick, his eyes a light blue, his fair complexion tanned from an ever-present California sun. He was the flip side of the coin to his sister, a coppery redhead with soulful green eyes. Shannon was the only woman he truly trusted and believed in. Without her, Devon would have written off the entire female population years earlier.

Devon swung open the door. Jay Lundgren, a stocky man with brown hair, hazel eyes and a sharp intellect that was hidden under a deceptively affable disposition, pointed a finger at him. "You, my friend, are in for a big surprise."

"Is that good or bad?" Devon asked, closing the door behind him.

"Depends." No humor lit up Jay's expression. In fact his eyes were sober, almost anxious.

"What's the problem?" Devon's gaze turned to the thick manila folder Jay held in his right hand.

"You know what you said about a Mexican connection? Well, I think you're right. There's a flight arriving from Mexico City in about an hour, and our boy's on it."

"Bingo," Devon said with satisfaction.

Jay hesitated. "But...there's an ironic twist here that I don't think you're going to appreciate."

It wasn't like Jay to tiptoe. Devon's brows drew together and he waited somewhat impatiently. Damn it all! He didn't have time to dally and Jay was the one person who should know that. Jay's ability to cut through all the garbage and get to the point was the quality Devon liked best about him—that and his unspoken loyalty.

"The plane, Jay..." Devon reminded him.

Jay glanced at the closed file. "Broderick's in the first-class section."

"Anyone else?"

"A few people. We've got the names. Several of them make regular trips to Mexico. And they use Mexico City as a gateway."

Devon drew in a long breath. "That makes it harder to pinpoint Broderick." He thought carefully, a grim smile forming on his lips. "But not impossible. Especially if he's got the gems with him."

"Do you really think he has?" Jay asked curiously.

Devon frowned and shook his head. "I don't know. But he's got to be bringing them into the country somehow. Someone is. And I'd bet money it's Broderick."

"If so, he's pretty wily."

"And lucky," Devon agreed. "But everyone's luck has to run out eventually." His gaze narrowed on Jay's file. He'd never been a fan of Grant Broderick's, though the man definitely had friends in high places. He was a well-respected investment broker with a who's-who list of clients. But Devon had suspicions that Broderick also had a very lucrative side business, one that walked the other side of the law. Smuggling. Devon doubted Broderick's clients would approve....

"What about these other people?" Devon asked.

Anyone making regular trips to Mexico City could theoretically be involved and Devon had to explore all the angles. But he had a gut feeling, an instinctive hunch that Grant Broderick was his man. The man's investment dealings revolved around gems; he could easily have a contact outside the U.S.

Jay hesitated again, as if he were reluctant to open the file. Devon stared at him, his impatience beginning to wane. A prickling along his nerves warned him. A surprise, Jay had said. He watched Jay open the folder with a feeling akin to dread.

"There's a Mexican couple who fly to the States regularly—the De Vacas." Jay flipped up a page. "And there's a young man, a college student from San Diego. His parents are wallowing in money and he flies all over. Mexico's one of his favorite places—he spends a lot of weekends there." Another page was turned. "There's Broderick, of course. And...there's a woman."

Jay's monologue stopped so abruptly that Devon looked up. He'd expected something far worse from the theatrical way Jay had built up the tension.

"A woman?" Devon repeated, frowning. At Jay's careful expression, Devon's face broke into a gleaming smile of understanding. "I'm not that down on them, Jay. I promise—" he raised a solemn palm "—I won't pin the blame on her just because of her sex."

The look Jay sent him was so skeptical that Devon's grin widened. Whoever this woman was, she'd obviously made a favorable impression on his friend. Devon began to grow curious, and he was suddenly itching to get his hands on that file.

"This is no ordinary woman, Devon," Jay warned.

"They never are, Jay."

Jay took a deep breath and looked around Devon's home, admiring, not for the first time, its style and atmosphere. What could have been sterile and uninviting—cream carpet, putty-colored walls, stark paintings—was softened by mahogany furniture and soft lighting. An overstuffed couch of striped, textured material reigned supreme in the center of the room. The balcony above was crowded with books, bookshelves, Devon's desk and an elaborate stereo system. Jay liked the apartment and he liked the man. He regretted what he had to tell him.

"This woman's a model," he said wearily.

Devon's face stiffened. Harsh lines formed around his eyes and jaw. With an effort, he got himself under control before Jay, who knew only part of his past, could see how much his words had shocked him.

Devon's smile was forced, but he managed to say, "There are lots of models in the world, Jay."

"No, Devon." Jay dolefully shook his head. "I'm afraid there's only one. The woman on that plane is Brittany Daniels. I'm sorry...."

Brittany stifled a yawn and handed her teacup to the hovering stewardess. The Fasten Your Seat Belts sign had flashed on. *Thank God.* She felt as tired and wrung out as her crumpled gray linen suit. The wait in Mexico City had seemed interminable; it was good to be back in Los Angeles.

Brittany wished her parents lived closer to her, but she understood why they'd chosen to live in Mexico: her father couldn't wait for the FDA to relax its rigid standards and put new drugs on the market. Now her father went regularly to a physician in Acapulco, and though Brittany was convinced the drugs he received were little more than a placebo, she wasn't about to argue with him about it. Maybe they made his life easier; she prayed they did. Whatever the case, she knew her parents would live in Acapulco until her father's death.

Brittany inhaled deeply, her eyes dropping to the copy of *Élégante* magazine lying open in her lap. She idly flipped through a few pages, trying to fill her mind with something other than her father's illness.

Suddenly there she was, smiling at herself from the slick pages of the magazine, back to the camera, a coy glance over her left shoulder—hips, thighs and legs encased in skintight designer jeans. The caption glared: "in your wildest jeans...."

Brittany made a startled sound and stuffed the magazine to one side, feeling upset. She'd modeled for the advertisement, yet had never seen it. Now she wished she hadn't.

Did you really expect anything different?

Brittany closed her eyes, then opened them again, staring out the window. The night was clear and bright, the lights of Los Angeles a flickering, limitless grid. No, she hadn't expected the ad to be different, but she'd harbored the faint hope that it would be. Bryant Berkshire of Berkshire Ltd. had apparently been more interested in selling sex than the quality of his designer fashions. When the job had ended, Brittany had sworn she'd never work again for the smirking, self-important little jerk; she hadn't wanted to in the first place.

Yet one couldn't live off noble intentions.

Brittany sighed. She'd done lots of commercials and magazine ads that hadn't turned out quite the way she wanted, and she would probably do lots more. Her agent, Jessica Barlowe, kept reminding her that she had to eat.

But she always tried to pick and choose her jobs carefully. It was just that sometimes circumstances were beyond her control. Like Berkshire Jeans.

Brittany wrinkled her nose in distaste. Bryant Berkshire hadn't been willing to listen to anything his model might say. He'd been positively appalled that she had an opinion at all.

"Look, honey," he'd said with extreme patience, "your check doesn't cover speech, okay? All you have to do is look pretty…and sexy. Pout a little, why don't you? I'm paying you a goddamned fortune for this, so get it right."

Brittany had been incensed, and if she could have got out of the contract she would have done so on the spot. Instead she'd made the best of a bad situation and given him only some of what he'd asked for. He hadn't been overly happy, but then Brittany hadn't exactly been pleased herself.

And what did it matter anyway? A feud with an egotistical designer—it was all so trivial and petty. Especially when she thought about her father...and even when she thought about Devon.

Brittany crossed her ankles and shifted uncomfortably. The stewardesses had buckled in, preparing for landing. For the thousandth time Brittany glanced at the silent man seated next to her. He was engrossed in a business magazine, his face grim, a five o'clock shadow already forming along his rigid jawline. There was something about him that reminded her of Devon and she couldn't seem to pull her eyes away. Ever since her mother had mentioned Devon's name she'd been fighting back memories of what they'd shared. And then she'd had the bad luck to be seated next to a near clone of the man!

It hurt to think about Devon; the memory brought back a bittersweet ache that Brittany didn't want to feel. She looked at the discarded magazine, then out the window, then at her hands. But she couldn't help herself. Of their own volition, her eyes once again sought the profile of her companion: Devon's profile.

This time the man caught her staring and lifted his brows, smiling. Brittany's fascination with him did a nose dive: he was nothing like Devon, after all. This man's eyes were dark and unreadable, cold and, she thought, unkind; nothing like Devon's impossible electric-blue ones. She could have drowned in *his* eyes.

"I know you," the man said, breaking into Brittany's thoughts. "You're that actress...." He snapped his fingers in recall, still staring.

Brittany smiled, wishing she hadn't invited this conversation. "I'm hardly an actress. I'm a model. I do some commercials."

"Some people would call that acting."

"Maybe."

A dimple dented her cheek as she remembered Bryant Berkshire's opinion of her skills. He'd been furious with her for not being unable to understand what he wanted. "I won't allow you to do my television commercial, little lady!" he'd fumed. "You can't even model! And I'll be damned if I'm going to waste time watching you try to *act!*"

Brittany had finally agreed to some of his requests—after they'd settled on the contract. But she hadn't played the part exactly as he'd wanted, and Berkshire had grumbled and complained all the way through about her. Maybe it had been bad public relations, sabotaging her own performance, but the result was still better than what Berkshire had planned. Berkshire would never understand that what he'd witnessed was a first-class performance of an actress playing the part of a beautiful but empty-headed model.

Her traveling companion stuck out his hand. "The name's Grant Broderick," he told her, his eyes sweeping her face with sharp assessment.

Brittany was surprised. "The investment broker?" she asked. She tried not to feel uneasy under his inspection; he was, after all, a powerful man in Los Angeles, and his clients publicly raved about the fortunes he'd made for them. She knew, too, that he was fighting to become part of California's political scene.

"One and the same. And you are...?"

"Brittany Daniels."

Brittany shook his hand, hiding her feelings. This man was Grant Broderick? She wasn't certain why, but she didn't think she would dare to put her financial future in his hands. There was something about him she instinctively didn't like. Yet many people swore he was an investment genius. Looks certainly could be deceiving, she thought wryly.

He pointed to her necklace. "I couldn't help noticing your pearls," he said, and Brittany's hand automatically went to her throat. "They're incredible. I deal in gems a lot myself, but I have a fondness for pearls."

Brittany swallowed with difficulty. She dropped her hand from the string of lustrous graduated natural pearls, wishing she had had the sense to sell them. "They were a gift," she said.

"From an admirer?" he guessed.

"Something like that."

"Are you interested in gems?" Broderick began fishing in his pocket and produced a business card.

"As an investment?" Brittany asked with a smile. She accepted the card.

"Naturally." His answering smile was full of ego. "What other reason would you buy them for?"

"Maybe because you like them?"

"Diamonds are a girl's best friend only if she buys wisely," he intoned.

Britanny was certain she was hearing a well-rehearsed line; she was getting a subtle sales pitch. "Well, if I'm ever in the market..." she said graciously, holding up his card.

The deafening backward thrust of the engines ended the conversation and Brittany bent to pull her carry-on bag from beneath the seat. Grant Broderick quickly came to her aid, grabbing her bag before she could protest.

"Let me get that," he said, and Brittany had no choice but to lean back and let him. For a man who'd ignored her presence during most of the flight, he was suddenly very attentive.

The Los Angeles airport was filled with people. Brittany maneuvered the best she could through the packed crowd, vainly hoping baggage claim and customs would have fewer people per square inch.

"Do you live in Los Angeles?"

Brittany inwardly sighed as Grant Broderick fell in step beside her. She didn't know how to tell him nicely that she wasn't in the mood to talk about investments. "All my life."

"What part? Beverly Hills? Bel Air?"

"Hardly," she laughed. "Try Redondo Beach."

Something shifted in his expression and she had to hide a smile. He was losing interest in her as a potential client.

She saw the number of her flight listed on the overhead monitor and went in search of her bags. Her twin canvas cases tumbled onto the carousel and she bent to pick them up. She rarely traveled so heavily but this last trip had been long. Long and depressing. She felt completely drained of emotion.

"Here. Let me get those for you," Broderick offered.

"No. Thanks. I'm fine." Brittany pulled the bags off, flexing unexpected muscles in her arms. Jane Fonda's workout had nothing on the rigorous routine she'd designed for herself. Brittany's body was curvaceous but as lean and strong as a whip. She spent at least an hour each morning and night working it into shape.

"A tough lady, huh?" Broderick said, smiling.

Brittany didn't answer. She started walking toward customs.

No, she wasn't tough. She was weak. And though she'd striven to make herself diamond hard over the years, she hadn't succeeded. She was still a pushover.

But there was one major difference between how she'd been before she met Devon and now: maturity. At least she knew her faults—and herself—and didn't try to be something she wasn't.

What she was—and had been ever since she'd blossomed from puberty into womanhood—was a woman with an intriguingly beautiful face. It was the kind of face that should be plastered over magazine covers—or so her parents had been told when she was fifteen. Softly curled black hair, violet eyes with long-fringed lashes, exquisite cheekbones, a wide expressive mouth: she was a photographer's dream.

She'd been picked up by an exclusive modeling agency at an early age, then been primed, coached, trained and hyped. She'd burst on the scene full of unrealistic expectations, half believing she truly was the beautiful seductive woman of her photographs. Enter Devon.... And Brittany, full of self-importance and confidence in her lures as a woman, had set herself up for a colossal fall. In all honesty she couldn't really blame Devon. She could only blame herself.

"Would you come this way?"

Brittany turned at the quiet authoritative request. A customs official in a dark blue suit was looking at her.

"Pardon?"

"Would you please follow me, ma'am?"

He was moving toward a door at the far end of the room. Puzzled, Brittany obediently lifted her bags from the back of the line and followed him, wondering what was up.

She'd never been singled out before. From the corner of her eye she saw Grant Broderick being pulled aside by another similarly dressed man and, at another table, a middle-aged Mexican couple.

The customs man held the door for her, pointed to the bare rectangular table in the center of the room and said, "The small one first."

Brittany lifted her suitcase onto the table, an uneasy feeling growing in the pit of her stomach. Why weren't they being examined in the huge room with all the other travelers?

Her imagination ran riot. She'd heard of instances where an innocent person was victimized by smugglers, an intimate search of their belongings revealing cocaine and other drugs. With growing fear she remembered her long wait in Mexico City's airport. She'd been jostled once or twice but had paid scant attention; she'd been too self-absorbed to care.

Her palms broke out in a sweat. Had she been an unwitting accomplice to a crime?

The customs official knew what he was doing. Expert fingers rifled through her clothing, touching, searching, then discarding. In fascination she watched him run his hands along the inside of her suitcase, tugging experimentally on the lining. Brittany was transfixed, aware that she'd never before witnessed such a thorough search.

He picked up her second suitcase. She unlatched the locks with quaking fingers, feeling inordinately relieved that nothing had come to light inside the smaller case. Once again he went through the same motions, probing and testing until she was sure he had a complete mental inventory of everything she possessed: two pairs of shoes, one black, one brown; three dresses; four pairs of slacks; silk underwear, off-white....

He turned her shoes over and examined the soles. *They need to be reheeled,* Brittany thought detachedly, watching him test the narrow heels. She half expected him to pull one off the shoe, but he suddenly stuffed them back, reclosing her case.

"The shoulder bag?" he requested politely.

Brittany had heard somewhere that it was easy to identify policemen: they had a certain look. Now she believed it. This man spelled government. He had the trained no-nonsense face of a professional. She was convinced he wasn't your average customs man.

Which was hardly encouraging, she thought with trepidation, slipping the bag from her shoulder.

He took it without a word, unzipping both sides before taking anything out. Brittany's throat went dry. She knew she must have looked guilty. Dear God, she *felt* guilty! She could only pray that the man was used to innocent people falling apart under stress.

He pulled a bottle of vitamins from an inner pocket of the bag, letting it roll across his palm, his scrutiny of the tiny orange pills intense. Brittany had purchased them on a whim right before her trip to Mexico, buying a cheap local brand in the hope they would give her added pep. Her meals had been haphazard for a long time; she'd been trying to do too much at once, catching a sandwich here, a pizza there. The vitamins were a salve to the guilt she felt about abusing her body. Now she worried that the customs man had never heard of the brand.

"I bought those in L.A.," she burst out. *Only guilty people break into confession,* an inner voice warned, but she couldn't help herself. "Century vitamins are distributed by G & L Markets. They're a local brand. I thought I might need some while I was in Mexico.''

He didn't bother acknowledging whether he knew the brand or not. He just set the bottle on the counter and systematically went through the rest of her bag. Brittany felt like a fool. If she hadn't been so anxious, she would have resented the way she was being treated. But resenting this man, she knew, would be an exercise in futility. He was armored with experience.

He did a cursory examination of her makeup, then unscrewed the top of her cold-cream jar. Brittany gasped when he suddenly jabbed one finger inside. *Do you know how much that costs,* she wanted to scream. Her makeup cost a small fortune, a price she gladly paid for its high quality. Being constantly under hot lights that prematurely aged the skin, she needed the best cosmetics, but she wouldn't use that particular jar of cold cream again.

Her shocked face didn't perturb him. He wiped his finger on a handkerchief and continued. When he'd exhausted every toiletry item he searched the set of clothes she'd packed in the shoulder bag just in case the airlines lost the rest of her luggage. Then he examined the bag itself again.

Brittany's confidence returned as he zipped it shut and stacked it with her suitcases. So, she thought with relief, she'd merely been letting her imagination run wild. He'd found nothing.

"You're looking for something, aren't you?" she asked, slinging her bag over her shoulder. "Something specific."

He merely smiled in a friendly distracted way. He pointed to the back of the room. "Just pass through those double doors and you'll be headed upstairs."

She hadn't really expected an answer.

Brittany sighed with relief. She couldn't wait to get home and throw herself into bed. What a day! What a night! There were only a few hours left before dawn.

She passed through the doors and wondered about Grant Broderick. She was fairly certain he was being subjected to the same exhaustive search. Why? And why the Mexican couple? Did the customs people suspect someone was smuggling?

Brittany shivered. Well, it wasn't her problem, she thought thankfully. She had more than enough of her own.

She tried to shake off her uneasiness but it persisted. The flight from Mexico, the grave problems affecting her father's health, customs, Grant Broderick... *memories....* Brittany sucked in a quick ragged breath and told herself she just needed to go home and forget. She wanted to burrow between the sheets and hold back the world, at least for a little while.

Shifting her large case from her right hand to her left, Brittany walked purposefully toward the stairs to the second floor, her steps tapping rapidly across the linoleum.

She felt someone's eyes on her and looked up. With a ruthless lack of warning, her eyes clashed with the hostile gaze of a man near the far wall.

Her lips parted in shock. The handle slipped from her palm. It couldn't be!

"Devon?" she whispered in disbelief.

She'd seen him on television, of course, but not in person. Not so close. Not for almost three years!

"Hello, Brittany," he said, the low timbre of his voice shockingly familiar. "It's been a long time."

Chapter Two

Brittany had never been the type to run from disaster, but seeing Devon hit her viscerally, memories tumbling down one upon another, like the after shocks of an earthquake. She had to get away.

Her palms were trembling, her eyes searching wildly for another exit. *I'm not ready for this.*

She turned blindly. With a brutal flash of recall she saw herself as she'd once been: vibrant, adventuresome, a bit wicked, full of unrealistic expectations. She'd been so foolish and so much younger in maturity, if not in age.

And Devon Gallagher was the mirror of her worst mistakes.

"I want to talk to you," Devon said, his tight voice drumming in her ear as she stumbled in search of another exit.

"No."

Coming face-to-face with him again unraveled years of carefully won hours and minutes of self-respect. As much as she'd loved him, as much as her father wanted her to forget the past, as much as she might like to forget, she still couldn't.

"Brittany—"

"I don't want to talk to you, Devon."

She'd imagined herself saying a hundred different things to him when, and if, she ever encountered him again. Most often she told him how great her life was going and how nice it was running into him and how much she enjoyed his newscasts. Always—*always*—she was in perfect control.

But all she could think of now was getting away.

"Well, you *need* to talk to me," Devon said grimly, stepping in front of her to halt her progress.

Head bent, Brittany got a clear glimpse of a hard flat waist, narrow hips, jean-clad thighs taut with well-defined muscles and a pair of booted feet before she stopped herself from running into him. She met his gaze fleetingly and something died inside her at his set hard face.

He inclined his head toward the stairs. "Upstairs there's a room that's more private."

His utter arrogance struck her momentarily dumb. Brittany felt her initial shock disappear beneath a wave of righteous indignation. Who did he think he was, popping up after all this time, acting as if she'd still follow him to the ends of the earth, expecting her to come with him like a well-trained dog?

"I'm sorry, Devon," she said shortly. "I've got things to do, and I'm really tired. I just flew in from Mexico."

"I know."

"You know?"

Devon's blue eyes were filled with steely determination. For a wild moment Brittany wondered if her father had contacted him. Then reason returned and she knew that if anyone had engineered this meeting it was Devon himself.

Brittany's eyebrows lifted as she realized this was not the random crossing of old lovers' paths. "You mean you're here to meet my plane?" she asked, her voice rising in disbelief.

Devon's jaw hardened, then relaxed. "Something like that. But believe me, lady, your being on it was a real surprise."

Brittany could barely breathe. He was radiating anger and animosity. It made her hurt inside in a way she couldn't define. "Then I don't see why you need to speak to me," she murmured, groping blindly for her cases.

"Would you just come with me? There are some things that need to be said, and I'd rather say them in private."

"I don't think there's anything left to be said." Brittany glanced toward the top of the stairway longingly. She wanted to go up there and out of the customs area, but she wanted to go alone. It was incredible! Since she'd left Acapulco, she'd half entertained the idea of attempting a reconciliation with Devon. Yet here he was! In the flesh. And she had no idea how to begin. She didn't even know if she could; she didn't know if he would let her.

Devon inhaled an impatient breath. "After all we've been through together, Britt?" His laugh was ugly. "There's lots left to say."

Brittany stopped herself just in time from wincing under Devon's attack. "I'm tired, Devon. Really. I've got other—things—on my mind."

"I'm not asking, Brittany."

His presumption infuriated her and she tilted her chin defiantly. "What do you want to talk about, Devon?"

Devon's smile was grim and purposeful. "Maybe we ought to talk about old times."

"I'm surprised you would want to," she said, her breath catching. She didn't think she could relive those unhappy moments right now, but if Devon wanted to...

"I don't." His harsh answer cruelly swept her flickering hope aside. "But I need to discuss something else with you and our past association will inevitably come up. Let's just make this quick and painless, okay?"

He reached for her cases and Brittany instantly grabbed them away. Moments passed, their hands locked in a brutal struggle, Devon's set face challenging Brittany's pale one. She nearly flinched at the simmering hostility she read in the vivid blue of his eyes.

"What are you afraid of, Brittany?" he asked softly. "Having to look at someone who knows the real you? Do you hate yourself that much?"

"No!" All limbs trembling, she jerked the cases away from him. She couldn't believe he could be so cruel, so cutting. For tortured moments she could only hear the sound of her ragged breathing, then anger rescued her. "You don't understand anything about me. You never have!"

"I understand you perfectly."

Brittany's legs shook as she climbed the stairs, her back rigid with rage. He'd never believed in her! No matter how many ways she'd tried to show him how much she'd loved him. And even today he still saw her as the mercenary thoughtless girl he'd believed her to be three years ago.

"Your opinions always were biased, Devon." Attacking her indefensible youth was one thing, but Brittany wouldn't let him put down the woman she was still struggling to become. "Frankly, you're wasting your breath trying them out on me."

"Really?" he drawled. "I always thought my opinions were justified, especially where you were concerned."

"Well, you were wrong."

At the top of the stairs Brittany turned to face him, her eyes narrowed to accusing amethyst slits. Devon's brows drew into a frown and he rubbed his face with his palm, his glance toward her suitcases making her realize his male pride wouldn't allow her to carry them much longer. In defiance, Brittany clutched the cases more tightly to her body.

Devon sighed. "Then convince me I was wrong."

Brittany's lips parted. Oh, how she wished she could! She was actually considering giving it a try when the stony implacability of his expression registered in her mind: she'd already been tried and convicted.

Her heart ached and she said wearily, "I don't think I can, Devon. You made up your mind about me years ago. Now if you'll excuse me..."

She hadn't really expected him just to let her go but she was amazed, when he grabbed her arm, that he would actually touch her.

"That's a cop-out if I ever heard one. You just can't face me."

"For God's sake, Devon. Not tonight!"

Brittany could feel her control rapidly deteriorating. She closed her eyes and tried to hold on to the rags of her self-respect, knowing tears would be the ultimate humiliation. Damn Devon! Damn his incredible timing! She wasn't up to facing anyone right now, least of all *him*. And he was battering her with psychological weapons that could destroy her.

"Why not tonight?" Devon asked quietly.

Even in her distracted state Brittany sensed Devon's increased awareness. Every muscle in his body seemed frozen, suspensed, poised in waiting....

Brittany struggled to get her throat working. More than anything, all she wanted to do was get away.

Devon moved instinctively in front of her, outguessing her intentions before she'd even moved. His eyes captured hers with an intensity that was frightening. "What were you doing in Mexico City?"

Brittany saw the color recede from his face and felt alarmed. "What was I...?" Her voice trailed off in bafflement. She thought she saw pain in Devon's gaze...and regret...?

"What's going on?" Brittany's nerves were stretched to the limit. "Is something wrong? What is it, Devon? You're beginning to really scare me with—"

Brittany inhaled fiercely. Dear God, she couldn't believe it! A shiver went down her back as she experienced a brutal déjà vu. It was her past all over again. The suspicions, the distrust, the disbelief—Devon was on some kind of assignment!

"Brittany—"

"Get out of my way."

All the hurt and anger Brittany had carefully hidden from herself over Devon's rejection came to the fore, blinding her, tearing her apart inside.

"Listen, Brittany—"

"Don't you hear, Devon? Can't you feel *anything*?" Brittany's chest heaved, her pain glittering through unshed tears. "Get out of my way. And get the hell out of my life." Her passion pushed her past him, away from him, away from customs, away from Acapulco, away from memories. *Away*.

Devon swore and Brittany heard him from the far end of the hall. She tossed her head up and glared at him, every nerve afire with a hot and hurting agony. "Go play your games with someone else, Devon. I have only one thing to say to the press. 'No comment!'"

Devon watched her walk away with a mixture of frustration and admiration. It didn't matter what he thought of her or how he felt about her. And it really didn't matter what she'd done. The plain and simple truth was that Brittany Daniels was the most beautiful woman he'd ever met.

He sighed wearily and ran his hand around the back of his neck, asking himself for the billionth time what he could have done differently. It was rare for Devon to find himself at a loss, but that was exactly how he felt now.

And he was filled with emotions he'd thought long dead.

With a self-deprecating smile forming on his lips, Devon reluctantly remembered his first reaction upon seeing her again: he'd had the passionate desire to strangle her! She was so utterly unchanged, so beautiful, so untouchable. One look at the slender form, the regal bearing, the vulnerability that lurked beneath the maturity of her gaze, and a deep angry part of himself had melted into quiet regret.

"Damn you, Brittany," he whispered, but the words were filled with more admiration than heat.

You might as well damn yourself while you're at it, he thought wryly.

To Devon, emotionalism was the bane of a good newsman. It was something he rarely fell prey to himself, or so he liked to believe. That time with Brittany...well, he'd deluded himself into thinking it was all a condition of his past, something he'd never be victimized by again.

Now he wasn't so sure.

But the Brittany Daniels of today couldn't be much different from the Brittany he'd known at nineteen. And that Brittany had been single-minded and determined and interested only in serving herself.

Still, it was hard to equate the cruel-hearted goddess from his past with the woman he'd just met....

Devon stared down the empty hallway. Could he have been *that* wrong about her?

Jay came through the double doors at the bottom of the stairs and Devon went down to meet him.

"I'm still waiting for Broderick," Jay said. "It's going to be a while yet; customs is tearing him apart."

"But so far nothing?"

Jay nodded grimly.

"Okay." Devon glanced in the direction Brittany had gone, feeling impatient. "Stick with Broderick and I'll catch up with you later. There's something else I've got to do."

"Good luck," Jay said, the corners of his mouth twitching as he watched Devon head upstairs.

With purposeful strides Devon ate up the distance between himself and Brittany. Hating himself a little, he could admit that seeing her again did strange things to his equilibrium. She intrigued him. She tantalized him. She'd matured into a very desirable woman.

Yet she was still remarkably the same. The vulnerability that had been his downfall in the beginning still remained; he'd seen it in her first startled look. And, just like before, he'd been gripped by the same crazy impulse to shelter her.

Devon ground his teeth together, remembering. The Brittany Daniels of his past hardly needed sheltering. He'd learned that the hard way.

And, he reminded himself with terrible logic, there was a possibility she was seriously involved in something dangerous, maybe even criminal. She'd been frantic to escape from him, and Devon had to ask himself if that desire could possibly stem from guilt. Devon was at the airport for a reason—to catch a smuggler.

And Brittany had suddenly become a prime candidate.

With a muttered imprecation directed solely at himself, Devon opened the door that led to the main airport, his gaze sweeping the near-empty room. He'd been the one who had tipped off customs to Broderick's possible smuggling, but now, with Brittany's involvement, Devon was consumed with vague anxieties.

Could she be involved? His senses cried out against it, but Devon knew better than anyone that Brittany's ethics didn't necessarily jibe with his own.

She was making her way toward the outside exit when he caught up to her, fatigue slumping her shoulders against the weight of her cases. Devon repressed the urge to offer help, knowing she would resist, and he frowned in annoyance at himself while a part of him noticed the smooth curve of her calf, the willowy beauty of her waist, the richness of her hair.

"Brittany...."

She stopped abruptly, shoulders straightening. Strain had painted dark circles around her eyes, and she looked weary and resigned as she turned to meet him. "I guess you didn't hear me, Devon. I'm not interested in furthering your career...again."

"Look, this'll just take a minute."

"No. It's late and I'm beat. Call my agent and make an appointment." She added flippantly, "We'll have lunch."

Devon could have laughed if he hadn't been so worried about her. Instead, taking refuge in professionalism, he said, "You came in on flight 108 from Mexico City. It's a flight you've taken before."

"No." Brittany's answer was short and succinct. She could still remember clearly the last time Devon had interviewed her. Now, like then, he'd been after a story; she'd been a fool to imagine there was something more between them.

"No?"

"I missed my flight from Acapulco. I was forced to take this one."

"You were on this flight three months ago," Devon pointed out, his face giving nothing away.

Surprised, Brittany matched Devon's stare. "I may have been," she responded slowly. "I've taken late-night flights before. Have you been checking up on me?"

"You were traveling first-class."

Brittany's eyes searched his stony countenance but she decided he wasn't trying to wound her. If he still felt she was a slave to the amount of money she could make from her career, he was careful not to show it. She nodded, knowing she should leave but held to the spot by Devon's powerful presence as much as by her own curiosity. "Is my decision to travel first-class relevant?"

Devon didn't answer. She really hadn't expected him to. She told herself she should be angry; he was interrogating her all over again. And this time she hadn't even asked for it.

Devon glanced at his watch and scowled. Brittany didn't even have to ask about the time; streaks of gray were lightening the night sky beyond the glass doors. She felt weary with muscle fatigue and wished she could work up the anger just to leave Devon hanging.

"What do you do in Mexico, Brittany?"

"What do I do?" She shook the tousled tresses of her hair and said softly, "You're pushing, Devon."

His tense expression eased a bit, an engaging smile briefly touching his lips. "Humor me. It's my nature. Remember?"

"I remember."

His eyes glinted deep blue between impossibly thick lashes, and Brittany wondered if his memories were as powerful as her own. She looked down at her forgotten suitcases, then smoothed her hands on her skirt. "Give me one good reason why I should explain what I've been doing in Mexico, and I'll tell you. What's going on, Devon?"

Devon shook his head and shrugged. "It's all merely guesswork at this point."

"Then you are investigating something or someone?"

"Yes."

It seemed the closest she would ever get to an explanation and Brittany considered herself lucky to get even that much information out of him. "I don't think I can help you, Devon."

"Maybe not. Tell me this, are these trips you go on for business or pleasure?"

Brittany bit down sharply on her lower lip. A vision of her father on the back deck filled her mind. She didn't want to answer. Throat aching, she managed to whisper, "Neither."

"Neither?" Devon searched her face, puzzled. He saw lines of strain appear briefly beside her mouth.

Brittany felt him grappling to understand and knew he never would; there was no way he could. He hadn't understood love before; he wouldn't be able to now.

The Mexican couple who had also been singled out by customs came into the room looking peeved at their delay. Before Brittany could protest, Devon grabbed her elbow and steered her toward a door marked Security.

"What are you doing?" she demanded.

"I want to talk to you alone."

"Let go of me. I've been pushed around enough, thank you very much."

"Just give me a few more minutes. That's all. I promise, Britt."

"My suitcases!"

"I'll get them."

She was deposited inside a bare room with metal folding chairs, and Devon returned for her bags. She rubbed her face with her hands and wondered what in the world she was doing here. What was Devon doing?

I promise, Britt....

Brittany's breath came out with a rush of suppressed emotion. She couldn't believe this was happening. It was like some kind of incredible replay. Because there was nothing else she could do, she dropped into one of the folding chairs next to the wall.

The door reopened and Devon came in, carrying her cases with remarkable ease. Brittany inspected the polish of her nails and tried not to think of anything at all.

"I'm really not trying to delay you any more than necessary," he said, examining the silky crown of her head. "But I am in the middle of something and I need your cooperation."

Brittany gave him a long look that said, *We've been here before,* and Devon inclined his head, accepting her censure. But it didn't deter him.

"How well do you know Grant Broderick?" he asked.

Whatever she'd expected, it wasn't this. "Broderick?"

"I saw you speaking to him. You were seated next to him on the plane."

Brittany paused, aware that Devon had to have been watching her from the moment she stepped off the plane. She answered carefully, "I don't know him well at all."

"Has he ever been on a plane with you before?"

Brittany looked askance. "Maybe. I don't know. I've never noticed him before."

"You've never been seated with him before today?"

"No."

"And you don't have any other connection with him?"

"No!" Brittany didn't like the sound of Devon's questions. "What's he supposedly done? Or is that privileged information, too?"

"He hasn't done anything. I'm just checking on him."

"Searching out a story," Brittany said flatly, feeling absurdly let down that Devon's interest had nothing whatsoever to do with her personally.

Devon shifted his weight from one foot to the other and Brittany's eyes were unwillingly drawn to his physique. He had a spare tough build, rugged shoulders and the overall look of a man used to power and respect—despite the jeans and navy jacket. His face looked older but it was still as handsome and compelling as it had been when Brittany had fallen in love with him.

"I barely know Grant Broderick," Brittany said again, responding to Devon's silence as if it were an accusation. "I met him on the plane today and spoke with him for just a few minutes."

"What did he say?"

"He said that he was an investment broker, which, in case you don't know, is true. I have friends who speak very highly of him."

Devon didn't betray his own intimate knowledge of Grant Broderick. "That's all he said?"

Brittany stood up. "As far as I can remember. Am I free to go now, Mr. Gallagher?"

Devon seemed to want to argue. Brittany waited and he lifted a hand. "Yeah. That's it."

Brittany was thinking back to the conversation with Broderick and it was then that she remembered the pearls. Devon's pearls. Her face flushed in embarrassment. He would have to realize what a sentimental fool she still was that she'd hung on to them.

"You remembered something." Devon was straightening, his features tense at the change in her expression.

"No. No." Brittany shook her head, gauging the space required to pass Devon. She would have to brush against him to get to the door. "Nothing important to you, anyway."

"What?"

"Nothing."

"For God's sake, Britt!" he exploded. "Everything's important!"

Brittany stared at him. "Just what do you think Broderick's up to?"

The thorough search at customs flitted through her mind and it dawned on her that only the first-class section had been singled out. Because Broderick had flown first-class? What had Devon expected to find in the man's luggage?

"You don't think—you *can't* think—he's smuggling. Can you?"

"I'm just following a lead," Devon said repressively.

"You mean a hunch. Oh, Devon...." Brittany tried to get past him. He was still trying to be the crusading white knight. "Grant Broderick's hardly the smuggler type, or haven't you noticed? He's got a successful business going. He's been described as a financial genius. And he doesn't strike me as the kind of man to blow his own fortune away by doing something illegal."

"I agree," Devon said, aware that he'd already said far more than he wanted to.

"Then why are you after him? Tell me, Devon. It was you who had us searched, wasn't it? What did you expect to find?" An ugly thought entered Brittany's mind and she tried to reject it outright. But she couldn't. Turning her eyes to Devon's she whispered, "Unless you're really not after Broderick at all. Do you think I'm involved in something, Devon?"

"No." Devon's tone was definite. More definite than he actually felt.

But Brittany's sensitivity to him as a man picked up on the lie in his words. "Is that the kind of woman I am, Devon? Unscrupulous? Untrustworthy? *Criminal?*"

"You're jumping to conclusions—again," he added harshly.

"I don't think so." Her throat was tight. Brittany didn't know why she should even care, but Devon's assumptions—because she knew him well enough to guess what he was thinking—hurt in a way she wouldn't have believed was still possible.

"I'm leaving now," she said, determined to push against the wall of his chest if he defied her.

"What was it you remembered about Broderick?" Devon asked, not budging.

"I told you. Nothing." She was so close to Devon she could feel the heat from his skin.

"You remembered something," he argued. "I could see it in your face."

"He just complimented me, that's all!"

She shoved her way past him, inadvertently touching the shockingly hard muscles of his upper arm. For a moment her eyes met his, seeing the stormy doubts that still clouded his blue eyes. Then his gaze dropped to the single strand of pearls nearly hidden beneath the collar of her dress, and his brows drew together. With an effort Brittany tore herself away, escaping to the cool safety of the waiting area.

"Brittany!"

Grant Broderick's delighted call made Brittany's steps falter. *Not now,* she wanted to scream, but she forced a smile to her lips and kept walking in the direction of the street.

He met up with her, a garment bag slung carelessly over one shoulder. Brittany wondered why Devon could be after him; he was too self-assured and carefree to be concerned about the customs search, and though Devon hadn't admitted to being the instigator, she was certain he was behind it.

Another thought crossed her mind. Could Devon's tip-off to customs have been merely a ruse? A way to look through Grant Broderick's personal papers?

"Do you need a lift?" Broderick asked, drawing nearer. "My car's in the lot across the street and I'd be happy to drop you in Redondo Beach."

"Thanks but I've got a car here, too," Brittany replied, spinning the small white lie to save herself from his company. She'd taken a taxi to the airport when she'd departed because she'd been unsure how long she would need to stay in Mexico.

Devon appeared at that moment, closing the door to the security room behind him. Broderick's eyes narrowed briefly, then he said, "Devon Gallagher, isn't it?" He glanced sideways toward Brittany. "I seem to be surrounded by famous faces."

Brittany wasn't certain whether Broderick would make the connection between Devon and the customs' search, but for reasons she would later wonder about, she sprang to Devon's aid. "Mr. Gallagher and I are old friends," she said, seeing the surprised lift to Devon's brows the instant before he recovered himself. "We met when I was still working for the Nora Castle Modeling Agency."

"Ah. I see."

What Grant Broderick saw, Brittany was afraid to ask. After a polite farewell to both Broderick and Devon, she walked the remaining distance to the doors and stepped out into early dawn sunshine.

"Customs didn't find anything. Or if they did they're not telling."

Devon acted as if he hadn't heard, his brooding perusal of the Pacific unchanging, his silence indicative of his mental state. Jay Lundgren kept his eyes on his friend's broad back, waiting. He'd expected Devon to be upset. He hadn't, however, expected him to be this upset. His knowledge of what had passed between Devon and Brittany Daniels was limited; he knew only that she'd scarred him in some deep, unforgivable way. Devon's few references to her had led him to believe she was coldhearted and ambitious, her career and everything that went with it coming before anything and anyone else. Devon had once wedged himself between Brittany and her career, and Brittany had had to choose.

Jay's private opinion had always been that Devon should just forget about her. She simply wasn't worth it. But seeing Brittany at the airport had given him a new perspective. Just for an instant, when she'd first seen Devon, her face was full of ravaged emotions, and Jay had decided whatever she'd done to Devon wasn't that far ahead of what he'd done to her. She was still hurting, too.

Getting no response from Devon, Jay went on, "Broderick's cagey. He hasn't booked another flight to Mexico Ciy yet, as far as we know. I'm still checking."

"The man has to work sometime," Devon commented.

It was Jay's first indication that Devon was listening at all. Encouraged, he said, "Maybe not. From what I hear, business finds him. He's had phenomenal success."

"When was his last trip?"

Jay heard the grim tone and knew Devon didn't share the public's general opinion. "About six weeks ago. And before that, sometime in June. He's pretty regular."

"And the other passengers?"

Jay hurriedly flipped open his folder, glancing at the copious notes. "The De Vacas live outside Mexico City. They've made three other trips this year. Eric Cordell, the college kid, has been in and out of Mexico about five times, maybe more. We're not completely sure." He paused. "Brittany's come through Mexico City twice. She's always gone to Acapulco first, though."

Devon turned, his brows drawn into a line. "Why?"

"We're checking now. She hadn't ever been on a flight with Broderick before," Jay added somewhat apologetically. He had the least information on her and she probably wouldn't even be seriously considered except for the coincidence of her past association with Devon.

"Well, find out. Right away." Devon was suddenly all action, pacing the room, his hands clenching impatiently, determination written in the thrust of his jaw. "I want to make sure she's not involved with him. She said she wasn't, but..."

Jay was too learned in the ways and means of Devon Gallagher to offer any comment about Brittany Daniels. He had great respect for his friend's judgment and intuition and generally understood all Devon's motives. He had to admit, however, that he had definite doubts about Devon's objectivity now.

"I'll get right on it," he said, slapping the file shut with brisk finality. "See you tomorrow."

"Right."

Devon heard the door click shut behind him. It was obvious to both him and Jay that Broderick was involved in some kind of clandestine activity, be it smuggling gems or just fencing them. He had the perfect front for fencing—his knowledge of gems and his own indisputable reputation.

Devon had tried to wangle information from the authorities but they were singularly closemouthed. So he'd struck out on an investigation of his own, intent on finding out how Broderick was fooling customs, the law-enforcement agencies and his clients, as well.

And Brittany...?

Devon sucked in a deep breath. Now there was a development he hadn't expected. A surprise. No wonder Jay had been so tentative. Devon himself wasn't sure how he should react. He'd told himself he hated her for a long, long time, yet after seeing her again, honesty made him admit that wasn't entirely true. And he'd been stunned by her totally unexpected charge to his defense when Broderick had appeared on the scene.

But he couldn't forget what she'd done.

With a muttered curse Devon strode to the bar, scooping ice into a glass and pouring a liberal stream of amber Scotch over-it. He shook his head and took a deep gulp.

You've got to get over her once and for all.

Devon sighed. For all his investigative technique he was still as powerless to understand her today as he had been years before. And he sensed inside himself a willingness to forgive that hadn't quite died, a disbelief in Brittany's total selfishness that wouldn't quite disappear. That was his vulnerability.

Whatever the case, he wanted her clear of trouble. Brittany Daniels was a distraction and a nuisance he couldn't afford.

The bar telephone rang.

"Devon Gallagher," he answered.

"Do you know it's impossible to catch up with you? For a week I've called every single day and night and you're *never* in. You also don't apparently return any calls. Out prowling, Devon?"

Shannon's dry voice eased some of the tension that had settled between his shoulder blades, and he felt a stab of guilt that he hadn't had time to answer the messages she'd left on his answering machine. His sister was his one link to the other world: the one full of love and family. She had a husband, two children, three cats and a dog, a house complete with a temperamental hot tub, and a teaching career to boot. She juggled and balanced, and though sometimes she was completely frazzled, she did everything and managed to stay happy into the bargain. Devon loved and admired her. He'd never met another woman like her.

"I've been busy," he replied enigmatically. "Business."

"Mmm-hmm. It's never anything else." In the background he could hear the computer music of a video game and pictured Shannon's eldest hard at work. "Thanksgiving's in three weeks. This is my final offer. Will you come?"

"I don't know. Some things are happening right now that I just can't drop." Devon felt regret slide over him. His holidays were bleak. Rarely could he just pack it in and fly to Seattle to be with his sister's family. "Sorry, Shannon. I'll have to let you know."

"As ever, Devon," Shannon replied with an undignified snort. "When was the last time you had a real vacation? I'd be afraid of burnout if I were you. And what's the point of having a famous brother if you can't show him off?"

"Ah-ha! Now I understand the pressure. You've already committed me to God knows what!" Devon's rare smile surfaced but was lost on the empty room.

"Just some friends of mine. Nothing big. But I've promised you to them for months and months and haven't been able to come up with the goods. Come, Devon," she urged, her tone turning serious. "Please."

"All I can say is, I'll try. I want to. You know that."

There was a pause at the other end and Devon sensed her struggling for the right words. He knew what was coming and said quickly, "Look, no lecture on my love life, okay? I really don't need it right now."

The steel warning in his voice was something he'd never used on his sister before, but right now he couldn't handle her misguided concern. Not after his recent run-in with Brittany. Shannon suspected a woman had turned him into an emotionally barren wasteland, but Devon had never given her the particulars.

"You do need it, Devon. Whoever she was, she should be drawn and quartered."

"Goodbye, Shannon."

"Devon! Don't you dare hang up on me! I swear, if you do I'll never watch 'Perspective' again."

Devon laughed, a deep rich sound that made his sister grin. "Oh, hurt me some more, Shannon. You probably have all my shows on tape."

"Arrogant bastard," she said fondly. "Be here for Thanksgiving."

"I'll try."

He hung up and poured himself another drink, feeling better. Thanksgiving was too far away to think about. He still had today, tomorrow and the rest of three weeks.

And a problem named Brittany Daniels that shouldn't have been a problem at all.

What had she been doing in Mexico? he asked himself again.

He walked back to the window, his face grave. He was afraid he might not want to know.

Chapter Three

Brittany pushed the button to her automatic garage-door opener and watched it slowly begin to close. She was balancing two grocery bags and attempting to unlock the door at the top of the stairs when her phone began to ring.

"Damn!"

Telling herself it was probably nobody important anyway, she forced herself to slow down, threading the key into the lock and twisting it open.

"Hello?" The sack to her right hovered on the edge of the counter and she thrust out a restraining hand. Two oranges tumbled to the floor.

"Oh, Brittany. Good. You're home."

"Barely." Brittany shifted the receiver as she attempted to corral the rolling oranges. For some reason Jessica Barlowe's voice, though one Brittany usually welcomed since her agent handled her career assignments, was a disappointment. She'd been hoping it was someone else calling. But she was too afraid to admit it to herself.

Brittany Daniels was an industry unto herself. No longer part of a modeling squad, she relied completely on herself and her agent. Jessica kept her name in front of interested advertisers and Brittany managed her business affairs herself.

"Well, I'm afraid it's bad news this time," Jessica said on a sigh. "The people from Body Language Shampoo don't like the commercial. They're redoing it."

Brittany frowned. She'd finished that commercial two days earlier, and everyone had seemed pleased with her performance. "What's wrong?" she asked anxiously.

"Oh, it's not you. They don't like the script. They want something sexier."

Don't they all, Brittany thought with twinge of regret. "Okay, so what's the script like now?"

"Basic. All you have to do is say, 'Shhh.' Narration takes care of the rest."

"Shhhampoo?"

Jessica chuckled. "Nothing that cute. I told the advertisers you'd be at the studio at 7:00 sharp, Thursday morning, okay?"

Brittany glanced at the calendar above her kitchen desk. She reflected that Jessica knew her schedule better than she did. "Fine. I'll be there."

Brittany penciled in the appointment, noting that Thursday was the only day she could have squeezed Body Language in. A look through the rest of the month wasn't encouraging. Back-to-back appointments on the seventh; three full days to shoot that diet-drink commercial—thank God; a smattering of publicity appearances...then two whole weeks at Thanksgiving.

One week would be spent in Acapulco with her parents. But the other week was free, a much needed rest period. It was that week that Brittany fixed on every time something went wrong. *Don't worry,* she would remind herself, *you've got a whole week coming with nothing to do.*

Now she reminded herself again, circling the dates with a red felt-tip pen.

"Oh, one more thing," Jessica said, just before hanging up. "Grant Broderick, the investment broker, has been trying to reach you. I was hesitant to give him your number, but if he calls again, what would you like me to do?"

So he'd found her agent. Brittany was surprised that he'd felt compelled to track her down. She hesitated briefly, then said, "It's okay. I met him on the plane coming back from Mexico."

"All right. Suzanne Peters swears by the man. She told me she made a hundred thousand last year, just on his advice."

"No kidding." Brittany wasn't certain she trusted all the glowing accolades to Broderick's success.

"Yes, well, Suzanne has been known for stretching the truth, too."

Brittany laughed. "And I'm a skeptic from way back. Broderick sounds almost too good to be true."

Jessica agreed. "Would you like me to scout around for you? Find out what others think about him—from the horse's mouth, so to speak?"

"Would you?" Brittany's curiosity was getting the best of her, and Devon's interest in Grant Broderick only made it worse.

"Certainly. You sound tired, hon. Get some rest, okay?"

"Will do."

"Bye-bye." Jessica signed off, and Brittany replaced the phone with a thoughtful frown.

Since she'd returned from Mexico her free time had been so limited that she'd barely had time to think. Her killing schedule allowed her only enough time to eat and sleep. Which was just as well, Brittany reflected, because she didn't want to dwell on her father's illness. And she didn't want to think about Devon, either.

Devon. Telling herself not to think about him just brought him to mind. She could remember very clearly how, intent on digging up a story, he'd dogged her while she was still with the Castle agency. A reliable source had alerted him to the fact that several of Nora's models were suffering from anorexia nervosa and bulimia, and Devon had been assigned to do a story about its frequency in the modeling industry.

Brittany had been fascinated by him. She'd never known a man so determined and persuasive. But after Devon had got all the information out of her that Brittany had to give, he'd moved on to the next source. Convinced of her desirability, Brittany had started a campaign to get him to notice her. Devon's amused tolerance had only made her redouble her efforts, and finally one night she was successful.

It was the night of the premiere opening for one of Los Angeles's up-and-coming fashion designers. Nora's models were on brilliant and expensive display. Moments before she was due to go out, Brittany had witnessed a scene that still made her shudder as much from the way she'd used it to her own advantage as the scene itself. One of the models, Tricia, had been in the bathroom forcing herself to vomit.

If she'd been a little older, Brittany reflected with sorrowful hindsight, she would have handled the situation far more tactfully. But at nineteen, empathy hadn't been Brittany's strong suit. Nor had common sense, she could now admit. Instead of reporting what she'd seen to Nora, she'd gone straight to Devon.

"That could be anything," he'd said slowly in the taxi that took them both from the premiere to his apartment. He'd been disinclined to believe Brittany, though he'd been interested enough to invite her to his place.

"It's true," Brittany had said honestly. "It's what I saw."

"Tricia's the tall blonde who was wearing the red sequined gown?"

"Yes."

Devon had been skeptical. "Are you certain it was her? I've spoken to her a few times, and frankly, she doesn't look as though she's starving herself."

Brittany had spent half the evening convincing him, and the more she'd talked about it, the greater her conviction had grown that Tricia was fighting bulimia. But she'd also come to realize that Devon would never be interested in her as anything but a source.

"I've got to get back," she'd said, concentrating on saving her pride. She'd convinced herself that given enough time, Devon might notice her. But she'd been wrong, and she was embarrassed.

Devon had glanced at the clock. "It is late," he'd admitted, reaching for her coat. He'd slipped it over her bare shoulders, his fingers trailing across her skin. Her

flesh had broken into goose bumps and her embarrassment had increased. She'd been so aware of him and he
hadn't even noticed her!

She had tried to salvage her pride by giving him her
honest feelings about Tricia. "I wouldn't make this
story up, Devon. You should really talk to Tricia...and
Nora."

He'd pondered that for a moment. "Maybe I will."
His blue eyes had captured hers and he'd smiled.
"Thank you, Brittany."

She'd flushed. "You're welcome."

Maybe it was her truthfulness, her dropping of all
pretention. Or maybe it was because she'd finally shown
him the real Brittany Daniels without all the trappings
of her profession. Whatever the case, it was at that
moment that Devon had finally seen her as a woman.

He'd looked at her with blue eyes that seemed to
reach into her soul. Brittany was breathless. Now that
she'd got his attention she hardly knew how to react.

"Devon...?"

"Hmm?"

Brittany was never sure later how it all happened, but
one moment she was going to ask him something, the
next she was leaning on her tiptoes to give him a fond
kiss of farewell. She'd never been particularly forward;
she'd never even had time to have a lasting relationship. But the discreet kiss she'd planned melted away
when he turned his mouth to hers.

It had started slowly, carefully. Brittany was inexpe-
rienced but aware enough of her body's signals to recognize the earthy sensation of true desire. And she'd
also felt Devon's passion. Her back had been against the
wall, Devon's body pressed urgently against hers. She'd
done nothing to stop the explosive need that took them

both by surprise, and after a certain point Devon couldn't, either.

Looking back, Brittany knew their affair had been inevitable after that first night. She'd been naive not to have realized that Devon hadn't felt quite the same way. Her pregnancy had brought everything to an instant and abrupt halt. Working up the nerve to tell Devon, she'd gone to Nora first.

"You'll have to do something about it," Nora had said flatly. "You're not working for me pregnant."

Brittany had been stunned and silenced. Later she'd made the mistake of breaking the news to Devon over the telephone; his own shock had been palpable even over the wire. In a grim voice he'd said, "I'll have to do some thinking, Brittany. I'll call you."

Until that moment she'd been sure he loved her. It wasn't a matter of words, it was the way he treated her, the way he needed her and had grown to respect her. But those brutally reluctant, carefully spoken words had opened her eyes.

Two days later she'd miscarried. She'd gone to the doctor in a panic and he'd confined her to bed, clinging on to the life of her baby. But it was already too late. She lost the child in the middle of a long, lonely night.

The next few weeks were the worst period of Brittany's young life. She was sick, miserable and filled with guilt and self-hate. She'd blamed herself for everything, no matter what the doctor and her parents said. She'd slipped into a black depression that she only later learned had frightened her parents enough to bring in a specialist. Brittany had refused to talk to him, preferring to be alone, but somewhere in her darkness she'd realized how terribly unfair she was being to the people she loved most. Using every ounce of willpower she possessed, she'd pulled herself together—but she was never quite the same.

Nora had been furious with her for missing so much work, but Brittany wouldn't tell her why; she simply couldn't. Her grief was too enormous. She couldn't face Devon, either. She'd shuddered at the thought of the relief that would surely cross his face when she told him she was no longer pregnant.

When she'd finally gone back to work, she'd realized Nora was on the brink of firing her. Brittany had told her that she'd been ill but didn't give any details.

"And the other problem?" Nora had asked, frowning at the evidence of Brittany's weight loss.

"It's been solved," Brittany had answered in a whisper. If Nora realized that Brittany had miscarried, she didn't say so; she didn't ask any questions at all. Which was just as well, as far as Brittany was concerned, because she didn't want to hear any false condolences. She didn't want to have to explain at all. The whole ordeal had been much too private, too painful for her to put in plain language.

A week later she'd got a call from Devon. His "How are you?" was so hostile that Brittany noticed it even through her misery.

"I'm terrible," she'd answered, even then wishing there was something left between them.

"Good." Devon's feelings had been painfully clear. "So am I." He'd hung up even before she could tell him about the miscarriage.

That was the end. The finish was so total, so shatteringly abrupt that Brittany barely had time to grieve. It was later—much, much later—before she could analyze the events and mourn for both the loss of her child and the man she'd loved.

But life went on. And as soon as she could, she made her break from the Castle agency. Much sadder but wiser....

Brittany could easily see her mistakes now, but she'd never forgiven Devon for abandoning her when she'd needed him most. Still, she'd hung on to the pearl necklace—a gift from him on her twentieth birthday. He hadn't said he loved her, not in words, but it had been apparent in his gestures, in the tender way he'd looked at her. She'd treasured the pearls and the memory of that night ever since. Sentimentality at its worst, she supposed.

The one thing the situation had taught her was to rely totally on herself. No knight in shining armor would defend her; no one would share the blame for her mistakes. She was on her own.

The phone rang early that evening, just as Brittany was getting ready to watch the news. She felt her pulse jump expectantly, and her brow creased. *Just who do you expect to call?*

"Hello?"

"Brittany, hello. I'm glad I finally connected with you. You're a hard woman to catch at home."

Grant Broderick's voice was full of pleasure. Brittany, however, felt let down, already forgetting that Jessica had mentioned he'd been trying to reach her. "I lead a busy life," she said lightly.

"Yes, I know. I saw this week's cover of *Metro*."

"Did you?" Brittany glanced at her own copy, deciding critically that it was one of her better photos. They'd let her smile—really smile—and she looked happy and sure of herself.

"Uh-huh. I had the gall to mention to some friends that I'd met you, and now I'd like to prove it by inviting you to a small party I'm giving."

Brittany instantly began thinking of a dozen reasons she couldn't go. Politely she asked, "What kind of party?"

"Nothing wild. It's mainly just people I know—and who know me—through business. Marjorie Vandoren of Vandoren Cosmetics specifically asked about you."

Broderick's words were deliberately casual, but Brittany's interest quickened. She knew what he was hinting at. Vandoren Cosmetics was looking for a new face to launch its multimillion-dollar advertising campaign for Toujours cosmetics, a new line made especially for the woman who leads an active life. Brittany, however, hadn't done much campaigning for the coveted position. She'd been too busy with her other obligations.

"I think you're trying to bribe me," she said, and Broderick laughed.

"I probably am," he conceded.

Brittany wondered just how badly he wanted her at that party. "What evening are we talking about?" she asked, glancing at her calendar.

"Friday the thirteenth. Good day for a party, isn't it?"

"If you're not superstitious."

"Not me," Broderick replied smoothly. "I believe you make your own luck, your own opportunities."

Vandoren Cosmetics was an irresistible lure, but Brittany didn't trust Grant Broderick's motives. And Devon didn't trust him at all. Which, Brittany decided, was probably a mark in Broderick's favor at this point.

"Maybe I could call you at the end of the week? I'll try to make it, but I've got a few things to juggle...."

Broderick's satisfied chuckle came over the line. He was convinced he'd really hooked her. Well, he hadn't, she thought with a smile, but she was willing to keep an open mind.

She hung up and immediately called Jessica.

"Vandoren Cosmetics?" Jessica repeated. "Brittany, sweetheart, why are you even consulting me? This is an opportunity you can't afford to miss!"

"I know. It's just that I'm wary of Grant Broderick. I'm sure he intends to turn me into his next client—among other things," she added dryly.

"Hmm. Well, as for being a client of Broderick's, you'd be in good company. From what I understand, the man has an incredible following." Jessica mentioned a few names and even Brittany was impressed.

Brittany had handled her own financial affairs from the time she'd left Nora Castle's agency and had carefully monitored each and every one of her investments. She knew that her only fault was that she may have been a bit too conservative, and she wondered if she was being overly cautious about Broderick's business sense. She didn't particularly like the man, but then she'd dealt with a lot of people she hadn't liked who had been successful in business—Bryant Berkshire was a prime example.

"If Broderick's after your body and mind, in addition to your bankbook, you're on your own," Jessica went on. "But I think you can handle him."

"Thanks...I think."

"Just don't let him get you to sign on the dotted line until you're ready."

Brittany was amused that Jessica was acting so motherly. "So tell me, what should I say to my host when he starts shoving contracts in one hand and a pen in the other?''

"Just say, 'I'll think about it.' He'll get the message."

"I hope you're right."

Brittany found herself longing to talk to Devon once more and was stunned by that revelation. What was she thinking of, asking Devon's advice?

She shook her head in amazement. Rationally she knew she could never trust Devon again, but her emotions weren't convinced. Seeing him again had awakened a storm of feelings she would rather have let lie.

Remembering her father's wish, Brittany sighed. Would she ever be able to put her feelings about Devon in perspective?

Grant Broderick's home was one of ten condominiums at the end of a sweeping drive lined with palm trees. It was above and to the north of Malibu Beach with a view of the curved crescent of city and sand that ended at the tip of the Palos Verdes Peninsula.

"A great investment," Broderick was saying to a sumptuous woman in navy silk when Brittany was escorted inside by a manservant. "There are still two left," he went on, guiding his attentive listener to the stucco balcony and pointing out a corner unit with a spectacular view.

Brittany listened in amusement. She was certain she was hearing a sales pitch; Broderick probably owned the whole block of condominiums personally.

She'd been doing some homework on her host since his invitation to the party. What she'd learned had elevated her opinion of Grant Broderick and made her wonder if Devon wasn't barking up the wrong tree.

Broderick's reputation was impeccable, his list of successes outstripping his losses by a huge margin. Although, like most investment firms, Broderick's urged its clients to diversify, gems were where most of his clients put their money.

Brittany had to admit she was intrigued. She'd never invested in precious stones before. Her main reason for coming to Broderick's party had been to meet Marjorie Vandoren, but now she realized she was no longer so opposed to the idea of talking to her host. Where her investments were concerned, she had to keep an open mind.

"Champagne?"

Brittany accepted the profferred glass from a woman dressed in a black uniform and wondered just how "small" Broderick's party was going to be. People were already filling the spacious rooms; some she recognized, all exuding affluence. Brittany wandered among them, chatting amiably. It wasn't really her type of affair but she decided to grin and bear it.

Marjorie Vandoren was a thin, sharp-faced woman who smoked incessantly. Brittany caught sight of her in the den but speaking to her privately looked next to impossible. Marjorie was surrounded by a group of incredibly chic women and fast-talking men, and Brittany didn't have the gall to push herself into the fray, hoping for a few minutes of the cosmetic heiress's time.

Instead she squeezed herself back through the crowd and walked onto the now empty balcony. Twilight was painting the horizon shades of lavender and silver, and she leaned against the wrought-iron railing, inhaling a long breath of sharp sea air. She felt stifled by the crowd and wondered ruefully if coming to Broderick's party had been such a great idea after all.

"There you are."

Brittany turned from her silent contemplation of the coastline to greet her host. Broderick was dressed in a pair of casual slacks and an open-throat silk shirt. He looked flushed with pleasure, and Brittany could only surmise that the party was a huge success for him.

"You have a beautiful view," she complimented him.

He nodded in satisfaction. "One of the best."

"I hear there are still two condominiums available."

He gave her a sharp look, but his heightened interest died as he saw the amusement lurking around her mouth. "There's more to you than meets the eye, Brittany Daniels..." he murmured. "I would love to work with you."

Brittany turned back to the view, watching the waves glide into shore far below them. "I'll think about it," she said with an inner smile.

"I'm serious, Brittany."

"I know. So am I."

Broderick looked very pleased with himself. "I'll take that as a positive sign. Before you leave, I'd like to talk business."

Brittany wasn't ready to get down to brass tacks. She shook her head apologetically and said, "I don't want to rush into anything. Why don't you call me? Say, next week?"

"Well—" he scowled, not altogether happy with her evasiveness "—I'll have to see. I might not be able to get to you so quickly."

"Anytime's fine," she assured him.

Broderick seemed about to say something else, but then he glanced through the sliding glass door and waved to someone inside. Brittany smiled at the thought that he'd found a new quarry, but the next second her smile fell as he said, "By the way, I took the liberty of inviting another guest, an old friend of yours. Oh, and here he is now...."

Brittany swung around before Broderick's words had completely registered, her eyes widening at the sight of Devon. Her throat closed in on itself. He was weaving his way through the crowd toward them.

Brittany couldn't speak. With an effort she dragged her eyes away from Devon, hoping Broderick hadn't heard her surprised intake of breath. There was a Machiavellian side to Grant Broderick, she decided. Somehow he'd sensed she wasn't as friendly with Devon as she'd implied at the airport and he was testing her.

"I didn't think Devon Gallagher came to this kind of affair," she managed to say.

"Neither did I," Broderick answered easily. "But he was more than willing."

I'll bet, Brittany thought. Devon wouldn't pass up such a golden opportunity to investigate. "I wonder why," she murmured.

"Maybe because you're here?"

"We're not that close, Mr. Broderick."

Grant Broderick's smile did nothing to ease Brittany's nerves. "I'm glad to hear it. More champagne?"

"Please."

Devon had been captured by a young woman with a deep tan who was elegantly wrapped in a flowing white gown. Both shoulders were bare and there was a slit from hem to hip. But as attractive as his companion was, Devon's blue eyes were focused determinedly on Brittany.

Feeling breathless, Brittany followed Grant Broderick. It would be better to meet Devon in the crowd, she determined, than be trapped with him on the secluded balcony. She might even be able to avoid him entirely.

That hope died when Devon detached himself from the lovely woman in white and came straight to her side.

"How's the party?" he asked.

Brittany tried to ignore her racing pulse. "Terminal. I was thinking of leaving." The woman Devon had walked away from gave Brittany a venomous glare, then caught the arm of another handsome man. Brittany called on her courage and asked, "Did you know I'd be here?"

Devon's brows raised at her directness. "Would it make a difference?"

The waiter offered Brittany another glass of champagne and she accepted gratefully, turning away from Devon's unnerving stare. She felt his eyes travel over her, glad that she'd worn a gown whose plunging neckline was covered by a short beaded jacket. Light flashed off the hundreds of crystal beads.

"Don't answer questions with questions, Devon," she said, avoiding an answer.

"Yes, I knew you'd be here."

Brittany took a long sip of champagne, wishing she didn't always feel so off balance around him.

"What are you doing here?" he asked, watching her with serious blue eyes.

There was a thread of hostility in his voice, and Brittany wondered what was going through his mind. "Oh, I don't know. I thought it might be fun."

Devon's mouth was grim as he slanted a narrow look at their approaching host. "I thought you and Broderick weren't close acquaintances."

Brittany's nerves were stretched to breaking. "We're not. I just accepted an invitation to a party. End of story."

"Oh, come on, Britt—" he said tensely, but whatever else he might have said was cut off by the arrival of their host.

"The waiter already found you, I see," Grant Broderick interrupted them, smiling at Brittany. "Would you care for a glass of champagne, Mr. Gallagher? I seem to have ended up with two."

"Thank you." Devon was polite but Broderick gave him a long look anyway.

"I saw your exposé on the rock band that died in an airplane crash," Broderick said. "There are a lot of questions still unanswered. Do you have any theories?"

"Lots of them. But no proof."

"A pity." Broderick turned to Brittany and touched her arm. "Marjorie Vandoren's asked about you, dear. Don't make yourself too scarce."

He smiled and turned to greet some of his other guests. Brittany tried to do the same but Devon caught her arm. She twisted to glare at him, but the look on his face melted her resistance. She saw lines of strain around his mouth, and his eyes were full of regret.

"What do I have to do to call a truce?" he asked softly.

Brittany's eyes flashed with surprise. "Are you sure you want to?"

"For the time being, yes. Since our paths seem destined to cross, I think it would save us both a lot of grief."

Brittany inhaled a deep breath, crystal beads dancing and reflecting light. She didn't know how good she looked to him at that moment, but Devon noticed everything about her, the sculpted cheekbones, the startlingly thick lashes surrounding amethyst eyes, the smooth skin of her throat and neck....

He shook his head and remembered whom he was with and what she'd done. The memory horrified him. Yet her beauty nearly knocked him off his feet. Why now? He hadn't really felt this way about her in the past.

"I don't know, Devon," she murmured, wishing she didn't feel so isolated even with the moving sea of people around them. She didn't know if she could meet his request. She was still healing beneath the fragile scars Devon's wounds had left on her.

His smile appeared briefly. "All right. But can't we make a stab at coexistence?"

"Brittany Daniels?"

Both Devon and Brittany turned at the sound of Marjorie Vandoren's voice. Marjorie shook Brittany's hand, her sharp eyes traveling critically over the younger woman's face.

"Grant said you'd be here," she said in a voice that was accustomed to being listened to. "You've heard, of course, of Toujours."

Beside her, Devon stiffened. Brittany looked at him. His cold expression reminded her of what he thought of her modeling—what he'd always thought of her modeling. *Some things never change,* she thought sadly.

"Of course," Brittany answered Marjorie. Toujours had hardly been a well-kept secret—more like a proclamation from the reigning house of beauty.

"Would you be interested in doing a photo session?"

Around her, murmurs of surprise blended with the subtle mood music issuing from the condominium's built-in speakers. Brittany's attention was distracted by Devon's dangerous stillness. She tried to ignore him as she said, "I'd be privileged, Mrs. Vandoren."

The news wove through the room as quickly as the juiciest Hollywood gossip. By no means had Brittany already been selected as the Toujours woman, but she was now a giant leap ahead of the competition.

Marjorie Vandoren acknowledged Brittany's companion with an appreciative lift of her brows. "Mr. Gallagher."

"It's nice to see you again, Marjorie."

She looked skeptical, and Brittany remembered the stock takeover that had been attempted by Vandoren Cosmetics—Devon's reporting had brought it to the public attention.

"What brings you here tonight, hmm?" she asked him.

Devon hesitated and Brittany waited, holding her breath. His presence at Grant Broderick's was so out of character that the gossip mill was revving up. But she knew he couldn't divulge his real reasons. To her horror, he slanted a lazy look in her direction, then planted her hand firmly in the crook of his elbow.

Marjorie Vandoren peered down her nose. "Be careful, Miss Daniels. This man's known for sifting through ashes to find a story. Be sure all your skeletons are safely locked away."

Brittany managed a thin smile and said, "I don't think Devon will find anything he doesn't know about already."

"Miss Daniels's closet is clean, Marjorie." Devon spoke with grace but Brittany could feel his tension radiating through the steel tautness of his arm.

Brittany didn't know how much more of this conversation she could stand. "Excuse me a moment, won't you?" she murmured, then headed for the nearest open doorway.

Devon caught up with her at the side door that led to the pool area.

Before he could speak, Brittany hissed, "Just what do you think you're doing?" She looked around, glad they were out of earshot of the group of wide-eyed watchers.

"Saving my cover." His smile was self-deprecating. "Bother you that much?"

"We were linked together in the past, Devon. Who knows? Someone might remember."

Devon shrugged. "So much the better."

Brittany could stand it no longer. She swept through the open door, thinking she was a fool to feel anything for him at all. He'd used her in the past; he was using her still. When she was younger she'd convinced herself he'd loved her, too. Now she knew differently.

A breeze from the ocean helped relieve the late-fall heat as Brittany walked down the steps to a central garden area that looked out over the ocean. Impatiens and oleander bushes, thick with white blossoms, lined the tile walkway, and at the end of the path stood a secluded cedar gazebo, its overhead lattice strung with hanging pots of fuchsia.

"I told you before," Devon's clear voice said, "you can't run away from yourself."

Brittany didn't turn around. She heard his shoes scrape on the step that led to the gazebo. "What do you want, Devon?'' she demanded, wrapping her arms protectively beneath her breasts. "I saw your reaction to Marjorie Vandoren's request for a photo session. Don't you think I know how you feel about my work? About *me*?''

The silence that followed could have meant a dozen different things, but Brittany took it as his unspoken agreement. She half turned, regarding him warily. She didn't trust Devon. And unfortunately she didn't quite trust herself where he was concerned.

Moonlight threaded through the latticed trellis, casting strange shadows across Devon's face as he walked the few feet to meet Brittany in the center of the floor. "You don't know how I feel about you," he said flatly.

"Don't I? It's written all over you." The last thing Brittany had intended to do was bring up the past. Yet now there seemed to be no escaping it. Since offense was usually the best defense, she said with remarkable poise, "You still haven't forgiven me for getting pregnant."

Devon caught his breath in surprise. Brittany turned away, hunching her shoulders. Inside she was hurting. She was no good at this. Wounding Devon was only wounding herself.

She had the feeling he wanted to say a hundred things—a thousand things—to hurt her back. He shifted and moved away. His restraint was even worse on Brittany, making weariness and pain fill her very soul.

"Your career's always been the most important thing to you," he said at length, his voice controlled.

Brittany's head turned sharply, moonlight catching the tiny diamond studs in her ears. "Am I supposed to feel guilty? Can you honestly say you're any different?''

"Yes." He ground out the word savagely, as if furious that she could even suggest they were alike.

"Well, forgive me if I don't see it, Devon. I remember how you pursued the story at the agency. I just got caught in the middle."

The sound of one of the condominium's windows sliding open shattered the cool silence. Music, voices and the occasional lilt of laughter floated outward.

"I don't want to talk about it anymore," Brittany said.

"Neither do I." There was a slight hesitation, then with a touch of weary humor Devon added, "See? We can agree on something."

Brittany wished she wasn't so aware of him. In the past she'd succumbed to his charm but she'd vowed that it would never happen again. Yet here she was, talking with him! It seemed so unreal.

He never really loved you, she reminded herself, yet she was aware that whatever she'd felt for him in the past hadn't truly died. It was still smoldering—buried but still alive.

Brittany exhaled slowly. "Why are you after Grant Broderick?"

Devon frowned, moving to her side. His gaze followed hers across the ink-dark Pacific. "I'd rather not talk about Broderick. I don't want to spread rumors and I don't want you involved."

Brittany's mouth curved. "I get the feeling I already am involved."

"No."

He was so positive that she turned to stare at him. "Is that what you really feel, Devon? Or is that just wishful thinking? Where do I fit in, according to you?"

"Your being on the plane with Broderick was just coincidence."

Devon's flat assessment made Brittany's inner hurt deepen. "You sound as if you're trying to convince yourself. You really have a lot of respect for my character, don't you?"

She would have walked away from him then, but he stepped in front of her. She glared at him, angry with herself all over again for letting it matter.

"I just don't want you involved with him. Especially right now."

"I'm not involved with him."

"Brittany..." Devon searched for the right words. He couldn't seem to find any that would come out the way he wanted. "Until this whole thing's over, the less you have to do with Broderick, the better."

"Just stay out of my life, Devon. I don't tell you how to run yours. Give me the same courtesy."

"I don't want to see you get hurt as a by-product of this investigation!" he threw out in exasperation.

Hurt? Brittany could scarcely believe her ears. "You have no right..." she whispered. Dear God! He'd hurt her more than anyone.

"I have every right," he growled back. After a pain-filled pause, he heaved a resentful sigh and amended, "I *had* every right."

Devon clasped his hands behind his neck and closed his eyes, squeezing tense muscles. His jacket gaped open and Brittany saw the taught fabric of his shirt stretched over his chest. With a stab at honesty he said, "But your career, your modeling, got in the way."

"I thought we weren't going to talk about the past," Brittany murmured. She looked down at the empty glass of champagne still clutched in her hand. She wished she had more. She wanted to find some kind of sweet oblivion and if champagne would work...

Why didn't you ever call me, she wanted to ask. *Why didn't you ask about the baby? Why don't you now? If we don't talk about it, does that mean it never happened?* Brittany formed the questions in her mind, trying to find a way to utter them aloud. But she couldn't. The words just wouldn't come.

Devon lapsed into silence. She didn't know he was fighting back a storm of emotions that left him amazed at the power of his feelings.

Their conversation had left her emotionally raw and bleeding. Brittany swallowed and shifted past him. "It's time for me to leave."

"Did you come by taxi?"

Devon's voice was drawn and tight. Brittany hesitated. "Yes," she admitted.

"Could I drive you home?"

Brittany shook her head. She could feel Devon's heat in the cool semidarkness, and it was as dangerously seductive as the drifting, fragrant scent of the oleander blossoms.

"Brittany..."

The haunted tone of his voice made her heart stop. She could see him looking down at her, searching her face. Her mouth was suddenly very dry.

"Why did you keep the pearls?"

The sound of enthusiastic clapping and the tinkle of piano keys said someone was warming up to play. Moments later faint music, soft and flowing, filled the night sky. Brittany found herself holding her breath.

She let the air out in a rush and wondered how truthful she should be. Setting her glass down a bit unsteadily on the gazebo's rail, she said simply, "Because you gave them to me."

A drowning sensation poured over Devon, a sensation that always preceded disaster. Emotions he didn't want for this woman, for Brittany, were stirring within him.

"Let me take you home," he said roughly, ignoring his own common sense. He put his hand to the small of her back, intending to guide her toward his car.

She turned suddenly, the softness of her breast accidentally brushing his chest. "I don't think it's a good idea, Devon. I don't want to fight...or talk."

Desire flickered through Devon, unexpected and unwanted. Rationally, he knew Brittany was the last woman in the world he should be thinking about in this way.

Yet she was different now from the woman she had been. More self-assured, yet less convinced of her feminine power. Had he done that to her?

He led her to his car, ignoring the rebellious line of her mouth. "Look, I don't want to fight, either. But we have a history, and I'd like to remove some of the bad feelings that have hung on."

Devon was a little amazed at himself. He was saying things he felt but hadn't actually formed into thoughts. He frowned. It worried him, the way he responded to this woman he'd hated for so long. Or was hate really the right word?

"Are you speaking for yourself?" Brittany asked, but she let him open the door of the tawny BMW.

"You don't have any bad feelings?"

"About you, Devon?" One look at the steely blue of his eyes and Brittany knew she couldn't fool him with false bravado. "Some," she admitted on a whisper.

She was leaning against the car, her hands braced on either side of her. Devon just looked at her, none of the hostility she'd come to expect evident in his expression. Brittany felt her own vulnerability and wanted to cry *I'm not in love with you anymore!* But she just stared at him through wide eyes, wondering what he could possibly be thinking about her.

"Brittany!"

Grant Broderick came down the tiered brick steps of his entryway, breaking the tension spiraling between herself and Devon. "You're leaving?" he asked, looking disappointed.

"I've got to work tomorrow," she apologized.

"Busy lady," he observed with a smile. He glanced casually at Devon, then looked back at Brittany. "I'll call you next week. Maybe I can squeeze in a lunch."

Brittany just smiled in agreement. She could feel Devon's disapproval, though he didn't move a muscle. She slid into the passenger seat of his car.

She waved at Grant Broderick as Devon closed the door very softly after her. For just a moment she caught his vivid blue gaze, the smoky passion and desire that hovered beneath his cool exterior. Her arms broke out in gooseflesh.

My God, she thought, as he climbed into the seat beside her and eased the car into gear, *what have I got myself into?*

Chapter Four

Brittany felt the silence between them as if it were another presence. It robbed her of speech, the words sticking in her throat. It ridiculed her one faint hope that this might be a chance to bury all the bad feelings between them, and at the same time it made the hopelessness of their situation all too clear.

There seemed to be no solution. The past was the past, and raking it up did nothing but cause more pain.

Brittany stared unseeingly out the window, acutely conscious of the man beside her. She shot him a quick surreptitious glance, the down-turned mouth and the lines of grim disillusionment bracketing it, leaving a deep impression on her mind. The past wasn't pleasant for him, either, she thought resignedly, and her mood of depression increased. It would be nice for both of them if they could clear the air once and for all. Unfortunately, the chance for any kind of reconciliation was practically nil. She felt it and apparently Devon did, too.

"Where do you live?" Devon asked, as he maneuvered the car back down the winding road from Broderick's condominium.

"Redondo Beach." Brittany frowned down at her hands. With Devon's connections he probably already knew exactly where she lived and which house was hers, unless his interest in her was less than he made out—something she would have banked on before their surprise meeting at the airport but now wondered about.

If he was interested in her now it was only because of Grant Broderick. Nothing more. *Devon stopped loving you years ago,* she reminded herself firmly. *If he ever really loved you at all.*

Brittany felt cold inside. That question was one she still asked herself.

"Do you live alone?"

Brittany jumped. The thoughts in her head made her feel guilty—like a traitor. Devon's dark head turned and he glanced her way briefly. Pulling herself together, Brittany answered, "Yes."

"So do I." Devon's gaze narrowed on the traffic. "It's a lot simpler than having to share."

Brittany could think of no answer so she turned her face to the side window. The smaller cities that made up Los Angeles—El Segundo, Venice, Manhattan Beach—sped by in a blur, blending unsung into one another as Devon drove the BMW south to Brittany's home. Again the car filled with silence. There seemed to be absolutely nothing left to say.

It hadn't always been this way. When they'd first met, both had been eager to share. Too eager, perhaps. Brittany had given him pieces of herself that couldn't be retrieved. Devon, too, had let her see his inner self—the blinding determination that drove him, the idealism that made him always seek the truth, the passion that was always carefully controlled. Yet Brittany had sensed his aloofness. She'd realized, with a woman's knowledge, how much he'd deliberately held back from her.

His love—if one could euphemistically call it that— and trust in her had been fragile. Her pregnancy had shattered both.

Brittany swallowed hard. As if she'd planned the whole scenario! She should be furious with him for such an outdated, unfair, chauvinistic viewpoint, but all the pain of her miscarriage had robbed her of wasted anger.

Brittany gathered her beaded purse into her lap and pointed to a side street. "Turn right up there, then veer to the left at the first intersection. My house is the one on the corner, above the beach." Devon followed her directions, pulling into the driveway of an eggshell-colored stucco house. The street was sloped upward from the beach, making the rear of Brittany's home one level. But the front was too full stories, garage underneath, living room above. A bank of white-paned windows wrapped around the entire upper floor and a tiled roof capped the house in the beautiful Spanish style so common to Southern California.

Devon parked in her driveway, pulling on the emergency brake to combat the steep grade. He looked upward at her home but said nothing. The lamp in the window seemed to glow like a warm invitation.

"Thank you for bringing me home." Brittany was anxious to get away. Being with Devon had a draining effect on her that seemed to sap all her self-respect and confidence.

"My pleasure."

The engine was idling and Brittany hurriedly felt for the door handle. Devon looked at her and for a moment she caught his brooding gaze. "Good luck," she said a trifle breathlessly. She was embarrassed that she could come up with so little to say. This might be the last time she saw Devon. The thought made her heart contract with pain.

Devon glanced past her, taking in her dazzling vista. "You've got the choicest lot around," he observed.

Brittany was stung. She inhaled sharply, knowing she was much too sensitive to anything Devon said regarding her career and money.

"It's not Bel Air," she replied shortly.

Devon's dark head turned around, his eyes shadowed but focused sharply on her face. "Is that where you want to be?"

"No. It's just...I sometimes..." Brittany shook her head and made an impatient sound. "It's just difficult to talk to you, Devon. Everything's so hard."

"It's no picnic for me, either." She heard the resignation in his tone but his eyes gave nothing away.

"Then let's not do it anymore," she suggested, unlatching the door and sliding across the seat. "Thanks for bringing me home. You didn't have to."

"I wanted to." His hands flexed on the steering wheel.

Brittany climbed from the car, leaning down to smile a goodbye, but the look on his face stripped her of speech. For just an instant he looked desolate, his face gaunt, his eyes filled with an emptiness that stopped her heart. Brittany's pain swelled in her chest. She reacted without thinking. "I'm sorry," she whispered. "I'm so sorry."

The change in Devon was instantaneous. His face closed up and a frightening hardness tightened the skin over his cheekbones. Brittany blinked, wondering if she'd imagined it all. Her face flushed with hot, burning color. She was horrified at herself, at how guilty he could make her feel. She turned blindly away but Devon's arm whipped out, his hand clasping her wrist.

"So am I," he muttered harshly. "I wish I didn't feel the things I do."

"I've got to go, Devon," she whispered. She moved a half step but his hand only tightened. A warm wind blew her dress against her legs, tangling her hair, turning the crystal breads on her jacket to flickering gems. But the tears that threatened the corners of her eyes were from within. She ached inside. She wanted to run away and sob forever.

"Brittany..."

She tore her arm away, walking quickly along the sidewalk to the tiered stairway that led to her front door.

Devon cut the engine to his car and the silence was shattering. He was out of the car and next to her before she could even think clearly.

"Wait. Britt, for God's sake..." Devon sighed and touched her arm, this time in entreaty. "I can't take this. It's driving me out of my mind."

Brittany's lips parted. She stared at him, seeing his misery, not understanding at all what forces brought him so much pain.

"I don't believe things can ever be completely forgotten between us but I'd like to at least reach a state of peace," Devon said heavily. "Wouldn't you?"

"I...yes." Brittany's emotions were churning within her. If she could, she realized in surprise, she would like a whole lot more than just that.

"Then let's take this opportunity. Would you like to go for a walk on the beach?"

Brittany looked past him to the night-darkened beach, the white-tipped breakers that turned into a spreading liquid blanket over the sand. She wanted to talk to Devon. And a walk on the beach was preferable to inviting him inside. She didn't think her nerves would be able to take that.

But what would it accomplish? She was already stripped raw and bleeding.

"All right." She heard her voice agree and berated herself for being such a gullible fool. But she didn't turn back. Instead she walked back down the steps, grateful that Devon stepped aside so she could get by without brushing against him. Devon thrust his hands deep within the pockets of his black dinner jacket, as if he didn't want to make the mistake of touching her at all.

They walked in silence down the small flight of cement steps that led to the beach, two people, formally dressed for an evening out, taking a stroll beside the sea. The scenario appealed to Brittany's sense of humor. She leaned against the rail and pulled off her sandals, dangling them from her fingers.

"Your shoes are going to get filled with sand if you don't take them off," she said.

"You're right." Devon looked at the pink-tipped nails of Brittany's bare toes and promptly sat down on the bottom step, taking off both shoes and socks. He left his shoes on the step and raised an eyebrow at Brittany, loosening the black tie above his snowy white shirt.

"I haven't walked along the beach in years," he admitted thoughtfully.

Brittany dragged her eyes away from the picture he made—black wind-ruffled hair, dark skin above a starched white collar, black jacket and slacks, a gentle, almost wistful smile. "You work too hard," she murmured, gathering up her long skirt and walking through the cool sand toward the water.

"So do you."

He caught up with her but kept several feet between them as Brittany stopped at the water's edge. "You didn't like it that Marjorie Vandoren offered me a chance at Toujours, did you?" she asked calmly.

Devon hesitated. "No, I didn't."

"Why?" The surf rushed inward, sweeping coldly over Brittany's bare feet. "Why does it matter to you at all?"

The sound Devon made was self-deprecating. "God only knows. But for some reason it does."

"And you wish it didn't."

"Maybe. Yes. It would be a lot simpler just to forget about certain...things."

His honesty made her feel worse. She was almost glad she didn't fully understand what horribly hostile feelings he had bottled up inside him, especially as she seemed to be at their root. What had she done to him that filled him with so much loathing? Surely her pregnancy couldn't be the only reason. Even given that Devon thought she'd tried to trap him (how could he think she would be so calculating?) his anger seemed way out of proportion. That was all in the past. Given the kind of monumental crises that happened in life, Devon's turbulent emotions over a long, nearly forgotten issue made no sense.

And his emotions were turbulent. One moment he was furious, the next his face reflected bittersweet sorrow. And before she could understand his feelings he would change again, sending off vibrant waves of frustration, anger and resignation.

"I don't know if there is any peace for us," she said softly. "Being with you is like walking through a mine field."

"Thanks," he said dryly.

"You know what I mean. I don't even know if there's a topic we can discusss freely."

Devon's mouth curved. "Oh, surely there's one."

"Then you pick it. I can't."

Devon pinched his nose thoughtfully. The loose ends of his tie flapped across his shoulder and Brittany curbed the temptation to smooth them back down.

"It's supposed to rain tomorrow."

Brittany regarded him suspiciously. "Oh?"

Devon nodded. "Uh-huh. A low-pressure area is moving down from the Canadian coast. We're to expect high winds and rain."

For a moment she stared at him in bafflement. Then she realized he'd picked his topic. She melted a bit inside. "I'm partial to stormy weather," she said softly.

Devon was looking at her not quite smiling, but indulgence twitched the corners of his mouth. "Then you should be in seventh heaven," he replied. "As long as you're insured."

"I'm insured. And I was reroofed a year ago."

"Then you can look forward to having the wind blow the smog away and the rain to clear the air. I like a good storm myself."

Brittany fought back a tide of feeling that had no place here. *Damn Devon*. He could be so charming when he wanted to!

"Devon..."

"Hmm?"

Brittany tried to speak but the words were lodged in her throat. In her mind she could hear herself saying, *I know we can't have what we once had, but I'd like to be your friend.* But the words were impossible. They seemed inadequate, pointless. Instead Brittany said, a trifle hesitantly, "We haven't seen each other for a few years. You've been busy, making a name for yourself. And I've been..."

"Doing the same?" he supplied quietly.

Brittany couldn't help blushing. He was right, of course. And she was painfully aware of what he thought of her career. "Yes, I suppose I have been. But not in the same way you have. You're a name on everyone's lips. You've made an impressive reputation for yourself by hard work, diligence and fair play."

Devon frowned, uncomfortable under Brittany's quiet words of praise. "You can save the accolades. I'm not ready for sainthood yet."

"I'm just trying to say...to apologize...for not realizing your dedication before."

Devon inhaled deeply. "Don't apologize, Brittany. There's no need."

"Yes, there is. I know that I nearly ruined your investigation into anorexia at the Castle agency—"

"You helped me with Tricia," Devon interrupted savagely.

"And I know what I was like. What I was doing. Oh, Devon, I've wished for a long time I could apologize." Once the words started tumbling out, Brittany couldn't stop herself. "If I could I'd change the way things turned out. I was young and silly, and I blame myself for—"

"Britt!"

"Devon, it's okay." She was incapable of understanding his terrible anguish so she did't even try. Instead she concentrated on saying what was foremost in her mind. "I just wanted to say—congratulations. I really am happy you've been so successful. And I'm glad I've had a chance to tell you." She smiled uncertainly. "That's all."

You've come a long way in a very short period of time, Brittany reminded herself wryly. It had been only a few weeks since she'd seen him at the airport, since the painful memories had been resurrected, since she'd been afraid to face Devon. Yet even then she'd wanted to explain herself. It was like a catharsis finally to speak her feelings out loud.

Devon was at a total loss. He had difficulty hiding the peculiar emotions her simple honest words inspired. He felt as though she'd bared some secret part of himself and torn it apart. He didn't know how to react.

He was still sorting through a dozen separate feelings when Brittany added lightly, "I didn't mean to break into confession."

The thought of what might come next burned through Devon and he said quickly, "Let's drop it, okay? I appreciate what you're trying to say but believe me, it's not necessary. It's all over and done with." His voice was flat and final.

Brittany's face fell into hurt surprise before she could get herself under control. Devon watched her fight vainly to keep from letting him see, hating himself for being the one to break the easy mood they'd both tried so hard to create. But he couldn't let her go on. He was shocked, amazed and sick with himself that he could be so easily taken under her influence. And he was afraid she might even convince him *she* had been the one who'd been wronged, not he.

Her eyes were wide open, unblinking. But her bottom lip was trembling. She wasn't as good as he was at hiding her feelings. Devon watched, his insides twisting in torture. God, but she was beautiful! Even in the darkness the perfect planes of her face were easily visible, the long sweep of her lashes an unconsciously seductive invitation.

The irony of it was that Devon had never been the kind of man to fall for a beautiful face. Before Brittany, he'd purposely steered clear of unusually attractive women, thinking—wrongly and rather chauvinistically—that beauty was in direct and opposite proportion to brains. In the past, he'd always been moved by the type of woman whose looks were secondary to her character and personality.

But Brittany had made a mockery of his theories. Her intelligence was on a par with her looks. He hadn't fully realized that in the beginning, when she'd been so eager to be involved in his investigation. But he'd gradually learned there was more to Brittany Daniels as a woman than he would ever have suspected, and his feelings for her had grown deep and impossibly strong.

And then—

Devon's mind snapped closed. He still felt betrayed. After all this time! What in the world was he doing with her now?

"Maybe we should go back..." Brittany suggested. She turned with that thought in mind.

"Are you ready to?" Devon's voice sounded odd to his own ears. Though he knew it was the sane decision to make, he couldn't let her go.

"Aren't you?" Brittany's eyes were troubled.

"I should be, but I'm not."

Brittany tried to smile, a dimple denting her cheek for a brief moment. "Then pick another topic, Devon. We seem to be getting into dangerous territory again."

Devon sighed. "I think it's your turn to pick."

Brittany hesitated. "You could tell me about your work. And I don't mean Grant Broderick," she added hastily. "I was actually thinking about Paul Geller Glade—the serial killer that you did the in-depth story on."

It was hardly light conversation but it was the first thing that popped into Brittany's mind. She'd seen Devon's report and been horrified that he'd been in such close contact with Glade, a man who'd reportedly killed more than twenty people. Devon had made contact with Glade's suspected girlfriend and had been partially responsible for the man's capture.

Although Devon's report had been after the fact, she'd found herself trembling with fear as she watched and listened. The danger had been evident; the risks Devon had taken had turned her inside out.

"You don't want to hear about Glade," Devon said repressively.

"Maybe not," Brittany agreed. She smiled slightly. "But it's my turn to choose, and I would like to know how you got involved."

Devon's smile was grim. "Luck of the draw, I guess."

"Because of Melina Sanders?"

"She wrote me a letter," Devon admitted. "She said she'd been involved with Glade and that if I wanted some information, she was willing to talk. At that time there was a nationwide manhunt on for Glade. I couldn't pass up such an incredible opportunity."

Brittany rubbed her elbows briskly. "It was risky," she said flatly.

"A lot of my job is."

"Yes, but you pick the risks yourself. You have a choice."

Devon shook his head. "Not in this case. She came to me."

Brittany made a frustrated sound. "Don't con me, Devon. You always have a choice. You could have turned her down or convinced her to talk to someone else. It didn't have to be you."

Devon looked at her oddly. "Do you wish it hadn't been?"

Brittany stopped short. The fears she'd felt for him were coming out against her will. "I think the police are better suited to deal with people like Melina Sanders," she answered evasively. "Why did she choose you?"

"She'd seen me on television," Devon said, his mouth twisting.

Of course. Devon was a powerful presence on the screen, even more so in person. "What did she say?" Brittany asked.

"A lot." Devon's eyes narrowed and Brittany got the impression that his memories weren't pleasant. "It was Melina's testimony to the police that had put them on Glade's trail, but now she wanted to tell her story to the world. She'd actually witnessed him kill someone."

Brittany had heard some of this before but her face drained of color. The story was horrific enough, but Devon's involvement made it seem so much more real.

"And she'd seen other things. I was prepared when I went to see her, but even so, her tale made my blood run cold."

Brittany's mouth went dry. "Yet she was his girlfriend?"

Devon nodded. "You have to understand about Melina. She's tough, impervious, totally without fear or empathy. Her emotions are completely repressed. They don't seem to affect her. The fact that she showed no horror or fear is probably what saved her from becoming a victim."

Brittany shivered. Devon's interview had shown some of those facets of Melina Sanders. She was an attractive woman but had the tough-eyed, street-mean look of someone who had seen the worst that life could offer and had somehow managed to survive unscathed.

"I don't think Glade knew what to think of Melina," Devon went on after a moment of thought. "She was a woman he couldn't terrorize and he was fascinated with her. But after she set the police after him, he was ready to kill her. He was actually at her house when the police caught him. I was there, too."

Brittany blinked. She didn't remember that. "With the police?"

Devon gave her a sidelong glance. "No..." he said slowly. "They were outside, watching her place. Apparently they thought he might come back. I was inside, going over some final material for the broadcast with Melina." He frowned. "She was as excited as I've ever seen her. After I'd been there about fifteen minutes she suddenly said, 'Guess what? Paul called tonight. I think he's in Los Angeles.'"

"Oh, Devon..."

"Yes, 'Oh, Devon,'" he laughed. "It took everything I had to contain my shock. God, but Melina was a cool one. It was an adventure to her. Period. She either didn't see or didn't care about the danger."

"Why didn't you leave?" Brittany demanded in a strident voice.

"I was getting a story," he said simply.

"Devon."

"I didn't realize how close Glade was," Devon went on calmly. "Otherwise I would have hightailed it out of there. I didn't have time to warn the police before he was suddenly in the room. I found out later he'd climbed in through a back window."

Brittany's eyes were round with horror. She couldn't speak.

"Everything happened so fast I didn't really have time to be scared," Devon explained gently. "He took one look at me, realized he'd been set up and lunged for Melina. She pulled out a gun and shot him. End of story."

Brittany was shaking. "You didn't report all of that."

"The police were there instantly. They handled everything. Melina told them he'd tried to attack her so she shot him. I said the same. When I reported Glade's capture I said I was on the scene—that seemed like enough."

Brittany inhaled shakily. "I just always assumed that you got that information later."

"It was Melina's story, not mine," Devon said dismissively. "She's writing a book now and she's been approached for the movie rights. I'd just as soon be removed from all of that." A faint smile flickered across Devon's lips. "Want to hear any more about my job?"

"No." Brittany was positive. "I'm lucky I didn't know at the time. I would have been out of my mind. I never dreamed you would take such risks!"

Devon searched her pale face for several moments, reading her fear for him. He slipped an arm around her quaking shoulders and stared down at her. Brittany felt the warmth and security of his arm and gradually calmed down. She looked up at him, seeing the light blue gray of his iris against his dark pupil even in the moonlight.

"Does it matter so much to you?" he asked curiously.

Brittany wanted to pull her gaze away but couldn't. "Yes. Of course it does."

"Do *I* matter to you?"

Brittany's breath caught. He was looking at her so intently. "Well...yes..." She found it impossible to lie.

"My job is rarely so dangerous. Most of the time it's just routine."

"And the Broderick case?"

Devon smiled. "As you said, he hardly seems the type to smuggle."

"But you think he's done something." Against her will her pulse began to pound.

"Maybe." Devon shrugged as if to push the whole issue aside. "But Broderick's not Paul Geller Glade, either. Don't look so concerned, Britt."

She hadn't realized her face was giving away her inner feelings until Devon's soft words and the feel of his fingers smoothing the lines of worry from her forehead brought back all the impossibilities of their relationship. She was stunned that he would touch her so gently; it felt like a caress.

"Now you look afraid," he chided softly.

Brittany shook her head. She wasn't afraid. But she was wary. She didn't know what Devon wanted from her; she didn't know what she wanted from him. But intimacy between them, understanding, love, was something that just couldn't be.

Or could it?

Had she fooled herself into believing she and Devon were a past chapter because she was afraid of loving him again? Afraid that, like before, he couldn't love her? He'd hurt her deeply. Abandoned her when she'd needed him most. Yet she could almost forgive him that if she could just know what his reasons had been.

Devon leaned down and Brittany knew he was going to kiss her. She stopped breathing. But she did nothing to dissuade him. She just stared into the liquid blue of his eyes and waited.

He tipped her chin up to his face, letting his gaze roam over her moonlit face with a certain curiosity. Then his mouth brushed hers, soft and mobile. It was a brotherly kiss, nothing more, and Brittany's insides responded with straining desire. Passion moved within her. It took so little to awaken it that Brittany was frightened.

He pulled back, his thumb rubbing her chin. "Was that a mistake?"

"You tell me," Brittany laughed shakily.

For answer he dipped his head again, his kiss stronger, longer. Her heartbeat quickened into an erratic tempo. Brittany tensed. She was plunged into a nightmare of the past but all she could feel was Devon—his mouth, his arms, his body—and she was trembling with her need of him, just like before.

Devon felt her melt in his arms. He explored her mouth gently with his tongue, his own blood pounding like the surf in his ears. He struggled to remain aloof but passion was flooding his common sense. Her willingness was a bright spark to his desire and Devon pulled her roughly against him, his lips hardening, tasting, exploring. He kissed her chin, the delicate bones of her cheeks, her ear, her neck. Brittany's eyes closed, her head tipping back in ecstasy, a soft sigh escaping from her lips.

As quickly as it began it ended. Savagely, Devon pushed her away. Brittany sucked in a sharp breath of surprise and hurt. She saw his clenched hands, his rigid muscles. She witnessed how hard he tried to stamp out his passion and it filled her with desolation. She didn't know that Devon was wallowing in the black pit of his memories, that he was trying to clamp his mind shut to them but failing. She didn't know that he was swamped once again with guilt and anger and bewilderment. But she could feel his rejection and it was devastating.

Brittany began to tremble as realization crashed over her. All he felt was lust and he didn't even want that. She was deluding herself to think that there was anything left between them.

When are you going to learn?

"I think we should go back," she managed tonelessly. She was dying inside. It hurt even to breathe.

One of Devon's hands raked through his hair and she saw the fine tremor in his fingers. Brittany longed to wrap her arms around him and end his torment but she was frightened by the depth of his resentment. What had she done to him? She wanted to ask him but was afraid to.

Devon turned away from the sea but didn't look at her. His face was closed and controlled as they walked back across the sand, each of them silent, lost in thought. He stopped at the stairs to put on his shoes and Brittany watched with anguished eyes. She had the feeling that if she just tried a little harder she could reach him, yet nothing about his shuttered face was the least bit encouraging.

They walked to his car and Brittany managed a "Goodbye, Devon," as he opened the door. The interior light threw his face into relief and she could see clearly the grim lines beside his mouth.

He looked at her closely and she sensed that he wanted to say something important. Her heart pounded unevenly, but after a long moment he said only, "Goodbye, Britt," then folded his lean body into the car and started the engine.

From her porch, Brittany watched him leave. Her throat was hot and hurting, her chest tight. "I don't love him anymore," she whispered as she saw his taillights disappear around the corner.

She unlocked her front door and closed it behind her, leaning against it for a moment, her eyes squeezed shut. She was a terrible liar, even to herself. She still loved Devon. It was as plain to her now as it had been three years earlier.

But he hated her.

Brittany felt her eyes burn. Oh, he was attracted to her, but she wasn't so impressed with her womanly charms that she believed it was anything more than that. A man could be intrigued by a woman and still resent her at the same time. She'd learned that lesson the hard way—from Devon.

With weariness settled in every bone and joint, Brittany took off the beaded crystal jacket and the soft white gown. Then she washed her face and brushed her hair and crawled beneath the comforter on her bed.

She stared at the ceiling for a long time knowing sleep was impossible. She'd been successful in many ways, but she'd failed miserably with Devon. Just desserts, some would say. A way of evening out all the advantages she'd had.

But she would give it all away for Devon's love and respect. She'd known it deep down all along. It was one of life's cruel ironies that the girl who seemed to have everything, in reality had nothing at all.

Chapter Five

Devon savagely cranked down his windows, drawing in a deep lungful of cool night air. He felt hot and tired and uncomfortable and he needed something to clear his head. A drink would be nice. Maybe even two. With that simple pleasure planted firmly in the forefront of his mind he drove up the coast to his Malibu home.

But he couldn't escape his thoughts, and the past seemed very close tonight. He was furious with himself for reliving those days, yet he couldn't seem to stop. Seeing Brittany had brought it all back, and the worst of it was that given half a chance he knew he could fall for her all over again!

His right hand balled into a fist and he thumped the steering wheel in frustration. How could he be so stupid? He wouldn't have believed it was possible. But there was something about Brittany Daniels that got in his blood, making him forget all his sane reasons for dropping her from his life forever.

He thought of the day he'd first met her. He'd gone to see Nora Castle, the sole owner of the Castle modeling agency, to ask her for permission to interview her models. Though he'd known Nora for some time, his idea to expose anorexia and bulimia at her modeling agency hadn't pleased her at all.

"I don't need this, Devon," she'd said in her short, flat way. "I've got a business to run. Go play '60 Minutes' with someone else."

"I'm not just singling you out, Nora," he'd answered with a smile, "but I thought I'd start somewhere and you were the logical choice. I'm not trying to come down on you. I'm doing a story about the unrealistic expectations the whole country has about staying slim. And people get their ideas from television, films, advertising and the media. Being thin is in vogue—if it weren't your models would be rounder."

Nora's lined face had scowled. "I don't give a damn. Today is today. I can't worry about tomorrow."

Devon had tried to explain that his motive wasn't to crucify her business. "Ultraslim models aren't the cause. They're just a symptom of the overall obsession. And there are problems with being too thin— health problems. That's the whole thrust of my story."

"What a crusader you are," she'd muttered, but eventually she'd given in and let him talk to her models. Her unwillingness, however, had been felt by the whole squad. Only a few of the women had been interested in talking to him. Brittany was one of them.

He'd first seen her when Nora had introduced him to a group of six of her top models. "This is Devon Gallagher," she'd said. "He's here to do a story on anorexia and bulimia in the modeling industry."

Her disparaging tone had caused suspicious murmurs.

"What for? What's he trying to do?" an angular redhead had demanded.

Nora's mouth had lifted in irony. "Make a living. Just like the rest of us. Go ahead and be nice to him but be careful of the printed word."

She'd left then, giving Devon an amused look as six pairs of gorgeous eyes turned his way.

Brittany had stood out even in that lovely crowd. Her black hair was pinned loosely on her head, dark tendrils escaping to curl gently against the pale skin of her nape. Her violet eyes were wide and serious, yet their depths simmered with a kind of innocent seduction that Devon had found intriguing.

"What do you want to know?" she'd asked him directly, dimples appearing beside the beautiful curve of her lips.

"Everything. Anything. Let's start with a regular day. What time do you get up, what do you eat, what's your daily exercise routine, what do you do with your time off...?" He'd trailed off and looked expectant.

The redhead had laughed. "We try to date beautiful men. Interested?"

Devon had lifted his shoulders. "As long as you don't mind being pumped as a source."

"Go ahead, Mr. Gallagher," Brittany had said, her smile widening. "Pump away. But I'm afraid all you're going to discover is what a boring job modeling is."

Brittany had been more than willing to tell him about her work. She was helpful and honest and not afraid to make her opinion known. Though often she made light of how vacuous her job appeared, Devon had sensed how much it meant to her, how determined she was to succeed. At the time he'd admired her for it.

He'd spent a lot of time with her, much more than with any of the other models. But he'd kept himself distanced. He hadn't been eager for a romantic entanglement with anyone, especially a woman as overtly beautiful as Brittany Daniels. But it had been hard to stay so aloof, especially when Brittany's attraction for him became obvious. He could see it in her eyes, in the way she looked at him, and though it certainly stroked his ego, he'd had no idea how to deal with her adoration.

The night Brittany and the other Castle protégeés were modeling at the premiere of one of Los Angeles's newest designers, Devon had already amassed most of his information and had determined that although the Castle models were superslim, none of them appeared to be anorectic. He'd reached a dead end. And while he watched Brittany pose in one diaphanous gown after another, he'd decided it was time to stop dreaming about the dark-haired beauty. He knew his feelings for her weren't the same as hers for him. It would have been cruel and pointless to let things progress any farther.

He'd been still trying to find the words to end a relationship that had never truly begun when she came to him, breathless with her news.

"I think Tricia's bulimic," she'd said, darting a quick look over her shoulder as she told him of the scene she'd witnessed in the bathroom.

Devon had been unconvinced. Brittany was so young and open and eager that he wondered if she were imagining or, at the very least, exaggerating what she'd witnessed.

But she'd been adamant, and before he'd had a chance to really think through the consequences he was seated in the back of a taxi with her, arguing about the possibilities. They'd ended up at his apartment.

That had been his downfall. Alone, with only his own laughable control standing between them, he'd given in to a desire that had been steadily building and had become virtually impossible to ignore. Brittany's beauty and vulnerability and her irrepressible nature were an intoxicating combination. In a blind, passionate moment he'd given up the fight and made love to her, overwhelmed by her sensual and giving nature.

Her love was addictive. She was open and undemanding. Devon had been powerless to stop the rollercoaster speed of their relationship once it had begun. He'd let himself be swept away, yet he was consumed with self-hate, knowing he'd taken everything from her and offered nothing in return.

He wasn't in love with her. He was attracted to her, entranced by her, totally caught up in her spell, but he wasn't in love. He'd never lied to her and if Brittany had felt his distance, she hadn't let on. Even so, she'd become an important part of his life, helping him with the rest of his story on anorexia, spending her free time with him, relieving the pressures of those especially exhausting days, loving him with a selflessness that made him feel like a fraud.

He'd given her the pearls because he'd truly cared about her, but her undiluted happiness had only made him feel worse. He couldn't give her what she so unreservedly gave him—all her love. Loving had always been hard for him. He'd learned when his parents had deserted both him and his sister that love was something rarely found or given, and Devon's love for others was zealously guarded within him. Shannon was the only person he loved openly and wholeheartedly.

And it turned out he'd been right to hold back.

Devon flexed his hands, his jaw tight, his neck corded with tension. When Brittany had called him and dropped the bomb about her pregnancy he'd been stunned. Immediately all his doubts had crytallized. Had she planned it? Was she using it as a weapon to get him to marry her?

But Devon had known enough about her by that time to realize his fears were probably unjustified. She was too ambitious to plan a pregnancy and purposely interrupt her career. And she'd sounded totally undone on the telephone. He began to regret how he'd put her off and after thinking it over, he'd gone to find her at the Castle agency.

"She's not here," Nora had told him. "She's gone, thanks to you."

Devon had been shocked and disturbed that Brittany had talked about her pregnancy to Nora. "What's that supposed to mean?"

"Damn you, Devon. Don't you see what's happened? You've forced her to do something she doesn't want to do!"

Devon's brows had pulled together into a frown. He hadn't understood what Nora was getting at.

"She's gone to get an abortion," Nora had said on a heavy sigh. "And she's really torn up about it."

"*What?*"

"Oh, for God's sake. Don't act so upset. You've hardly been a pillar of support," she'd said scathingly. "I should never have let you in here in the first place. None of this would have happened. But I made the mistake of thinking Devon Gallagher would have more sense.''

Devon had reeled from shock. Abortion? The word wasn't in his vocabulary. ''I don't believe you,'' he'd said tautly.

''Well, you'd better. She's coming back to work tomorrow and I told her she couldn't come back if she was pregnant.''

His emotions were on a roller coaster. He couldn't take it all in. He'd never dreamed Brittany would make such a decision. But he'd called Nora's agency the next morning and found out that Brittany was indeed back at work.

Nora had refused to let him speak to her. ''Leave it alone for a while,'' she'd suggested in a subdued voice.

''If you don't let me talk to her now, I'll come straight over there and deal with Brittany in person!'' Devon had told her furiously.

''She's a wreck, Devon. She's just made the most important decision of her life and she's barely twenty years old. Give her some time....''

''What decision did she make?'' Devon's fury had sliced through Nora's pleas.

Nora had sighed unhappily. ''The problem's solved,'' she'd said in a subdued voice. ''That's what she said: 'The problem's solved.' I am sorry, Devon, but maybe it's all for the best.''

''It'll be a cold day in hell when it's for the best, Nora!'' Devon had snarled unmercifully. Damn Brittany! Damn himself! He couldn't believe she'd thrown away a human life for her career.

Calling Brittany then had been something he just had to do. He hadn't known what to expect but the sound of her anguish had only turned his stomach. It was a

travesty, a colossal joke on him. He'd always understood her ambition...at least he'd thought he had. But
she'd taken that ambition beyond the laws of decency
and he hated her for it.

Except that now, three years later, he found himself
drawn to her again and it was a force that both infuriated and frightened him.

He clenched his teeth together and turned the BMW
into his driveway, parking it beneath a clematis-trellised
carport. He tried to clear his thoughts but Brittany's
ivory skin and seductive dark-lashed eyes were im-
planted in his inner vision.

Devon strode purposefully down the tiled walkway to
his condominium. He shook his head. He didn't understand himself at all. When he'd interviewed the
coldhearted Melina Sanders he'd been repulsed by her
lack of empathy, her self-interest. Even though she'd
probably saved his life there was something about that
woman that had made his skin crawl. Brittany, by all
standards, should make him feel the same way. She was
the same type of woman—self-serving, ambitious, one-
dimensional, driven by greed and acquisition and fame.

Why then did she burn in his system like a tantaliz-
ing flame? Why should he even care that she might be
involved in the Broderick affair?

Why did he care about her?

Devon sighed, unlocking his front door. He didn't
know why his feelings were so wrapped up with Brittany; they just were. And he was going to have to face
facts and do something about them before the whole
situation got totally out of hand.

Devon rewound the tape on his answering machine.
He listened to the messages dutifully. Nothing important. His mind was elsewhere, full of images of a beau-

tiful lavender-eyed woman who could be as warm as summer rain and as cold as winter ice.

"Devon?" Jay's voice came after the last beep. "Call me as soon as you get in. Broderick's planning another trip to Mexico at the end of November."

Devon inhaled sharply.

"I don't know whether this is good news or bad," Jay's voice went on, "but Brittany Daniels has scheduled another trip for around the same time."

The message ended with a click but Devon let the tape run soundlessly on. He stared sightlessly at the machine. Brittany was going to Mexico? Again? With Broderick?

He shook his head. That was jumping to conclusions.

But if she wasn't going with Broderick, why was she going? What was it that pulled her back to Mexico over and over again?

Devon switched off the machine and poured himself the longed-for drink, scowling. He had to know what was going on with Brittany once and for all. He would never get any peace until he did.

And if you don't like the answers...? an inner voice taunted.

Devon took a long swallow of Scotch, then gritted his teeth. Well, then he'd know for certain about Brittany one way or the other. It might not be what he wanted to believe but at least the torment would be over.

The storm Devon had predicted came on ferociously. The wind howled around the eaves, shaking the palm fronds so loudly they sounded as if they were chattering in fear. Rain poured from the sky and Brittany could see it falling in sheets from the leaf-choked

gutters. By morning, however, the storm had blown itself out, and Brittany walked along the rain-rinsed
beach with only an occasional stiff breeze to remind her
of its fury.

Six A.M. Not a soul for miles. Brittany walked
thoughtfully between the debris the waves had deposited on the sand: broken fragments of shells, tangled
ropes of seaweed, shiny black and gray pebbles, a small
forlorn-looking crab. She picked up an unbroken sand
dollar and tried to think about anything but Devon.

She made a face at herself. Weekends were the worst.
During the week she worked so hard she barely had time
to eat and sleep. But on weekends, though she still spent
time planning, telephoning and trying to maintain her
sorely neglected personal life, Brittany too often found
time to worry. And she had too much to worry about.

Her father. Brittany bit into her bottom lip and felt
helpless. She would do anything for him, yet there was
so little she could do. In a few more weeks she would be
going back to Acapulco but for now all she could do
was wait and worry.

Unless she could grant him his one solitary wish:
putting Devon and her miscarriage firmly behind her.

Brittany watched the sky lighten, turn from darkness to dawn-streaked gray. She'd always considered
herself a realist, and being so, she'd tried to put her past
with Devon in perspective. She'd thought she'd succeeded. Then Devon had walked back into her life and
everything had gone haywire.

So much for trying to fulfill her father's wish. She
couldn't forget Devon no matter how hard she tried.
Worse yet, she suspected she was still in love with him.

Brittany wandered aimlessly for another twenty minutes, then headed back to her house. She was treading

barefoot up the stairs to her porch, sand gritting beneath her soles, when she heard the phone ring.

Her heart stopped. No one called her this early. Not unless it was an emergency.

She raced through the house, the door slamming loudly behind her, sand scattering unheeded from her bare feet as she ran across the plush white carpeting of her living room. Her stomach dropped with dread. She snatched up the receiver. "Hello?"

"Hello, sweetheart," her father's gentle voice answered her. "I'm sorry to call so early but it's hard to catch you home. I hope I didn't wake you."

Brittany collapsed in a chair. She went weak with relief. *Thank God.* Her worst fears weren't realized—yet. Her father was just checking in. "You didn't wake me," she assured him. "I was just out on the beach."

"Such an early bird—and here we thought you'd be sleeping in."

"Tomorrow," Brittany said lightly, her pulse returning to normal. She knew she was going to lose her father soon but she couldn't bear thinking about it.

"You work too hard, Brittany," he admonished. "Sometimes I think it was a mistake letting you get into modeling so young."

"No. No." She wasn't going to let him ride on that guilt trip. "It was my decision. You both just went along with it."

The silence on the other end was heavy. "You were so young. You were exposed to situations and people you shouldn't have been exposed to until you were older."

Brittany's chest tightened. "Dad, I'm fine," she said firmly. She gathered her courage and added softly, "Stop taking the blame for what happened between me and Devon."

"Oh, I'm not," he protested. "Did I come off like that?"

"Mother told me what you said to her. And I want you to know, I'm fine. Devon...and everything...that's all in the past," she lied gently. "That woman was a different me. Stop worrying, please. I'm tough. I bounced back, didn't I? And it was eons ago."

"You can't fool me, child," he said quietly.

Brittany's eyes instantly filled with tears. "Would you stop that?" she scolded, relieved at how normal she sounded. "I'm a grown woman with a fabulous career. I don't have anything to complain about. You're overplaying this father bit. You just take care of yourself."

"I know. I know." Her father sighed deeply. "I didn't really intend to bring all this up, but I just thought you looked so unhappy when you were here last." ·

"Don't you think that has a little bit to do with you?" Brittany managed to choke out.

Her father's soft laugh was poignant and she wanted to cry out loud at his bravery. "Oh, honey, I just want you to be happy. That's all."

"I'm trying," she whispered, hating herself for being the weak one.

"Devon's just one man, you know. The world is full of them."

How could her father understand her so well? He'd zeroed in on Devon, though they hadn't discussed him in years. "I've seen Devon recently," she admitted. "I'm really working on putting the past behind me and that includes straightening things out between us."

She sensed her father's surprise. "You mean you're talking about it?"

"Not exactly. He resents me, probably more than I do him, and every time I get close to mentioning what happened he shuts me out."

"Maybe he feels guilty," her father offered thoughtfully.

"Maybe."

Brittany privately felt that Devon blamed her entirely and guilt wasn't an issue at all. But she didn't really want to go into it all with her father. The way he faced his illness made her feel her own problems were petty and unimportant. She changed the subject as soon as she could.

"Your mother wants to talk to you now," her father signed off. "See you soon."

He sounded so tired that Brittany got worried, and her mother's anxious "We'll see you the week before Thanksgiving, won't we?" didn't help at all.

"Absolutely. How are things going?"

Her mother understood implicitly. "Not too bad. We're both looking forward to seeing you again soon. I'll cook a turkey with all the trimmings and we'll celebrate big."

When Brittany hung up she walked to her front windows, now bright with sunlight, and stared across the glittering sea. She debated packing right then and there and catching the next flight to Acapulco. Her mother was concerned; Brittany could hear it in her voice.

Jessica's call forced her to change her mind. "The Crestview Cola commercial has been moved up to Monday and, if you run over, Tuesday, too," she said without preamble. "I've already juggled your interview with *In Touch* magazine and your two-o'clock photography session with Ramon was already cancelled by the Sheik of Sweat himself."

Brittany smiled in spite of herself. "Has Ramon re-scheduled?"

Jessica snorted. "He wanted you for the next day. I told him to wait in line like everyone else."

"Did you really?" Brittany couldn't imagine that a man as used to people scrambling for him as Ramon would take Jessica's message lying down.

"Yes, and he was quite articulate about what I could do with my business. He didn't say anything about you, however."

"The coward." Brittany laughed.

"He wants you for that leotard spread. He's not crazy enough to sound off when it could really affect his pocketbook. Good luck with Crestview Cola. Talk to you soon."

Brittany's good mood vanished with Jessica. She felt pressure building on all sides. Her father...the holidays...Devon...

She walked to the bathroom, slipped off her clothes and turned on the shower. With an effort she pushed thoughts of her father and Devon to the back of her mind and concentrated on the one thing that took away her self-doubts and helplessness: her work.

Brittany closed her eyes and let the hot water cascade over her head. *If only it was Monday already,* she thought. *Too bad the work week is only five days long.*

Brittany's hair was wet and oiled back from her forehead to keep it in place. Her body had been given the same treatment and her long arms and legs glistened. A skimpy white bikini covered the only parts of her skin that were oil-free, but she'd been sprayed all over with water and tiny droplets clung everywhere.

She lay back on the striped canvas beach chair and tried not to think that beyond the scattered sand and backdrops was a high-ceilinged room with wires that hung like tentacles and people scrambling madly about to create a grand illusion. She needed to believe she was idling away a lazy, hot summer day and to do that she had to forget all about the props, noise, director and the dozen or more top personnel from Crestview Cola Light.

They'd already shot the first scene, where Brittany played the part of a bespectacled, prim-suited secretary who wore a severe chignon at the back of her head. Her eyes had traveled from a computer screen to a clock and back again. When the hands reached five o'clock she'd raced out of the office and literally let down her hair. Now she was at the beach savoring one of Crestview's flavored diet colas.

"Look dreamy. Look satisfied," the director said again, and Brittany closed her eyes and tried to blank Devon completely out of her mind. It was an impossible task. As impossible as forgetting about her father. For once she couldn't lose herself in her work.

"You're frowning," the director chastised, and Brittany opened one eye to see his impatient face.

"Sorry." She tilted her chin up and curved her mouth into a sybaritic smile. Her fingers trailed in the sand, half an inch from a red-and-gold can of Crestview cherry-flavored diet cola. Terrible stuff, Brittany secretly thought. Thank God she didn't have to drink very much of it.

After another hour of changing lighting and camera angles, a break was called. Brittany wrapped herself in a towel and headed for the dressing room.

"There's a phone message for you," a young mop-topped assistant said, handing her a white slip of paper.

"Thanks." Brittany looked at the name and number. Grant Broderick. With all that was on her mind she'd forgotten about him. Resignedly, she called him back.

"Brittany." His smooth voice greeted her warmly. "I've been trying to reach you for two days. Your agent finally told me where you were."

Jessica had grown more and more impressed with Broderick's list of successes, but Brittany hadn't had time to contact him. "I've been busy," she said apologetically. "Really."

"I know. You're the worst workaholic I've met, and believe me, I've met a lot. Is it possible to steal just an hour of your time? I'd like to take you to lunch at Pavilon's."

Pavilon's was a chic restaurant whose clientele included celebrities and the extremely wealthy. Brittany had been there several times but had found it a bit too flashy for her liking. Yet she wanted to go to lunch with Grant Broderick and have that obligation out of the way. She felt she owed it to him since he'd invited her to his party and therefore opened the door to Toujours.

"When would you like to go?" she asked.

"How about today? Can you get away for a while?"

Not a chance. Brittany was about to decline when it occurred to her she might be done by midday. They were already a day over schedule; the Crestview people were hard to please. But the whole group had begun checking their watches a little more regularly and Brittany guessed they were worried about the cost of running over much farther.

"If you wouldn't mind a late lunch I could maybe meet you after I'm done for the day. If all goes well, that should be around two."

"Perfect." Broderick was eager. "I'll meet you there?" Brittany readily agreed. She didn't want him to have to drive all the way to the small studio where she was working just to pick her up. Besides, she liked the independence of having her own car.

It took another three hours before everyone was satisfied with the commercial and by the time Brittany was finished it was half past one. She'd arranged to meet Grant at two and now knew she'd be late. She raced through the shower, scrubbed off the oil, managed to dab on a bit of makeup, then looked in dismay at her wet and crinkly hair. As a last resort she grabbed a fawn-colored wide brimmed hat with a black band and shoved all her hair up inside. She tilted it for some sophistication, surveyed the results and shrugged. Her tan-and-cream skirt and blouse would have to do. By the time she finally got to Pavilon's it was nearly two-thirty.

"I'm sorry," she apologized to Grant after the maître d' had directed her to his table. "It ran longer than I expected and I couldn't get away. I should have probably made our lunch for another day."

Grant wasn't alone. A man Brittany recognized as one of prime-time television's top producers was seated opposite him.

Grant was already waving Brittany's apology aside. "Don't worry about it. I ran into Sam and we started discussing business."

"You're having lunch with a financial genius," Sam Walters said as he firmly clasped Brittany's hand in greeting.

"So I've heard," she said with a smile.

"It's not just rumor. It's fact. He certainly showed me the error of my ways. Seriously." He threw out an encompassing arm. "Look around this room. Everyone who's willing to talk about their investments will tell you the same."

Pavilon's was known for its late-lunch crowd and most of the tables were still full. Brittany saw several well-known and important faces scattered among the clientele.

"I think that's enough of the glowing accolades," Broderick interjected modestly.

"Not by a long shot," Sam disagreed. A group from another table got up to leave and he added, "Looks as though it's time for me to go. It was nice meeting you, Miss Daniels. You're in royal company."

"It was nice meeting you."

He dropped his hand on Grant's shoulder for a moment. "How's it going with Senator Burgess?" he asked. "Need any help there?"

Broderick smiled. "Not right now, Sam. I seem to be making some inroads."

"Let me know if you do. I'll be there." He gave Brittany a friendly wink, then left to catch up with his group.

Grant watched him for a moment, then turned back to Brittany. "You look lovely," he complimented her.

Brittany laughed. If he only knew what she'd gone through to look halfway presentable. "Thank you. I didn't think I would get myself together in time."

"Well, you did a remarkable job. Of course—" he toasted her with his wineglass "—you have wonderful raw material to work with. With a face like yours, you should wear more than just pearls. Diamonds and sapphires would suit you. And emeralds.''

"You spoil my image of you, Mr. Broderick," she said lightly. "I thought you were only interested in gems as an investment—not for their esthetic value."

"I am. But I can appreciate beauty, too. And you're a very beautiful woman."

Uncomfortable, she murmured, "Be careful, you might turn my head."

"I don't think so." His smile was warm. "You seem to have a remarkably down-to-earth opinion of yourself and your job. It's part of your intrigue. So much," he added thoughtfully, "all in one package."

Brittany smiled in embarrassment. She appreciated people who were direct but Grant Broderick had the knack for making her uneasy. Still, it seemed his business acumen couldn't be faulted. And just because Devon didn't like the man certainly didn't mean he was a criminal. God knew Devon's judgment wasn't anything to go by. She knew that from firsthand experience, she reminded herself grimly.

Devon's recommendations or not, Brittany wanted to make certain her relationship with Grant Broderick stayed strictly professional. She might listen to his business advice, but she wasn't interested in him as a man.

"You certainly have a fan in Sam Walters," she observed.

Broderick smiled faintly. "Sam was wasting more than half the income he made," he said quietly. "He thinks I'm his savior for putting his money in safe places."

"That's a talent in itself."

"Not enough to get myself elected, I'm afraid."

Brittany looked at him. "Is that your goal?"

He shrugged modestly but nodded. "It takes more than just talent. It takes cultivating the right friends...and lots of money."

Broderick's eyes gleamed and Brittany saw how keen he was on joining the political scene. She wondered if that was why Devon was so determined to pin something on him. It hardly seemed fair. "I think you're well on your way," she told him seriously.

The waiter came to take their order. Several other people stopped by their table to chat and Brittany began to realize fully the man's tremendous impact on the whole Los Angeles community. She thought he was probably closer to fulfilling his political dream than he knew.

It wasn't until coffee was served that Broderick overstepped his bounds.

"Could I ask you a personal question?" he inquired when they were alone again.

"Sure," Brittany said warily. "But I won't guarantee an answer."

"Ahh." He rubbed his nose thoughtfully. "So you're as cautious as you are beautiful. Well, I think I'll take a chance and get straight to the point. What is your relationship with Devon Gallagher?"

Brittany had expected something of the sort, though maybe not put quite so bluntly. She'd been seen in Devon's company both times she'd been with Broderick, and she'd sensed how interested he was in that fact. "As I said, we're old friends."

"Lovers?"

Brittany waited a heartbeat too long. "Devon's a past chapter," she said firmly.

"Then am I to assume you're not seeing him anymore?"

. He was signing the check as he carefully chose his words but Brittany knew he was closely tuned in to how she answered. "I'm not seeing Devon anymore," she agreed quietly. "But I'm not looking for any other relationship, either."

"Ouch," Broderick murmured.

Brittany flushed. "I thought this was supposed to be a business meeting," she said to change the subject. "I'm disappointed. You didn't even give me the hard sell."

He laughed, letting the tender issue of Devon Gallagher slip aside. "Would it have done me any good?"

"No. Probably not."

"Well, then I haven't wasted my time." He paused, then eyed her intently. "If you are interested in investing in gems, I could give you the name of a reputed gem-brokerage house. Free advice."

"Nothing's free."

Broderick shook his head. "Window-shopping is." He searched through some business cards in his wallet, then handed one to Brittany. "Go and look if you want. Gems are appreciating in value right now and the ceiling's a long way away." He leaned toward her and said in a stage whisper, "It's my hot tip."

Brittany smiled. Without the come-on, Broderick wasn't half-bad. "All right. I'll check it out."

"Good girl. You won't be sorry."

Brittany drove home lost in thought. She still didn't feel entirely secure about investing money with Grant Broderick—Devon's influence, she was sure—but as he obviously wasn't personally benefiting by offering her his free advice, she couldn't see how it could hurt to explore investing in gems. Besides, no one could force her to put her money down. She always relied on her own instinct.

She was turning the corner to her house, one finger on the button to open her automatic garage door, when she saw a familiar tawny BMW, Devon's car, parked in her driveway. Devon was sitting inside.

Chapter Six

Brittany's heart leaped to her throat. She didn't think she was up to seeing Devon again so soon. But it was too late to drive by without turning in; the garage door was already lifting, a dead giveaway to her whereabouts.

Brittany drove into her driveway, past his car and into her garage. In her rearview mirror she watched him unfold his lean body from the BMW. Her pulse was pounding in excitement, every nerve on alert. She was kidding herself, she realized ruefully, if she believed she could stop caring for him. He was a part of her, and in a way she was a part of him. He might not love her, he might not even like her, but he wasn't indifferent to her. He was drawn to her, as she was drawn to him.

And what that meant for the future was anyone's guess.

Brittany cut the engine and noticed the fine tremor in her fingers as she pulled the keys from the ignition. She made a face at herself. Her reactions were embarrassing!

"What are you doing here?" she asked as Devon approached.

"Looking for you." He glanced toward the wooden stairway at the back of her garage that led inside the house. "Could I come in for a while? I'd like to talk to you."

Brittany's brows laced together in a frown. There was something detached and professional in his voice that she didn't like. Some of her excitement faded. "Sure," she said, and led the way upstairs.

The stairs from the garage opened directly into Brittany's kitchen. She walked in with Devon right behind her and flipped on the overhead track lights, the room brightening cheerily. The walls and cabinets were white, the floor deep blue tile. For lack of anything better to do Brittany started making coffee.

Devon was standing in the middle of the room, silently surveying the interior of her home. Just having him here made her throat dry. Brittany wished he would say something, anything.

She watched the coffee drip through the filter. "Was there something specific that you wanted?" she asked, turning to see him.

He was dressed casually in a pair of jeans and well-worn boots, a heavy blue-green sweater and a rust-colored leather jacket. But he possessed that indefinable attraction that was purely male, purely Devon, that always affected Brittany no matter what he looked like, no matter what he did.

He sighed and pulled his shoulders back, as if his forthcoming task gave him no pleasure whatsoever.

"Coffee will be ready in just a minute," Brittany said. "You still take it black?"

"Yes, but I don't want any, thanks." He prowled around the confined space of the room, looking tense and uncomfortable. "I've only got a few minutes. I just need to ask you something."

"Go ahead," she said slowly.

She waited expectantly. Part of her couldn't help hoping that he'd come to finally straighten things out between them. He'd balked the other night when their conversation had headed in that direction, but maybe now he was ready to go farther.

Devon hesitated, scowling down at the scuffed toes of his boots. Brittany had never seen him at such a loss. After a moment he cleared his throat and said, "You're going to Mexico again at the end of this month. Does your trip have anything to do with Grant Broderick?"

Brittany blinked, her heart plummeting. Why had she thought Devon would be interested in talking to her? She was a source. Nothing more. All he ever wanted from her was a blasted story.

"Well, does it?" Devon demanded aggressively. He was leaning against the counter, his fingers curled tightly around the edge, his face grim. "Damn it, Britt. If you're involved, I've got to know!"

Brittany found her voice. "*You've* got to know," she said bitterly. "Everything always revolves around you, doesn't it?"

"I'm trying to save your neck. I've warned you about Broderick but you're too stubborn to listen!" He was practically shouting at her. "I don't have time to dance around with you on this. Are you going to Mexico with Broderick, and if so, why?''

Brittany's insides burned with fury. Some things never changed! "It's none of your business," she said tautly.

Devon swore under his breath. "You are going with him, aren't you?" His jaw tightened perceptibly. "Tell me, Britt."

"I don't owe you an explanation, Devon. You don't need to know anything about me—where I've been, whom I see...." Brittany clenched her teeth together, biting back her anger. As irrational as Devon's possessive streak was, she didn't want to jump into a full-scale war over it. She hated fighting with him.

Devon's face was dark and dangerous. He pointed a condemning finger in Brittany's direction. "That man is in serious trouble. And I'm going to make sure he pays for it. But I'd just as soon not stumble over you on the way."

"You won't."

He looked at her pinched white face. "I wish I could believe you."

Brittany's lungs were drained of air, empty. He'd never trusted her. Never! To him, she was still the same mercenary child he'd always seen. She could never rise above it. "You're just looking for an excuse to hate me," she told him flatly. "Don't pat yourself on the back as if you're some sterling knight out to save me. I know differently, Devon."

He moved abruptly but she continued relentlessly, "You're harboring a vendetta against me for God knows what reason. And you keep slashing away at me. Well, I haven't hurt you, Devon!"

"The hell you haven't," he snarled.

"How? *How?* You tell me how and maybe I'll understand!"

"Damn you..." Devon muttered.

"And damn you, Devon," she said in a low voice. "For hating me because I got pregnant." Her words were cruel but she forced them out. He needed to know how unfair he'd been to her...was still being to her. "Well, it takes two, you know. I couldn't have done it alone."

For a moment he looked violent. Then, realizing he was slipping the leash on his control, he visibly pulled himself together. "Tell me why you're going to Mexico and then I'll leave," he said with admirable control. "For good. I won't bother you again. But tell me the truth because if you don't, I'll find out in the end anyway."

"And do what? Hate me some more? Go find your truth, Devon. You can't threaten me, because I've got nothing to lose."

He swore angrily and growled, "What are you hiding this time?"

Brittany turned stony eyes on him. Inside she was fragmenting into a thousand pieces. She didn't know why she took such abuse from him. The way he felt about her, about what she was capable of, made her want to shrivel up and die.

He stared back, fury burning like a dangerous flame within his bright blue eyes. Brittany felt the trembling in her lower lip and tried to fight it. She couldn't show any weakness now. She couldn't let him see how much he could still hurt her.

The anger tightening his mouth slowly receded. His lips changed from thin lines of contempt to weary curves of sensuality. "What am I going to do about you?" he muttered, and passed a hand across his eyes.

He was completely unaware of the vulnerability that showed through, making Brittany's anger dissolve into a throbbing ache, her outrage turn to desperate yearning.

"I didn't come here to fight," Devon said heavily. He made a self-deprecating sound and added, "Really. I just don't want to find out too late that I've hurt you as a by-product of this investigation."

Brittany turned away. She couldn't look at him. "I won't be in your way," she said quietly.

"Just your being involved makes this case very...difficult for me."

Devon's words came carefully, haltingly, as if saying them aloud could reveal a part of himself he needed to keep hidden. She didn't know how to answer him, what to say. He was invading a very private part of her life, and though it would be simpler for her in the long run, she couldn't tell him about her father's illness.

Her heart was heavy. She couldn't give him what he wanted because of a need to protect her privacy. And his high-handed manner didn't deserve an answer anyway. Yet she could forgive him that because of the pain that shadowed his eyes, a pain that seemed to be due to her.

She tried to think of a way to explain about her father but words failed her. Her reasons for silence were so much more complex than he could ever imagine. She shook her head and offered nothing.

Devon sighed, and though Brittany prepared herself, his anger didn't return. Instead his expression was a mixture of resignation, frustration and another, indefinable, emotion. She would have called it passion except that Devon felt nothing but disgust for her.

Brittany's eyes were full of pain and a love that wouldn't quite die. "I don't know what to say other than I'm not involved with Grant Broderick. And I know that's not good enough for you."

"But it's all I deserve?"

She bowed her head. "My reasons for going to Mexico have nothing to do with Grant Broderick," she stated in a tone that warned him any more questions would be futile.

For long moments he said nothing and Brittany hoped he understood that she wasn't trying to be evasive. She didn't want to fight, either. But he was bulldozing his way into the darkest corners of her life and she refused to open herself up and wait for him to tromp all over her.

She was aware of the conflict that raged just beneath his grim surface. He was empathetic enough to want to respect her privacy even though he had doubts about her as a woman, as a sincere, feeling human being. She understood how he felt but it hurt.

"You can't trust me at all, can you?" Brittany asked miserably. "I didn't turn out to be that china doll you thought I was, and because of that you think I've deceived you."

"That's not true."

But Brittany knew it was. He'd answered too quickly. She was hitting too close to the truth. "Someday maybe you'll tell me what I did to make you hate me so much."

A terrible pain crossed his face. "You already know," he said roughly.

"No, I don't." Brittany felt a strange invisible barrier between them, one that kept breaking apart, one that Devon desperately tried to keep intact. She didn't understand it any more now than she had when he'd first put it up. But it was there, and it was becoming imperative that she find out why.

Devon exhaled sharply. "I don't want to talk about this."

Brittany shook her head, looking up at him from beneath the slanting brim of her hat. "Now who's evading whom? You expect total capitulation from me, yet you hide all those secrets of our past. Was it my pregnancy, Devon? Well, was it?" He tried to step away from Brittany but she moved in closer, cornering him. "Tell me, please. I've never understood."

"Christ, Brittany!"

"Well, what is it? Just tell me!" Brittany was desperate. She had the horrible feeling that Devon's contempt was from something else, something she had no control over.

His palm warded her off. "I don't hate you," he said in a tortured voice.

"I can feel it, Devon." Her voice was small, anxious. "It radiates from you in waves."

"I don't hate you," he repeated, and the look on his face almost convinced her he was telling the truth.

And if he was...

Brittany's eyes were eloquent with longing as she stared into Devon's beloved face. She was so close to him, as close as he would allow. And if he didn't hate her, then there was a chance for them. Maybe not love but at least understanding, respect, acceptance.

"I've wanted to hate you but I can't," he said hoarsely. "Not totally. Not honestly."

Brittany swallowed hard. "What does that mean?"

She sensed that he wanted to touch her, to hold her, to share the burden of his incredible pain. But his control was so strong and cold that it frightened her.

"You and I have different morals, Brittany. It's something that can't be changed. And maybe I can't hate you for what you are...but I can't forgive you, either."

The words were forced from him. Brittany was still sorting through what they meant when his palm came up to rest gently alongside her cheek, a tender gesture, a final goodbye. Panic moved through her. She cupped her hand over his and said fervently, "Devon, I don't know what you're talking about. Believe me. Please, please believe me. Don't stop now." She struggled for the words. "We're so close."

Emotions rippled through him, a desperate battle she could feel in her own heart. He tried to break contact but she wouldn't let him. "Devon..."

Brittany's plea wrenched Devon's heart. His forehead dipped down to rest against hers, his hand sliding from beneath her small palm to the nape of her neck.

This tiny weakness gave Brittany courage. Gently she touched the strong line of his chin. When he didn't pull away, she braved a light kiss, her lips dusting briefly over his. "I may be masochistic, Devon," she whispered, "but I'd like another chance." She was surprised at how easy the words came to her, how right they sounded. "I haven't ever got over you. You're still a part of me."

Devon's muscles quivered. "No. You had a part of me, Britt, and you threw it away!"

The words were torn from deep within him. Brittany was bewildered. Then, with a blast of sudden insight, she knew he was speaking literally. "The baby?" she asked, swallowing. "You blame me for losing the baby?"

Devon's head came back with a snap, knocking the brim of Brittany's hat. It tumbled from her hair to the floor, releasing a tangle of black curls that spilled in wild abandon across her confused eyes.

He threw out an arm in dramatic disbelief. "Of course I blame you!" he shouted. "For God's sake, you didn't even consult me! You may have knocked me off my feet when you announced your pregnancy, Britt, but my God—" He broke off, breathing hard. "I wouldn't have changed things!"

Brittany brushed back the curls, her brows laced together. Devon's pain and anguish were a palpable force. She stared at his taut face, at the cords that stood out in his neck, at the working of his throat. Something clicked. Something her subconscious had considered and rejected straight out. Suddenly she saw herself through his eyes, his perspective. A tremor went through her and she stopped breathing altogether.

"You think I had...I got—" She broke off, appalled. "You think I deliberately got rid of our child— *my* child!"

Devon went very still.

"How could you?" Brittany hissed, her fist clenched. "My God, I—" Brittany broke off as the weight of what she'd learned crashed down on her. Her face became a pale mask of itself. Her insides were tearing apart in agony.

"Britt...?"

She faintly heard the question in Devon's tone, but it was far away and unimportant to her. "I understand now," she whispered in a voice that echoed strangely in her ears. "You thought I got rid of the baby because of my career."

Brittany's strange calm alarmed Devon. He gripped her shoulder with hard hands. "Are you saying you didn't?"

There was something wrong with the room. The corners seemed to move, the walls buckled and swayed. "You don't know me at all, Devon," she said tautly, fighting back an oppressive darkness. "You don't know me at all."

Her senses were turning in on themselves but her mind was startlingly clear. She saw Devon as she'd never seen him before, and a whole host of disturbing anxieties suddenly crystallized into painful reality. "You thought I was trying to force you to marry me by getting pregnant," she said in a thin disbelieving voice. "And when that didn't work, I had an abortion."

Devon's grip on her shoulders tightened. She was pale as a wraith. He felt a mounting concern and wild disbelief at that she was implying.

"Brittany..." He tried to guide her to a chair but she wouldn't move. She stared at him through cold lavender eyes, her small body rigid.

"You can take your hands off me. I won't fall apart."

She'd retreated to some place he couldn't follow; he could see it in her eyes. Devon gripped her harder, feeling her small bones beneath the rich silkiness of her blouse. He felt as oddly disoriented as she looked, trying to find something solid to hang on to in a world turned suddenly upside down.

When his hands didn't move she yanked herself from his reach, quivering with emotion. "You're not worth that much, Devon," she whispered harshly. "Don't fool yourself that you are."

An ache spread through Devon's chest. He recognized Brittany's pain. But what was she saying? He couldn't believe the simple answer. He wouldn't believe it. He knew better than to believe it!

"You didn't have an abortion?" he asked tautly.

"Why ask?" Brittany's lips were tight. "You've already figured out the whole scenario. Why ask me anything? I wouldn't tell the truth. I'm just a mercenary, selfish bitch who would kill her own..."

"Brittany! Dear God, I can't—" Devon's voice broke.

"Get out of my life." Brittany's lips were pressed together, all her features tight and pale. "I mean it this time. It took a lot, Devon, but you've managed to destroy my love for you. Goodbye."

"Did you miscarry? Tell me, for God's sake!"

Through the numbing darkness that was closing in on her, she saw the twisted agony on his face. But she wouldn't rehash the most horrible moments of a past best forgotten just for the sake of easing his mind. She wanted to hit him, wound him, flail at him with the built-up anguish of those three long, pain-filled years. How could he? *How could he?*

"Nora told me you had an abortion," Devon said in a strained voice. "She told me, do you understand? There was no time to speculate on why you weren't pregnant after you said you were. I was *told*. Nora said you had a choice and you chose your career."

"Nice of you to talk to me, Devon," Brittany gasped in bitterness.

Devon's hands seemed to have a will of their own. He reached for her again but she backed off, her eyes deep and wary. *It isn't true,* Devon's mind warned him with cool logic. *Nora Castle wouldn't lie to you.*

Brittany stumbled and weaved and Devon sprang to her aid, catching her before she fell. Her hands were balled into tight fists against his chest and a dry sob was wrenched from her throat.

She hit him with one small fist. "You bastard," she cried. "Why didn't you talk to me? Why did you cut me off? I could have told you what happened. I wanted to! How could you talk about us to Nora?"

She struck his chest again, then again. Devon didn't even feel it. He pulled her into his arms, crushing her to him, holding her so tightly that her breath came out in a rush. His own breathing was harsh and labored. He understood how betrayed she felt, but God forgive him, he still couldn't fully believe her. He'd lived for too long with the pain of thinking she'd purposely rid herself of his child. He still couldn't believe she'd miscarried, though that was her unspoken claim.

Her blinding anguish seemed to be the real thing, but Devon couldn't make himself believe that all his years of anger and resentment had stemmed from a simple mistake. It was too easy, too pat. Or had he been the one who'd made it all so difficult?

Brittany was crying softly, her body limp now against the comfort of his. She was so tired she couldn't even fight him, though that was what she burned to do. She was stunned and wounded that he had accepted someone else's theories without asking her. It explained his antipathy but it also brought her emotions sharply into line. He'd believed Nora. He'd believed Brittany would have an abortion for the sake of her career! She didn't even care to speculate on why Nora would tell him such a terrible lie. Devon should have known she wouldn't have harmed his child.

Brittany knew now that he'd never truly loved her. He'd been looking for an excuse to drive her from his life and Nora had handed it to him on a silver platter.

Dusky twilight filtered through the kitchen windows and Brittany suddenly realized how long she'd been huddling weakly within the security of Devon's arms. She disengaged herself and turned away without looking at him. At least she hadn't fainted. For a moment or two she'd thought she was going to.

"Do you want that cup of coffee now?" Devon asked her.

Brittany straightened her shoulders and faced him. His blue eyes were dark and serious, his expression still grim. She studied him dispassionately for a moment, wondering how someone so familiar could look so alien.

"No, Devon," she said quietly. "What I really want is for you to go. I've had enough postmortems on my pregnancy....and my miscarriage," she added deliberately, "to last me several lifetimes. I should probably have guessed what you thought, but it never entered my head because I would never..." Brittany swallowed.

Devon winced. He felt ripped in two.

"I thought you knew me better than that," she finished.

"I'll go," he said, then didn't move.

Brittany waited in weary acceptance. Deep inside she knew she'd lied to him about one thing—he hadn't destroyed her love. It had a life of its own, beyond all reason and common sense. No matter what he thought of her she still loved him, and she knew that she always would.

"I can't leave you like this," he said helplessly. Before Brittany had time to react he was holding her again. Her pride, her need for self-preservation, warned her to push him away but she was too weak to do more than rest her cheek on his shoulder.

Then he was kissing her with rough passion. Brittany's eyes fluttered closed and her breath escaped on a wispy sigh. She didn't mean it to sound like unconditional surrender but that's how Devon took it. His lips were everywhere, on her mouth, the high slant of her cheekbones, the translucent loveliness of her eyelids, her lashes, her earlobes.

He was pressed against her, her lower back wedged against the edge of the counter. His mouth was ravenous, his tongue probing the interior of her mouth in a bone-melting way. This wasn't the Devon from her past, she thought vaguely. That Devon had been wary and careful even in his passion. This Devon was hungry and dangerous and out of control.

She tried to pull away but his desire had awakened an answering passion deep within her. An untamed part of her sang in ecstasy and when he moved his hips against hers once, hard, she couldn't hold back a moan of yearning.

"I've wanted to touch you for so long," he said in a rough whisper against her ear. "But I couldn't. I've wanted you so much."

Brittany tried to form a response but the trembling in his hands as he molded her soft curves against his hard ones splintered her thoughts. She forgot that she shouldn't be with him and succumbed to the pleasure of his touch and taste. Her tongue tentatively searched the warm interior of his mouth and he responded with a groan of desire.

"Britt, oh, Britt..." He pressed his face to her throat and her head lolled back.

It seemed more like a dream. She'd loved only one man in her life, Devon, yet the man she was with seemed an intoxicating stranger. She tried to be rational, to state clearly and emphatically that she couldn't let herself love him, but the words tangled on her tongue, sounding more like the plea of a starving woman.

Devon inhaled deeply, then reluctantly pulled back, staring into the shadowed depths of her eyes. His hunger made her feel weak. His gaze dropped to her neckline, then with shaking fingers he undid the tiny silk-covered buttons of her blouse. Breath ragged, face intense, he jerked her blouse free of her skirt.

For a moment there was absolute silence. Brittany's breasts trembled with her uneven breathing.

With the tip of his finger he touched the rope of pearls that had been hidden beneath her blouse. "You say I've destroyed your love for me, yet you kept it alive all these years. Is it really gone?"

It was so unfair of him to ask. She said the first thing that was on her mind. "I don't want to love you."

"That's not an answer." His mouth quirked at the corners. "Although I can relate to the sentiment."

"We're not good for each other, Devon." Now it was Brittany trying to erect walls. "All we ever do is hurt, hurt, hurt. There's got to be a better way to love."

"There is."

She heard the humor but also saw the flame burning in his eyes. "I mean, besides the physical."

For answer his fingers twisted the front clasp of her bra, his eyes locked to hers. She felt her breasts expand, heavy and eager. With infinite patience Devon pushed her blouse and bra over her shoulders, baring her from the waist up. His eyes never left her face.

"The physical isn't so bad," he said, then his gaze dropped. His lips slackened at the sight of her and Brittany dissolved inside. She gave a thin cry when his mouth closed over one nipple and her hands clenched and wove through his thick hair. She should stop him. *Stop him*.

"Devon, I don't think I can..." she gasped.

"Neither can I."

His voice was thick and heavy. Brittany felt her knees tremble uncontrollably. His mouth was hot and warm; the weight of his body an aphrodisiac. Her mind swirled with memories that didn't seem real; the present was dramatically different from her past.

They were falling, sliding down the counter as one. Brittany tried to stop their descent but it was a futile effort. Only the feel of cold tile against the bare skin of her back awakened her to danger.

"I'm not kidding, Devon. I *can't*." She began struggling in earnest.

He pinned her easily, his brows drawn into an angry line. "Why not?"

"Because..." Brittany glared at him in exasperation. "Oh, don't be dense. There are a thousand reasons."

"None that make a helluva lot of sense at this point," he said with utterly convoluted reasoning. He dropped a kiss to one rose-tipped nipple and Brittany's skin shuddered involuntarily. "See?" A smile touched the corners of his mouth. "You agree with me."

She closed her eyes. "I haven't slept with a man since you," she admitted.

Devon's eyes widened in amazement, then they narrowed. He couldn't trust her and she saw it instantly.

"There would be no reason for me to lie to you," she said between her teeth. "Now let me up, before we both do something we'll regret."

"I won't regret it and neither will you." He shifted his weight, making his intentions vividly obvious. His hips were hard against hers.

"You're such an egotist!" Brittany wriggled beneath him but he made a sound of mock ecstasy and she stopped moving instantly. A second later he burst into laughter.

"Damn you, Devon!" she hissed, but an unwilling smile curved her lips. Something had changed, she realized. Devon might not admit it but his perception of her had changed. He wouldn't be able to laugh if it hadn't. Maybe he did believe her, at least a little.

"I'm freezing to death down here," she said, and Devon placed his palms on either side of her shoulders, lifting his chest. They were still touching in very strategic places and she saw the humor lurking behind his blue, blue eyes.

"I did miscarry," she said softly. "I wanted the baby. Our baby." Devon stiffened but she went on anyway, "I wanted to die when I lost it. I would have done anything to save it, Devon."

He rolled away from her onto his back. "I thought you didn't want any more postmortems."

"You needed to know." Brittany propped herself up on one elbow, wishing with all her heart that he could see the truth.

His jaw worked. "You won't understand this. Hell, you'll tell me to get out of your life again, but damn it all, Brittany..."

He didn't need to finish. She knew exactly what he was going to say. "You find it impossible to believe me." At his startled look she sat up, vainly trying to adjust her clothes. "I guess I can't really blame you. It's too hard for you to admit that you might have been wrong."

Devon grabbed her hand before she could get to her feet. "Don't," he ordered harshly. The muscles of his throat worked. "I want to believe you. You don't know how much."

"Not enough, Devon. Or you would."

She was buttoning her blouse but he swept her hands away. "I don't know what I want," he admitted in frustration. "You make me crazy. I don't know what I'm doing with you." His eyes traveled to the tempting opening of her blouse. He could see the gentle, lush swell of her breasts. "Give me one good reason why Nora would lie to me. Convince me, Britt. I want to be convinced."

Brittany glared at him. "I don't owe you anything, Devon! I don't have to explain. You're the investigative reporter. Go out and ask someone else. You will anyway," she murmured, mimicking his earlier tone.

He yanked her down to him. "Damn it all to hell," he muttered, and his fury could be felt in the ravenous crushing of his mouth against hers. Brittany struggled to right herself but the way his hands moved over her was breathtakingly familiar. They slipped beneath her blouse, caressing her breasts, then moved down her waist, her hips, finding her trembling inner thigh exposed by her tangled skirt.

Her sparking anger became a dull yearning ache once more. Brittany squeezed her eyes shut and held her breath. She couldn't allow herself to give in; she wouldn't.

"Either you trust me now or you never will, Devon," she said with regret.

Devon sighed, pressing butterfly kisses against the pale skin of her neck. "I trust you."

"No. No, you don't." She had to get away from the feel of his virile body beneath hers. She wouldn't allow herself to make love to a man who thought so little of her. "But I understand you better now than I have since we broke up," she went on. Brittany shifted but Devon's strong hands held her tightly in place. It was impossible to think while his smoky eyes were mirroring her own feelings.

But she had to think. She'd made a mistake with Devon in the past; she could make a bigger one now. "Understanding you hasn't changed anything. Knowing why you hated me is hardly the reason to start a new affair."

"I didn't hate you," he denied vehemently.

"Close enough."

His palms held her face in gentle conquest. "Oh, Britt, what I've felt for you all this time has torn me apart. It's been agony. Torture. Not hate."

"Then you deserved what you got," she said, trying to keep up the barriers.

"Probably," Devon agreed, his eyes solemn. "If I've been the bastard you say I have."

She heard the big "if." "I can't love a man who's so unsure about me," she whispered before she thought.

Devon's thumb caressed her cheek. "I want you, Brittany. I've always wanted you."

She twisted sharply, managing to half escape from his grip. "Now that's a bald-faced lie. Don't try to con me, Devon."

She was on her feet again but only because he'd let her go. He rose beside her, tall and intent. "I'm not conning you. I might not have wanted to admit it all this time, but I *have* wanted you. Only you," he added thoughtfully.

It was too easy to see where this kind of talk could lead. Devon's desire hadn't faded just because he'd set her free. They were both emotionally heated, and yes, physically, too. Wrapping her arms beneath her breasts, tugging her blouse together, Brittany backed away from Devon. She turned blindly in the direction of the living room, her steps tapping rapidly across the oak-parquet hallway. She needed time to herself. Time to think clearly and objectively. He was making her crazy.

The carpeting muffled her footsteps but she heard Devon's tread in the hallway, the soft deadening as he, too, stepped onto the plush-pile carpet. Brittany didn't turn. She gazed out the window, her eyes caught by the dancing sunlight on the slate-blue Pacific sea. She was in over her head with Devon. She knew it and he knew it. But all he wanted was a quick affair. If the past had taught her anything, it was to be realistic about other people's motivations. Maybe he even wanted to rid himself of her. It almost made sense.

Brittany screwed up her courage and turned to face him. What she saw was hardly encouraging. Devon was a man used to having his way and now he was standing aggressively in the center of the room, booted feet apart, hands on hips.

She remembered his last words and said softly, "You've always kept love and lust very separate. I can't. I mix them up all the time where you're concerned."

Devon crossed the distance between them in two strides. His strong hands enfolded hers and he pulled her away from the window, against the potent contours of his body. Brittany tried passively to resist but his hands were warm and urgent, his body tense with repressed passion, his breathing rapid.

"You're the only woman I've ever wanted like this, Britt. Believe that. Since seeing you again I haven't been able to sleep."

His voice was rough and terse and sent a thrill of pleasure skittering down her spine. When he parted her blouse again Brittany melted against him. There was no room left inside her to say no.

Devon led her to the couch and before she could offer any comment his mouth had found hers, his tongue insistent, tense anticipation radiating from his flesh to hers. The air felt electric. Brittany's eyes were wide, her lips parted. She felt so new with Devon that she hungered to look at him, to assure herself that this was the man she'd loved before. That past they'd shared together seemed ever more distant.

Her clothes were being removed with wild abandon. Her heart was pounding in heavy beats that threatened to leave her deaf. Brittany was powerless to resist. She was mindless, boneless, her cheeks flushing with an anticipation that drew a groan of desire from Devon.

I want you. I want you. I want you. The words circled her brain in a wondrous litany. She held his face, brought his lips back to hers when they threatened to stray, felt the cushions of the couch caress her back and succumbed to the heady sensation of his weight dropping passionately over hers.

"Devon—"

His lips had found the secret pleasures of her breasts but now they returned to her mouth, cutting off whatever she'd been about to say. If he thought she'd been trying to voice a protest he was wrong. She wanted only to share her excitement.

He moved with a recklessness and urgency that left her breathless and floating on the rim of reality. Hot currents of need ran from his veins to hers, stoking desires that Brittany hadn't known existed. It hadn't been this way before, she wanted to say, but the only sound that passed her lips was a soft, lusty moan.

Her skirt and blouse were gone; so were her shoes and nylons. Only the filmy wisp of lace that was her last protection remained but Devon slid it over her hips with a gentleness that had her flesh trembling.

"Believe in me, Devon," she managed to whisper. "Please, please believe in me."

He couldn't answer. She felt him struggle for the words. Part of her died inside at his inability to see her as the woman she truly was.

"I want to..." he whispered, throat taut. "I want to...too much..."

"Then do," she urged, soft and yielding against his rigid hardness. She sensed he really was trying to believe in her anew. It was enough. It would have to be.

She helped him undress with hands that shook with tremors. What laughable control! She hadn't been with a man since Devon and though she'd never given much thought to sexual fulfillment in the interim, now she burned with a blinding passion that would have embarrassed her in a cooler state of mind.

Devon's bare chest lay upon hers, his heart beating hard and strong. His pants were undone, half off his body, and Brittany helped remove the rest of his clothes, overwhelmed by a glorious déjà vu that didn't remember any pain.

She felt his sudden silence, the curious tightening in the air, and her eyes flew to his controlled face. Something wasn't right. "What is it?" she whispered. "What's wrong?"

They were naked now, Devon's breath wafting warmly against her breasts, his hands stroking her in ways that had her moving against him, abandoned and eager.

His lower jaw moved, then locked firmly into place. "Are you...will you...get pregnant if we make love?"

Something inside her shattered. Brittany shuddered beneath his powerful frame. "No," she said weakly. Then, more firmly, with just a trace of bitterness, "No."

He looked at her questioningly, regretfully. "You said there had been no one else...."

"I'm not about to make another mistake, Devon. *We're* not about to."

He kissed her and she felt the unspoken apology. But she could hardly be angry. He had a right to know. Even she had done a quick mental calculation to make certain that history wouldn't repeat itself.

"I never wanted either of us to get hurt," he said softly. "If I'm to blame, I'm sorry."

Brittany's eyes closed and his lips brushed her lashes. She felt the smooth planes of his taut shoulders, the muscles that moved like liquid beneath. She would have no regrets when this night ended, she told herself. She expected so little that whatever happened afterward could not be a letdown. She would love him, physically and wholly, reveling in his scent and texture, and not be afraid to face the morning.

His tongue found her nipple and she felt it bud to life under his ministrations. "Devon..."

"Yes," he said against her soft skin. She clung to him, straining against him, her body moving restlessly.

She touched him everywhere and he groaned, trembling with urgency. "It's been too long," he murmured, positioning himself quickly, as if afraid she would change her mind if their lovemaking continued too long.

Her hands found the hard muscles of his buttocks just as he thrust into her in one powerful deliberate movement. Brittany was shocked by his entry and let out a small cry of surprise. But then Devon was soothing her, kissing her, caressing her, apologizing for the roughness of his need.

I love you, she thought as a small spark of desire fanned into a searing flame within her. She let out a faint moan of passion and Devon urged her further, tempting and enticing her with slow, fervent movements.

"I want..." She couldn't speak, couldn't remember.

"What?" Devon's voice didn't sound like his own. She could feel the effort he was making to restrain himself but she thrilled to the fact that he was perilously close to satisfaction.

Brittany's passion suddenly exploded. She cried out, pulling him into her, and Devon groaned thickly a moment before he, too, tumbled into the same chasm of desire.

The world seemed to slow, drifting into a liquid haze, and finally begin rotating again.

Brittany opened her eyes to see the dark top of Devon's head resting against her pale white breasts. Her breathing, like his, was fast and irregular. She didn't have time to think before he lifted his head and gave her an indulgent smile, his blue eyes still lazy with satisfaction.

"You've never looked more beautiful," he said, trailing a finger down one flushed cheek. "Your eyes, your hair...you look wild."

Something about the words, loving though they sounded, reminded Brittany of what he really thought of her. She'd been wrong, she realized too late, to think she could rationalize that hurt away, grab whatever meager love he could give her and be satisfied. He made her feel like a prize, an object of admiration that could never engender real feeling. She'd heard too many photographers tell her how beautiful she was to consider his compliment as it was intended. Brittany was exposed, vulnerable, and she responded to him as if he'd insulted her.

"I'll tell Ramon I need sex to achieve that 'just-loved' look next time he asks."

Devon's expression altered. "Who the hell's Ramon?"

"Jessica calls him the Sheik of Sweat. He's a photographer. He's known for preferring women in bikinis and lingerie rather than dresses and slacks. But he's good."

"Oh, Lord."

Devon lay against her once more but she could feel his tension. Instantly she regretted spoiling the moment. It had been a self-protective device, a way of distancing herself from him. Instead, she'd reminded Devon of all the traits he liked least about her.

Before she could open her mouth to explain, he'd rolled away from her, snatching up his clothes and thrusting his lean muscled legs into his jeans.

"I've gotta go," he muttered. "Goodbye."

Chapter Seven

Devon, wait!"

Brittany scrambled to her knees, grabbing for his arm. But Devon was already on his feet, zipping up his jeans, savagely searching through the tangled disarray of their clothes for his shirt.

"I'm sorry. Devon—" Brittany's throat closed in on itself. Why had she spoiled the moment? "I don't know what to say...except that I'm afraid."

His jaw clenched, Devon didn't answer. But the angry furor of his dressing slowed and he let out a long breath.

"I can't help it. I need to protect myself from you," Brittany said in a small voice. "It's automatic. I'm scared that it'll hurt all over again."

Devon's shoulders tightened as he met her wounded eyes. "There are no guarantees, Brittany," he said, looking away from the picture she made. Completely nude, with her face still flushed a delicious rosy pink, her lips swollen, her eyes deep and shadowed and her hair in the kind of fantastic abandon photographers died for, Brittany was a sensual landscape.

"Oh, Devon..." She stood and wrapped her arms around the broad haven of his back, her cheek pressed against his shoulder. "I should despise you for what you've thought of me, but I can't. I should tell you to get out of my life and mean it."

"Why don't you?" Devon was completely still.

She shook her head, her voice muffled, her mouth warm against his bare skin. "Because I'm crazy. Because loving you is worth the chance of hurting again."

Devon couldn't accept that. He moved sharply but didn't pull away. "You don't love me."

"Maybe I don't," she answered after a pause, her honesty making his chest fill with a kind of dull ache. "But what I feel for you is deep and you feel it, too. Otherwise we wouldn't be here like this now."

Devon looked down at the shirt in his hands. "What are we doing here now?"

His question could have been translated to "What am *I* doing here now?" but Brittany chose to answer it as it stood.

"Maybe we're just trying to understand each other."

Devon pressed her hands against his waist, feeling the heady weight of her breasts flattened against his back. "I'm on overload, Britt," he admitted. "You've piled a ton of information on me and I'm having trouble coping."

He was beginning to believe her. Brittany's breath shortened in a combination of excitement and hope. "Then let's take it one step at a time, Devon. I'm willing to wait."

"And if it all blows up in our faces?" His head was cocked, tuned to her response.

"Then I'll pick up the pieces again. I'm resilient. I'll survive."

His head swiveled, his sexy blue eyes assessing her over his shoulder. "And what about me?" he drawled.

"I could never hurt you the way you think I have. And you survived that."

Brittany was a little surprised at her own diplomacy and wisdom. The words seemed to come from deep within her, from some part of herself that had dispassionately assembled her thoughts and feelings.

"I'm not certain I did survive," Devon said with a touch of humor. "I'm in shell shock."

The heat of his body felt wonderful. Brittany could have stood all day in just that position, letting his broad back bear her pain and love.

He disengaged himself gently, turning to drape his white shirt over her bare shoulders. It hung on her lithe frame, the arms far too long, the tails sweeping over the luscious curves of her buttocks and thighs. Devon pulled his sweater over his head, letting Brittany stay protected beneath his shirt. He liked the way she looked. A hot possessive streak stirred within him at her tumbled sensuality and the lavender innocence in her wide eyes.

"I do have to leave," he said, unable to control a self-satisfied smile at the disappointment that clouded her expression. "But I want to see you again. Soon."

"My weekends are free."

"That's all?"

Brittany smiled, then said diffidently, "I'm working. And I have a ton of things to do before Thanksgiving."

"Such as?"

Brittany was aware that, where her career was concerned, she had to be careful with Devon. "I've got some photographic sessions and a couple of meetings."

Her tone begged him not to delve into it any farther. Devon scowled but said, "Do you work all night, too?"

His hands were on her waist, his fingers nearly spanning her. She felt their heated movement and an unconsciously seductive smile flickered across her lips. "No-o-o...."

"Then you might be free in the evenings?"

"Yes, but, Devon, sometimes my schedule gets moved around and I can't be certain until almost that very day."

Devon sighed, easing her anxieties. "I hear you. I've got a little problem that way myself."

Reluctantly he let her go, his hands trailing over her smooth skin. Thinking of his work reminded him of Broderick, and, coming full circle, thinking of Broderick reminded him of Brittany's involvement.

He tilted up her chin with his finger. "I won't ask you about Mexico. I'll believe you're not involved with Broderick. But tell me someday, okay? No—" he placed his fingers over her mouth "—you don't have to now. If it doesn't have anything to do with Broderick it's your business. *Comprendes?*"

"*Comprendo.*"

Brittany was swept up in the kind of happiness she'd been afraid to allow herself to feel. Trust. That was Devon's gift. Not totally, not entirely, but it was a start, a giant leap from where they'd been an hour earlier.

He picked up some of her clothes, eyeing the sheer nylons and frivolous lace undergarments. "I think these are yours," he said gravely.

"I wish you didn't have to leave," said Brittany, clutching the pile of clothes tightly.

"I wish I didn't have to, either. But don't you think it's for the best? I couldn't stay here and not..." His gaze was riveted on the proud beauty of her long-limbed body. He shuddered dramatically, then pretended to pull himself together, a smile hinting at the corners of his mouth. "Well, you get my drift. And if things continued as they have...I'd never get out of here."

He kissed her on the mouth. Brittany's lips molded softly to his and Devon let out a groan of torment. "Enough already," he begged, giving her a chaste peck on the forehead and promising, "I'll call you."

"I'm counting on it."

Devon grinned, flashing a shaft of sunlight across the grim contours of his face. It was like seeing a rare gem, one that had been hidden beneath layers of darkness. Brittany, on a wild whim, grabbed the lapel of the shirt she was wearing and flashed him a glimpse of the taut glowing skin and lush curves that had helped make her famous.

"If I had a camera," Devon observed, "I could make a mint off that view." His grin was very nearly a leer.

Brittany laughed. "That goes two ways. I'm sure your female viewers would be interested in seeing all of you."

"I'm not as breathtaking."

"That," she said softly, "is a matter of opinion."

They looked at each other for long moments, then Devon shook his head. "I'll call you very soon."

Brittany nodded.

"Don't worry, Britt," he added gently, witnessing the anxiety that flickered across her face. "You'll probably be hearing from me before you want to."

She walked him to the door, keeping her thoughts to herself. There was no way he could call her too soon. She already missed him and he hadn't even left yet.

Brittany bent double from the waist, touching her toes, turning her head toward the camera. She had to control an inappropriate chuckle at the sight Ramon made: upside-down with hands on hips, his comic face tight with intense thought, three earrings dangling from one ear, leather jump suit and a sharp-lensed Pentax held carelessly in his right hand.

"What is with you, Daniels?" he demanded, and Brittany abruptly lifted her head. "This god-awful happiness has got to quit."

Happiness. Brittany rolled the word over in her mind, unused to the sound of it. Did he really see her happiness? She straightened in surprise and Ramon's meager good humor vanished altogether.

"Bend over!" he bellowed, and to his total frustration Brittany started laughing in earnest.

"Okay. Okay." She made motions of waving an imaginary white flag and resumed her position. The shimmery gray leotard clung like a glove, hugging each curve as Brittany bent down and brushed her hair away from her eyes. Damp black curls hung down in a billowing curtain, brushing her aerobic-shoe-clad feet. Her tights were a pale dove gray interwoven with sparkling silver threads. A red belt and headband completed the outfit, and for effect, a barbell had been placed within her reach.

Ramon, grunting his grudging approval, took several shots. "That little smile's great. Keep it up. For once in your life you look as if you're enjoying yourself."

Ramon had been making cryptic remarks along the same vein all morning. It was a revelation to Brittany that her face was so expressive. She'd been congratulating herself on being able to hide her feelings all this time when in reality she'd been an open book.

"Now put your hands on the barbell. Don't pick it up. Just look as if you're going to."

"Ramon, no one would pick up a barbell in this position. It would be murder on your lower back."

"Shh." Ramon, the artist, allowed no arguments.

"Second Skin Sportswear will probably get sued for false advertising," she warned.

"Well, I'm not going to have you squat and hold that monstrosity," Ramon shot back, curling his lip at the equipment. Ramon was constantly battling his own weight but an exercise regimen had never been something he'd ascribed to. He was horrified at the idea.

Brittany couldn't resist temptation. Shifting her weight to her legs she lifted the black barbell. It was heavy, but not out of her range. She looked proudly at her muscles, then grinned outrageously at the plump photographer.

Ramon looked pained. "I think I liked you better when you were all haunted eyes and silent suffering."

Subdued, Brittany followed the rest of his orders to the letter, glad when the session was over. It was disturbing to realize how she'd been before her reconciliation with Devon.

Devon. She was still in a state of shock over what had happened between them. But she was happy. Deliriously happy. Too happy, perhaps. A cautious inner voice warned her about believing in silly dreams and rainbows. Especially with Devon.

She should, she knew, be furious with him for all the unnecessary pain he'd caused for both of them. She had been furious. She was still furious. But her fury was tempered by emotions that ran as deep and untamed as the earth's core. She loved him, and loving him could make up for a lot of unhappiness.

Brittany stepped out of the dressing room, her pearls lying white and lambent against the rich cloth of her royal-blue linen dress. She sketched a goodbye to the mercurial Ramon, hurrying lest he should come up with another reason to reshoot the last sequence. The man was impossible, mean tempered and immovable. She sometimes felt his reputation was what put him in such hot demand with the manufacturers; there were other photographers with as much talent but without Ramon's flamboyance. People remembered Ramon. His name surged to the top of every list.

And his pictures were excellent.

Brittany flipped through her appointment calendar, assuring herself that she did indeed have several hours free. With a vague feeling of guilt hovering in the back of her mind, she pulled out Grant Broderick's card, memorizing the address of the gem-brokerage firm he'd recommended.

Partly because Broderick's reputation had convinced her he knew his stuff and partly—in a perverse sort of way—because she needed to keep some independence from Devon, Brittany had decided she would look into investing in gems. An investment was an investment, Grant Broderick or no. She wasn't about to let anyone lead her by the nose but she was interested in diversifying. The idea of making a healthy investment in gems was very appealing. .

The woman at the reception desk of Marcel & Kingston brokerage firm looked up expectantly as Brittany walked through the door. She smiled and stood, the simple lines of her caramel silk dress mirroring the understated elegance of the whole reception room.

"Could I help you?" she asked, her eyes silently admiring Brittany's pearls.

Beyond the receptionist's desk was a hallway, on either side of which were offices with glass fronts opening inward. Brittany could see several people talking on telephones.

"I'd like to speak to someone about investing," Brittany said. "Grant Broderick suggested I stop in."

"You're a friend of Mr. Broderick's?"

Brittany smiled. "I suppose I'm more in the potential-customer line. I just met Mr. Broderick a few weeks ago."

"We sell most gems wholesale but we specialize in diamonds," the woman said with a return smile, reaching for a folder on her desk and handing it to Brittany. "This is our brochure. It lists the size, cut and clarity of each of the gems now available from the overseas wholesalers. If you buy now it will take several weeks, maybe even a bit longer, before you receive them." Leaving Brittany to look at the brochure, the woman punched a button on her phone and asked one of the brokers to come to the reception area.

Brittany was impressed with the brochure. A dazzling array of gems was fanned out on a black velvet background. Topaz, emerald, sapphire, ruby: an artist had arranged the spectacular rainbow of stones, their sparkling beauty alive even on the two-dimensional surface. In the center, its size outranking the more brilliantly colored gems, was an exquisite teardrop diamond.

The door of the nearest office opened and a young man in a Gucci suit walked briskly toward them. He, too, noticed Brittany's pearls. "Beautiful," he complimented her, then lifted his eyes and smiled, holding out his hand. "I'm Jace Segal. How can I be of help?"

"Brittany Daniels. I'm thinking of investing in gems. Probably diamonds, but I'm not ready to commit right at the moment."

"Fine." He swept his arm in the direction of his office and Brittany led the way inside. She saw several orders on his desk, and the amounts other customers were putting down on gems staggered her.

The receptionist tapped on the glass door, poking her head in for a moment. "Mr. Broderick suggested Miss Daniels stop by," she said.

Jace Segal's expression changed. "I see," he said slowly, giving Brittany all of his attention. "Is Mr. Broderick your investment adviser?"

"No. I manage my own money. He just knew I was interested in gems and recommended your firm."

"Mr. Broderick gives excellent advice," Jace Segal said with mock gravity, and they both chuckled.

"You're interested in diamonds," said Jace thoughtfully. "You've come to the right place because diamonds are our specialty. We have direct links with the European diamond-sales companies."

"When an order's placed, are the diamonds shipped direct to the customer or to you?" Brittany asked.

"Either way. We normally ship direct."

Jace proceeded to give Brittany an in-depth speech on gems as investments. His enthusiasm was genuine and

Brittany warmed to him. "Generally we don't keep any gems here, but one of our buyer's gems just came in and she hasn't picked them up yet. They're sapphires and they're absolutely stunning. Would you care to see them?"

Brittany was surprised. "May I?"

"Certainly. They're in the vault." He rose and gestured toward the back of the hallway. A uniformed guard stood by a huge walk-in vault. Marcel and Kingston might generally ship direct, but they were obviously prepared to house the gems if necessary.

Brittany wasn't interested in buying jewelry for jewelry's sake but she wanted to see the quality of Marcel and Kingston gems. She followed Jace to the back of the vault, to a case with hundreds of tiny drawers.

"They're practically all empty," Jace explained. Unerringly, he chose a drawer that to Brittany's eye was in no way different from any other. But when he pulled it open blue light flashed and gleamed as the gems tumbled over one another, a rainbow of azure, delft and cerulean on white satin.

The sight took Brittany's breath away. "It's such a shame to keep them in a vault."

"How true. They're appraised at $200,000," Jace said with a touch of pride. "Right now we're in a period of stable inflation, so their value will stay about the same. Gems, however, are very sensitive to inflation. As it goes up, so will their value. Now is a good time to buy."

Light shimmered and seemed to tremble off the many-faceted sapphires. Brittany had never thought much about gems other than her pearls, and then only for sentimental reasons. She'd worn some horrendously expensive necklaces, bracelets and earrings during her modeling career, but she'd never considered the stones themselves; not personally, not for herself.

"Which gems are the best investments?" she asked.

"There's nothing wrong with diamonds. I've bought them myself, and yes, I've made a profit. A substantial profit. I used to be a stockbroker but I prefer dealing in gems." He shut the drawer with a certain amount of reverence. "They're my one great love."

Brittany could understand what he meant. There was something binding about precious stones. They were real, lovely, pleasurable. One could hardly grow rapt over stocks and bonds, but gems were beautiful and fascinating.

"I'll give the investment a great deal of thought," Brittany said, shaking Jace's hand at the front door.

"Do. Give me a call when you've decided."

Brittany was halfway home when she realized how certain Jace Segal was that she would make the investment. *Give me a call when you've decided.* Had she seemed that eager? She didn't think so. The investment was riskier than most she'd made and Brittany was extremely careful with her money. She could, however, afford to gamble some of it.

She was still mulling over all the pros and cons while she made dinner later that evening. She hadn't yet come to a decision when she heard familiar footsteps on her porch. A second later the door bell chimed.

Devon.

Brittany looked down at the apron tossed over her sweater and jeans, fumbled with its knot, swore, then laughed and finally gave up, hurrying to meet him. She swung the door wide, her face flushing with pleasure at the sight of him leaning negligently against the porch rail, booted feet crossed at the ankle, arms folded across his chest.

He straightened, a slow smile lightening his controlled expression. "I wasn't entirely sure of my reception," he explained. "I thought you might have changed your mind."

"About what? You?" Brittany stepped back and bade him enter with a flourish of her hand. "Never."

His answer wasn't completely encouraging. "You're young. You've got lots of time to change."

"Not about this, Devon." Brittany was positive, her face serious. "Not about you."

Devon was silent as he followed her to the kitchen. Brittany picked up the knife she'd been using to dice an onion and worried again about what Devon was thinking. She cut with extra vigor, an eloquent display of her frustration with the difficulties he imposed on both of them.

"I went to see Nora today," he said suddenly, the words cool and careful.

Brittany's eyes flew to his face. She stopped chopping, a feeling of dread settling between her shoulder blades. "You checked up on my story?"

Devon shifted uneasily. "I told you I would."

Brittany could scarcely believe her ears. Every time they seemed to be pulling away from the miserable shackles of their past, Devon added another weight. "Your trust in me is staggering," she said bitterly.

"I know." The corners of his mouth slanted downward. "I'm one of those people who can't believe anything at face value."

"That's a cop-out, Devon." Brittany was angry.

"Don't you want to know what Nora said?"

"No."

"Why not?"

"Because she didn't know anything about what happened to me!" Brittany's eyes filled with instant, unexpected tears. Her lungs hurt for air.

"I figured that out right away," Devon said heavily. "She never knew, and she never wanted to know. And she didn't want you to have anything to do with me."

Brittany tried to pull herself together. "If you're trying to shove the blame on Nora..."

"I'm not. I'm at fault. Totally." His blue eyes were clouded with anger, an anger that was entirely self-directed. "I made mistakes and blamed you for them. An apology probably isn't enough, but it's all I have to offer. I'm sorry, Brittany."

She swallowed, stunned. "It's okay," she said in a small voice.

A shudder went through his large frame. "Okay? *Okay?* What do you mean, *okay?*" he thundered. "I've hurt you, wanted to hate you, blamed you, wished to ruin you. Damn it, Britt! Don't be understanding!"

She was weak with relief. He knew. He finally knew. "What do you want me to be?"

"Smug. Judgmental. Self-satisfied. Tell me, 'I told you so,' with great relish."

"I told you so," Brittany said with a huge grin. She loved him more at that moment than she ever had. She wanted to cradle him to her and tell him it was all right, that she understood.

Devon groaned and dropped his head into his hands. But her humor over the matter lifted his spirits. "Whip me, beat me," he pleaded, then at the trill of her laughter he added gravely, "but put down the knife, please."

"Not on your life. I may need it to defend myself."

Devon looked at her in a way that made her heart somersault. "I wanted out, Brittany. You scared me."

Brittany turned back to the rest of the salad greens. "I know," she said softly.

"I couldn't give you what you were so uninhibitedly giving me."

"I know, Devon. Really I do." Brittany didn't want to hear any more. The depth of Devon's feelings was still a worry to her, and if now he was about to bare his soul, revealing that he still couldn't love her, Brittany would just as soon he kept quiet. She wanted to dream for a while longer.

He came up behind her, wrapping his arms around her waist, his chin resting lightly on her shoulder. "Then why...?"

Brittany's hands were trembling. She laid the knife down carefully. "Because I loved you," she said with humbling honesty. "And now, I don't know. I think sometimes that maybe I still do. There's certainly something between us that's powerful and consuming."

"I don't deserve you."

"You're right," she said lightly.

"I mean it, Britt."

His arms tightened, as if she might listen to his warning and finally take heed. But she couldn't. "Are you staying for dinner?" she asked.

"Are you asking me?"

"I thought I told you to stop answering questions with questions."

"Yes," said Devon. "I'm staying for dinner."

"Then stop bothering the cook and let her get to work."

"Hmm." Devon nuzzled her neck, smelling her sweet scent, pushing aside his own self-recriminations and allowing himself to be drawn into her mood. "You're getting bossy in your old age."

Brittany was glad the other conversation had been laid to rest. "I've always been bossy but I've never been much of a cook. If you want something besides a green salad you're going to have to let go of me."

"A green salad and thou," he quoted, badly. "I'll help. What would you like me to do?"

He stepped back and regarded her seriously. Brittany hardly knew how to react to this side of Devon. He was treating her kindly, tenderly, even controlling the smoky passion that seethed in the blue depths of his eyes. His control, she knew, was partly due to contrition—he felt terrible for not believing her—but it might also be a protective mechanism. It was possible he regretted their abandoned lovemaking a few nights earlier.

"You can stir the stew," Brittany told him, pointing to a copper-bottomed pot that was just beginning to simmer on the stove.

Devon's gaze dropped to her mouth for a split second. Then he turned to do as she'd asked, but Brittany was devastated. In that moment she'd seen his hunger, his need. She went back to her task with clumsy hands, her appetite completely gone.

She fantasized about the night ahead, then shook her head in dismay. It would be so easy to fall into a pattern of loving him. Yet she knew he didn't feel the same. And she'd learned the hard way that you couldn't make someone fall in love with you simply by loving them.

Brittany tossed the salad, then relieved Devon of his duties, serving the stew in blue enamel bowls. She uncorked a bottle of red wine and poured two glasses. As Devon accepted the outstretched glass, his fingers closed around hers for a heartbeat too long.

"It's been three days," he remarked.

Brittany managed a tentative smile. Three days. It seemed like a thousand eternities.

Devon's attitude bothered her a little. She could feel the way he'd withdrawn, the dissatisfaction that laced that comment. *You're borrowing trouble,* she chided herself, but she couldn't shake off her uneasiness.

Brittany sat down but before she could pick up her spoon Devon reached for her hand. A frown creased his brow as his fingers meditatively massaged hers. "Things are happening pretty fast. Sometimes I think..." He inhaled slowly and Brittany's heart stopped. *Here it comes,* she thought helplessly. *Here it comes.*

"I don't even know what you want, where you're going," he said. His jaw worked as he carefully considered what he had to say.

Brittany looked down at her bowl. "I'm not going to worry about that now."

"You have to." Devon was blunt. He waited until her eyes met his again. "Once before we let the future just come. *Que sera, sera.* And look where it got us. I can't work that way. I'm a planner."

"Well, so am I."

Devon made a disbelieving sound. "Forgive me, Britt, but I've never seen that side of you."

She winced. It was easy to understand what he meant; all she had to do was remember the way she'd been before, willing to take Devon on any terms, anxious only to love him and hope that he would someday love her, too.

Wasn't that what she was doing now?

"I couldn't have got where I am in my career without some planning," she told him, blindly hiding her doubts.

"True," Devon conceded thoughtfully. "But you and I..."

"How come I get the feeling an unprecedented decision is about to be handed down?"

Devon had the grace to smile. "Nothing so terrible. I'd just like to slow the pace a little."

She could have reminded him that it had been his idea to come over tonight, but she didn't. "Meaning?"

"Meaning I have to leave in a few minutes. Don't look at me that way, Britt," he added gently. "I've done some serious thinking the past few days, and I'll be damned if I'm going to let us make the same mistakes we did before. The biggest problem we had was that we didn't know each other very well. Not really."

Brittany couldn't argue with him on that. She hadn't bothered to learn all the ins and outs of Devon Gallagher. At nineteen she'd known she loved him. Period. That had been all that mattered.

"I'm going to Seattle for Thanksgiving," Devon said, "to visit my sister, Shannon. She's the only family I have left."

Family. Her father. Brittany's throat felt dry and stiff. Thanksgiving. Devon was leaving her.

"Will you come to Seattle with me?"

Brittany blinked. "Come with you?"

Devon nodded, completely serious.

Surprised and pleased, Brittany said, "I'd love to." Her voice was breathless and full of amazement. She'd never dreamed Devon would ask her to meet Shannon, the only person he'd ever spoken about with any degree of love. She knew both Devon and Shannon had been abandoned as children, but even so, he'd kept that part of his life mostly hidden. He'd never once, during their first affair, made any mention of Brittany's meeting his sister.

With a dash of reality, she remembered Mexico. She'd promised her parents she would be there the week before Thanksgiving. But she had another empty week after, a week she could spend with Devon in Seattle.

For the first time, Brittany seriously considered telling Devon about her father. But before she could get up the courage, the phone rang.

"Excuse me." She dropped her napkin on the table and walked to the opposite wall, picking up the receiver from the wall phone. "Hello?"

"Hello, yourself," came Jessica Barlowe's voice. "Sorry to call so late but I just got off the phone from Marjorie Vandoren's right-hand woman. They want you to do the Toujours photo session ASAP."

Though Devon was watching her with only mild curiosity, Brittany was afraid his expression would turn to condemnation if he knew who was calling and what the phone call was about. A silly paranoia, she knew, but she was careful with her answers anyway. "I don't think I can do it before Thanksgiving."

"We'll have to change something in your schedule then. It'll take a couple days with the Toujours people. How about the end of next week?"

Brittany licked her lips. "I can't. I'm leaving for Mexico."

Devon laid down his fork and picked up his glass of wine. He looked over the rim at her but Brittany, after one look into his purposely neutral expression, avoided his eyes.

"Oh, no. So soon?" Jessica did some quick mental calculations. "All right, then we'll have to cancel that interview on Wednesday with *In Touch* magazine...again. They'll probably flip out. And the publicity appearance with Crestview Cola's got to go, too."

"They won't like it," Brittany warned.

"They don't have a choice. If I have to, I can tell them the reason you're going to Acapulco."

"No." Brittany was adamant. She didn't want her father besieged with publicity. It was the last thing he needed and she knew there were gossip reporters hungry for that type of story. Thank God Devon was of a different caliber, yet she couldn't even tell him!

"All right. Your decision. Leave these arrangements to me. I'll get it all worked out. When will you be back?"

Brittany found herself sweating. She could hear the sounds of Devons' eating behind her, yet his gaze seemed pinned to the space between her shoulder blades. "I may be going to Seattle for Thanskgiving," she told Jessica. "So I'll be out for two weeks."

"Seattle?"

"Don't ask."

"Hmm. This doesn't have something to do with Grant Broderick, does it?"

Brittany was surprised. "Heavens, no. I barely know him."

Jessica's other line started ringing. "Gotta go. Take care. I'll fix it for Toujours."

"Your agent?" Devon guessed as Brittany sat down again.

"Uh-huh. Jessica's having trouble with my schedule."

Devon finished his wine and stood up. Brittany saw how little he'd eaten and watched him with anxious eyes. Was he so negative about her career that he couldn't bear to listen to her make plans?

Devon thrust his arms through the sleeves of his jacket, the leather straining across his back as he flexed his shoulders.

"If you can't make Seattle—"

"I will, Devon." Brittany practically willed him to see what was truly important to her. "My career isn't everything to me, contrary to what you might believe."

He sighed, shoving his hands in his pockets, lines etched beside his nose. "I know."

"You don't really," Brittany disagreed.

Devon tried to rationalize away all his doubts but it was impossible. They were still embedded too deeply. "No, I don't."

Brittany's meal was forgotten. She pushed her chair back and walked over to him, so instantly and completely forgiving of his faults that Devon couldn't stand it.

"You shouldn't put up with me," he said tightly.

"You're telling me."

"Don't joke. It's too important."

She stared at him, unaware of the yearning that Devon could see, which made him feel even worse. But Brittany had heard his warning: *Don't love me too much, I don't want to hurt you again.*

She walked him to the door, knowing that if she tried very hard he would stay, but also aware that that would be the worst thing she could do at this juncture. Devon was a man used to knowing his own mind, and with Brittany, he was ravaged by indecision.

She kissed him lightly on the mouth. "One day it'll all come together," she said softly.

"Your certainty frightens me, Britt." Devon held her face in his palms and she knew fear of a different kind. He wasn't denying that he had feelings; he was denying what those feelings meant. Maybe he didn't love her, couldn't love her. She might very well be left high and dry in the end.

"I'm good at taking chances," she whispered.

Devon gave her a seaching look before he left. Brittany watched him walk down the stairs, mesmerized by his confident easy grace, flooded with more emotions than she could name.

She would have to be good at taking chances. Loving Devon was a risk any way she looked at it.

Chapter Eight

You can't be certain there's a connection between Eric Cordell and Broderick," Devon said with unusual testiness into the phone. He shifted the receiver from one ear to the other and searched through the papers on his desk for a pad and pencil.

Jay Lundgren thought carefully. "You still think Broderick's working alone?"

"Hard to tell at this point. What about the other people?"

"The De Vacas are definitely out," Jay said. "We've dug and dug into their history. There's nothing on them."

"But why Cordell?" Devon scowled at the broken tip of his pencil.

"A matter of elimination. Who else do we know who could be involved? Unless you're still considering Brittany Daniels."

Devon had to fight himself not to answer too quickly. He was already being a bit unreasonable; Jay's conclusions made perfect sense. It worried and perplexed him that his objectivity was in jeopardy where Brittany was concerned. Championing her innocence now would only destroy his credibility with Jay and lessen his self-respect. "I don't think Brittany's a likely candidate," he said with restraint.

Jay made a sound of agreement. She'd never been a suspect with him at all.

But Devon, who was afraid of being blinded by his feelings for her, wasn't as certain as he sounded. Rationally, he didn't believe she had anything to do with Broderick. She'd said as much and Devon had known she wasn't lying. But emotionally...

Why the hell hadn't he let her tell him about Mexico when she'd been willing?

"Broderick's partner, if he has one, doesn't have to be one of the first-class passengers," Devon pointed out, deliberately changing the course of the conversation. "It could be anyone who travels regularly from Mexico City to the States."

Jay was silent. He and Devon had gone over this before. When Broderick was last in Mexico, Devon had hired a private detective to record his whereabouts. No one Broderick contacted had made any trips to the U.S. and deliveries from the companies Broderick visited had been quietly searched by customs.

It made sense that either Broderick was bringing the gems across the border himself or someone else was doing it for him.

If gems were being smuggled. And Devon's gut instincts told him they were.

"No one flying coach has flown that regularly, as far as we know," Jay said, recapping. "It makes sense that it's someone in first class. The more you need to fly, the more you want luxury, especially if you can afford it."

Devon didn't want to agree with Jay's philosophy. Brittany had been in the first-class cabin on Broderick's last flight. "Flying first-class is like waving a red flag. People remember you."

"If you don't have anything to hide it doesn't matter." Jay's words were an echo of Devon's own. They'd covered this territory too many times. Devon had even argued Jay's side in the past. But having Brittany in the picture made Devon doubt his own instinct. He was too afraid for her. Too afraid for himself. An error in judgment now could prove fatal.

He knew she always flew to Acapulco, whether she stopped in Mexico City or not. But he didn't know what that meant.

"I'm going face-to-face with Broderick pretty soon," Devon said. "I want to press him real hard. But I need a few more facts or else I'll just tip my hand."

"What do you think he'll do?" asked Jay.

"Make a mistake, I hope." The thought of Brittany flying to Mexico around the same time as Broderick made Devon's mouth go dry.

"Why don't you follow up on Cordell?" Devon said to Jay. "And I'll work the other end. There's got to be a way he's pushing those gems through, and my money's on Marcel and Kingston. He's been bandying their name around at every opportunity. If he isn't a silent partner in that firm, he's a major shareholder."

Jay coughed lightly. "I wasn't going to say anything about this, Devon, until I got all the facts because I was afraid you would..."

"What?"

Devon heard a tense silence, then Jay said quietly, "Brittany Daniels went to Marcel and Kingston this morning. Probably at Broderick's suggestion."

Dread uncoiled in Devon's stomach. He didn't want to hear any more. "Did she buy anything?"

"This hasn't been verified yet, remember, but the first report is that she bought fifty thousand dollars' worth of diamonds."

"Holy God...." Tremors ran under Devon's skin. He pressed the heel of his hand against his forehead.

"I don't think she's involved," Jay went on unhappily, "but I do think she's been suckered."

"I'm gonna kill Broderick with my bare hands," Devon rasped.

"Well, you're going to have to work fast. Broderick's been making dozens of flight reservations to Mexico. He's double-booked all over the place and each reservation is for some time within the next few days."

Devon felt a rage of confusion. It didn't take Jay or any private detective to tell him something else he already knew—Brittany was scheduled to leave for Mexico tomorrow. Her plea of innocence was getting harder and harder to believe. Yet he had to believe it.

"I'm going to see Brittany tonight to find out what she can tell me," Devon said heavily. "Innocent or guilty, she's involved somehow. I've got to know."

Jay made a sound of agreement. "I'll follow up on Cordell."

"And I'm going to the authorities on Marcel and Kingston. If Broderick's on his way to Mexico, something's up. We'll let the police take care of it and hope they see fit to give us the exclusive."

"Thank you, Jace...yes, I'm really happy I decided to buy." Brittany shifted the receiver from one ear to the other, trying to master zipping up the sides of her blue canvas suitcase and talk to the delighted salesman at the same time. "You said it would be a few weeks, right? Good, because I'm going to be out of town for a while."

"We'll send you a note when the diamonds arrive," Jace replied. "You'll have to make security arrangements to transfer them. We can do that for you if you'd like."

"I'll think about it. Thanks again."

Indeed she would think about it. Brittany wasn't interested in transporting the gems herself; people had been killed for a lot less than fifty thousand dollars' worth of cut diamonds.

Devon will probably throw a fit when you tell him, Brittany reminded herself, grimacing at the thought. But there was nothing he could do now; she'd bought the diamonds two days earlier. She'd considered the purchase carefully and had felt that, regardless of Devon's instincts regarding Broderick, the investment was sound.

Resolutely pushing thoughts of her purchase aside, Brittany stacked the zippered suitcase beside its matching partner. All she had to do was pack her shoulder bag and she'd be ready. Tomorrow was her last photo session for Toujours, then she'd be on her way to Acapulco.

She prowled around the house, stopping in the living room to look out at the sunset, watching the water turn to molten gold, amber rays slanting through her windowpanes to cast strange, bright shadows over the furniture and herself. It was a brilliant last hurrah from the fiery orb, but Brittany barely noticed it. She glanced at her watch in frustration.

Devon had kept out of her way all week. He'd called her twice, but the distance in his voice had irritated and deflated Brittany. He was setting the pace and it was much too slow for her.

With determination she walked to the phone, hesitated, then stabbed out his number before her courage deserted her. Two rings. Three. After the fifth ring she hung up, hunching her shoulders miserably. She hadn't even had the opportunity to tell him when and why she was leaving.

Brittany ran a hand through her hair, removing the ivory combs that kept her tangled tresses out of her eyes. She rubbed her scalp and wondered why she was such a masochist.

"If you had any sense at all," she told her reflection in the hall mirror, "you would just get on with your life. Devon even said as much."

On the other side, the pale-faced woman with the dark curtain of curls didn't agree. Her face was set and determined and ready to fight tooth and nail.

A corner of Brittany's mouth lifted unwillingly. Her reflection did the same. Then she was grinning like an idiot.

She raised her palms in surrender and walked to the kitchen. She wasn't about to give up on Devon; telling herself she could was just so much wasted effort.

Brittany picked over a meal of leftovers, washed her plate, looked at the phone longingly, then grabbed a half-read novel. She read another chapter before giving up; she was far too restless to sit still.

Her restlessness was due mostly to Devon but partly to the Toujours assignment. She'd spent two days with the people from Vandoren Cosmetics and had learned a great deal about their upcoming line of products. It had been more of an indoctrination than an employment interview, as far as Brittany could see, yet she'd never once got an inkling as to what Majorie Vandoren's people thought about her potential as their new "face."

Tomorrow would be the big test, the clincher. Brittany had a photo session at 6:00 A.M. Actually, it sounded more like a screen test since she was to be photographed and filmed for a mock commercial. Marjorie Vandoren wasn't taking any chances with her newest baby; Toujours was going to be the cream of her business.

When the session was over, sometime late in the afternoon, Brittany would head straight for the airport. She wouldn't have time to pack, so she'd had to get her suitcases ready tonight.

She was anxious to see her father. Ever since his last phone call, when she'd heard her mother's uneasy voice, Brittany had been on pins and needles. So far she'd resisted the temptation to drop everything and fly to her father's side, knowing she was being ridiculously sensitive and paranoid. But after the photo session tomorrow there would be no stopping her. She had to see him. Even Devon didn't have the power to alter her plans.

Brittany had just grabbed her sweater and started toward the front door for a dash of brisk, head-clearing sea air when headlights flashed through her front windows. She stepped onto the porch. Devon's BMW was slowing to a stop in her driveway.

"Well, it's about time," she said with a soft smile. "You have this terrible habit of running out on me."

Devon didn't respond. It was difficult to be certain in the evening shadows, but Brittany thought she saw a flicker of annoyance flash across his face. She had the feeling that something had changed, that some new, dark doubt had taken over. "What's happened?" she asked, the happiness fading from her face.

Devon came up the stairs two at a time, his hard body lithe and in control. When he reached the top step he just stared into her eyes, his scrutiny intense, as if he wanted to pass through that beautiful amethyst screen and search inside her mind.

Brittany felt deeply uneasy. "What are you looking for?" she asked in a low voice.

"I don't know," he said, and he sounded as if he didn't.

"Then what's wrong?"

Devon glanced toward the horizon at the pale violet brush strokes that lay against the darkening sky, the only thing left between day and night. He tried to let the peaceful serenity ease his anxiety. He wasn't looking forward to the confrontation that was coming. And he dreaded losing her trust again.

He noticed the sweater draped over her arm. "Are you leaving?" he asked quickly.

"Just for a walk on the beach."

"Could you postpone it?"

"Sure," Brittany agreed slowly, opening the door. "But tell me what's happening, Devon. You're scaring me!"

"I don't mean to." Devon shut the door behind them and stood beside her in the entry hall. Brittany waited, fidgeting nervously, but Devon was too self-absorbed to notice.

After a long, terrible moment, he put his palms on her shoulders and drew her to his chest. Brittany moved woodenly, listening to the fast even beating of his heart, awed by the emotions she could feel racing through him.

"Are you having second thoughts?" she asked, her face pressed against his shirt, her voice small and muffled.

Devon realized the mental torture he'd inadvertently put her through. "No. Oh, no." His breath wisped through her fragrant black curls, his arms tightening convulsively. Tremors raged through him. He realized with dawning surprise that he couldn't let her go.

Brittany exhaled in relief. "Devon, I—"

"Shh."

He didn't want to spoil the moment. He didn't want to have to tell her about Broderick or about the diamonds he suspected she'd purchased. He didn't want to, but he would. Later, much later.

His hand wound into the thick mane at her nape, tilting her face upward. Brittany was open and ripe for the taking, her face aglow with a love she couldn't hide. Devon's innate honesty filled him with regret that he couldn't offer her the same. A sweeping sadness spread through him, followed by the earthier sensation of desire. In the space of a few heartbeats it was burning heavy and hot through him, thickly expanding to a painful pleasure that brought his mouth to hers.

Brittany's hands gripped the hard swell of muscle on his upper arms. His hunger reached out and touched her, enfolded her. She reveled in it, her fears forgotten. With a soft, breathless moan she let his mouth devour hers.

They moved in a lovers' haze toward her bedroom. Brittany's blood pounded at the fierceness of Devon's desire. Her heart took wing and her ego soared. With a controlled frenzy, they stripped each other of their clothes and sank onto the satin comforter, arms and legs locked tightly, hungrily together.

"I'm not myself when I'm with you," Devon muttered, almost angrily.

Brittany smiled to herself. He didn't like being out of control. "Then tell me who you are so I can remember later," she teased.

Devon's body was all male, heavy with tightly packed muscles. Brittany let her hands slide over his back, feeling the ripple of pleasure that moved beneath his skin.

"You don't know what you do to me," he muttered.

"Don't I?" Brittany's eyelids fluttered closed at the sensual invasion of his hands sliding down her thighs.

"I don't want this night to end," he said fiercely, and before she could question his savage intensity, his fingers were stroking her into a mind-numbing ecstasy.

Brittany let her hands answer. Devon shuddered under the sweet agony of her touch. She could feel him resisting her even now, and she wanted to break his awful control once and forever. A person could be too cautious, too careful. She'd gone that route once and been miserable. She wouldn't do it again and she didn't want Devon to do it, either.

Her tongue lightly licked the edge of his ear. She kissed him tenderly, her own body quivering beneath his male heat. She wanted to prolong the ecstasy of the moment.

Devon was kissing her everywhere, his tongue sliding over her, raising tiny goose bumps in its wake. Brittany was breathless.

She moved to accommodate him, negating his attempts to slow the pace with one small twist of her body. She was stretched taut, her back bowed, a sacrifice for the taking.

Devon's control collapsed. He groaned in need and slid his hips between her legs, taking her offering. He fit her perfectly, hot and very close, and moved with an exquisite restraint that had Brittany softly moaning for more.

He didn't ask this time about an unwanted pregnancy. He obviously trusted her. Brittany loved him for that. Even in passion he trusted her not to make the kind of painful mistake they'd made before.

His movements were slow and deliberate, his breathing ragged.

"I love you," she said.

The words were torn from her. Brittany heard them with a kind of detached surprise and felt Devon's involuntary movement.

But he said nothing, nor did he draw back. Instead Brittany felt them both begin to move with a rhythm as old as time itself and she wrapped her legs around him instinctively preparing for the storm.

She saw the rigid, straining cords of his neck, the slackening of his lips, the glaze that turned his sight inward. And she felt the same desire in herself as the heat and intensity of their movements increased. A lusty cry escaped from Brittany's lips, followed by a deeper one from Devon. In that moment, she felt herself melt and expand, felt Devon shudder in sweet release, and she knew that her soul had been joined with his forever.

He sank down upon her, kissing her neck and the sheen of perspiration on her collarbone. Brittany held him to her fiercely.

Quiet moments passed as they savored the lethargy that followed their lovemaking. Brittany let her senses take over, smelling his scent, feeling his weight, hearing the slowing of his breathing, his steadying pulse. He moved slightly and she felt a subtle change in him. His lashes swept against her skin and she knew his eyes were open.

"Does it bother you that I told you I love you?" Brittany dared to ask.

"No."

Devon levered himself onto his elbows, regarding her seriously. Brittany licked her lips, still tasting the saltiness of his skin.

"I find it hard to believe that you still do, after all I've done to you," he said with a touch of amusement.

"I've been in love with you from the start. There's no use denying it. I think it's pretty plain to see."

Devon's finger smoothed the hair at her temple. "I don't want to hurt you again, Britt."

"I know. It's not really in your nature."

Devon looked at her in surprise. "I think it's amazing that you can feel that way."

"You haven't done anything to me."

"Oh, Britt..."

"It's true. if I'd had more courage I would have faced you with my pregnancy straightaway. I could have saved us both a lot of grief. But I was so afraid."

Devon moved himself carefully away from her, one arm still slung across her waist. "God, but you're good at shifting blame to yourself!" he muttered in exasperation. "Stop it. I've been a bastard to you for years. Don't whitewash the past. I'm not proud of it, but at least I can face up to it. The last thing I need is a woman who tries to protect me."

"Protect you?" Brittany turned until her nose nearly touched his. She saw hostility simmering in his blue eyes, knew he was still furious with himself and would be for a long time to come. "How can I protect you, Devon? The shell you've got around yourself does that already. I'd like to rip it down and see the man you really are, open and naked and hungry."

He looked at her as if he was seeing her for the first time. "You amaze me."

"Sometimes I amaze myself," Brittany admitted with a laugh. "But the one thing I know about myself is that I'm no good at hiding from the truth. It just festers inside; it never goes away. Facing it is a thousand times easier."

Devon inhaled through his teeth. "You're one of a kind," he said with bitterness.

She shrugged. "I love you. That's all that matters."

Devon rolled onto his back, staring at the ceiling. "You may not feel that way soon."

"Why?"

"I didn't come her to fall into bed with you."

She remembered the way he'd looked at her when he'd first arrived, the way his eyes had tried to look into her very soul. "Has something happened?"

"You could say that." His voice was wry. He slanted her a look that wasn't meant to be sexy, but to Brittany's way of thinking, it was. She curled next to him, refusing to let her insecurities spoil the moment.

Devon meditatively touched the swollen curve of her mouth with the tip of his finger. Brittany waited, watching his eyes narrow.

"Did you make a fifty-thousand-dollar purchase of diamonds this week at Marcel and Kingston Investments?"

It was so unexpected that Brittany blinked, then recoiled. He couldn't have said anything that would make her reject him more quickly. The Broderick story. Devon was still on the hunt. And he still intended using her as some kind of source.

His face said he knew just what she was thinking. She saw his regret, his sadness, but she also saw that same old steely determination.

"You don't give up, do you?" she said on a sharp breath.

"Never."

"Well, in this case, I wouldn't call it an attribute."

"Brittany, I've got to know," said Devon quietly.

"What?" She had to keep herself from shouting. Her whole body was trembling. "Whether I invested in diamonds? That's what you have to know?"

Devon's face paled. "Did you invest?"

Brittany pressed her lips together. She tried to contain the churning anger within her. "Yes."

"Fifty thousand?" Devon was tense, eyes fastened on the rigid planes of her face.

She swallowed. "How do you know so much, Devon?" Then, when he refused to answer, she said thinly, "Are you having me followed?"

He just stared at her through defeated eyes. "My God...."

Brittany rolled off the bed and onto her feet in one fluid motion. Devon hadn't come over because he wanted to see her, he'd come to pry information out of her. As always.

She yanked a robe from her closet, savagely wrapping its red velour folds around her. He'd even warned her. She wondered if that eased his conscience.

She whirled to face him. For a moment, Devon's sprawled male beauty stole her breath, then she clamped her mind shut to the man she saw and concentrated on the man he was. "You think this has something to do with Grant Broderick, don't you? Well, you're way off base this time, Devon."

"How do you know?"

Devon was merely curious, lost to some inner line of thinking. He seemed oblivious to the fact that Brittany was shaking with emotion. It made her want to scream.

"Don't try to use me as a source," she warned. "I'm as hysterical over that as you are about my career!"

That got his attention. With a supple movement, he twisted his body off the bed and reached for his clothes. Raising one eyebrow, he asked, "Still think you're in love with me?"

He was maddeningly calm. Whatever thoughts were occupying his attention left no room for her. "Loving someone doesn't mean you can't be furious with them when they deserve it!"

Devon frowned. "Did Broderick tip you off to Marcel and Kingston?"

"You damn well know he did." Brittany's eyes glittered. "Why are you watching me so closely? You still don't believe me, do you? You still think I'm having a love affair with Grant Broderick, or worse!"

Devon's eyes narrowed. "Nothing could be worse than that," he growled.

"Not even smuggling?"

Devon sighed, buttoning his cuffs. He looked at Brittany with a mixture of frustration and regret. "I've never thought you were a smuggler."

"My mistake. You thought I was a—" Brittany cut herself off just as Devon's hands crashed down on her shoulders. She felt tears burning behind her eyes. "Damn you, Devon. Damn you."

"Yes, damn me."

He was kissing her again, raining soft, anguished kisses on her forehead, her cheeks and her mouth. She wasn't going to let him get away with it. He needed to know that she wouldn't swoon at the first sign of tenderness from him. But she was powerless to move under that gentle assault. She stood motionless while his hungry lips searched the texture and fullness of hers, his tongue flicking inside her mouth. Her ears filled with the deep groan of his apology.

When the telephone rang it startled them both. Devon stilled, then drew back, his eyes darkened to a smoky midnight blue. "That might be for me," he admitted diffidently. "I told Jay where I'd be."

Brittany stepped toward the door. "Business as usual?"

Devon's face darkened. He swore softly as she skimmed down the hallway to the comparative privacy of the kitchen phone.

She felt utterly betrayed. She picked up the receiver feeling oddly out of joint. "Hello?"

"Brittany...?" Her mother's voice was trembling with panic.

Brittany's breathing stopped. "Mother?"

Devon heard the worry in her voice from the bedroom. He pulled on his boots and walked to the kitchen, instinctively moving to Brittany's side.

"They've taken your father to the hospital," Mrs. Daniels quavered. She was trying to maintain her composure and failing utterly. "I think he's...I think...you should come."

"I'll be there." Brittany choked out the words. Her ears were buzzing and her lungs were starved for air.

She wasn't aware of hanging up the phone. She wasn't aware of Devon, until she whirled and cannoned straight into him.

Devon grabbed her arms and steadied her. "What is it? What's wrong?" He was alarmed by the pallor of her skin.

Brittany felt faraway and alone. She was trembling and each breath was a shaking rasp. "I...uh..."

Devon shook her once, hard. She was falling apart before his eyes and he had no idea what was wrong. "Tell me what's wrong. Who was that on the phone?"

"My mother. My father's dying."

"Dying?"

Devon had met Cal Daniels only once but he'd liked the man immensely. Brittany had inherited his humor, his uncomplicated openness. It was inconceivable that such a robust, irrepressible man could be dying.

"I have to catch a flight," Brittany murmured, looking around vaguely. "Tonight." She puckered her brow and stared into Devon's tight face. "Will you help me?"

Her plea nearly broke him in two. "Of course," he said hoarsely, and after assuring himself that she was all right and would be able to gather her things, he rushed to the telephone to call directory assistance for the airport.

"Where do your parents live?" Devon yelled, punching out the number.

Brittany came to stand in the doorway, her face blank. "Acapulco."

A distinct shock went through Devon as he stared blankly at her, but she was beyond seeing him. "Go and finish," he urged gently, and Brittany moved like an automaton down the hallway.

There was only one flight left with a reasonable connection to Acapulco. Devon booked Brittany a first-class seat, his face set grimly. Then he booked another seat for himself.

Brittany carried her suitcases from the bedroom to the kitchen, her knuckles white from the convulsive grip she had on them. Her face was white, too; white and pinched. Her beautiful eyes dulled with worry and a kind of weary acceptance that Devon didn't understand.

"The flight leaves in an hour," he said tersely. "We have to hurry."

Brittany nodded. "I think I have everything...." She looked around vaguely.

"What you don't have, you don't need." Devon propelled her toward the front door with supreme gentleness.

The ride to the airport was a blur to Brittany. Devon didn't ask any more questions and for that she was grateful. She couldn't talk. The urgency she felt was matched only by her bottomless regret and helplessness. It was so unfair!

She came to herself when the ticketing agent produced a record for Brittany Daniels and Devon Gallagher. Her head jerked to meet Devon's impassive gaze. "You can't come with me," she said.

"Why not?" Devon ignored her, nodding to the agent.

"Because I need to go alone. Devon—" Brittany's calm facade began to crack, her voice thrumming with tension "—I don't want you to come."

"Your flight's already boarding," the ticketing agent said. He pretended not to hear the urgent whispers that passed between them, but Brittany felt the quick side-long glances he tossed in her direction. Devon didn't bother answering. He waited until the two tickets were in his hand, one palm under Brittany's elbow, guiding her toward the gate.

At security check she balked. "My father's dying of cancer," she said in a low, penetrating voice. "You're the last person he needs to see."

Devon felt as if she'd slapped him. His shoulders slumped at what Cal Daniels must think of him. "I don't have to see him," he said softly. "But I want to be there for you."

"Not now, Devon," Brittany pleaded. Her eyes begged him to understand.

"I don't like the idea of your being alone."

Brittany didn't know how to get through to him. As much as she loved him, as much as she might want to bury herself in the protection of his arms and let him shoulder her burden, this was something she had to do on her own. She'd scraped rock bottom in her fight to become an independent woman. She owed her parents the strength she'd achieved. She owed it to herself.

"I'll call you. As soon as I get there," she promised.

"Britt—"

"Devon, please! This has nothing to do with what we talked about before. My family needs me. Just me." She glanced urgently at the flight monitor, searching through her purse for a note pad and pencil. She scribbled the name of the hospital and her parents' address. "This is where I'll be. Please, Devon, tell me you understand."

He didn't understand. Not totally. It went against all Devon's instincts to let her go but he couldn't argue with the stubborn thrust of her chin. He felt helpless, ostracized. He saw the faint suspicion that clouded her lovely eyes—suspicion that he'd put there—and hated himself.

"Looks as though I'll have to," he said curtly, drawing her into a tight, supportive hug before releasing her. He walked with her down the concourse, carrying her shoulder bag. With the solemnity afforded a religious ceremony, he handed it to her at the gate.

Even in her despair Brittany struggled to make him believe in her. "This has nothing to do with what we talked about before."

"I know, damn it!"

"Do you, Devon?" Brittany was miserable. "I'm afraid of what you think of me."

He swore violently. "God, what I wouldn't do to make you see...."

Brittany was the only passenger left outside the plane. The gate agent gave her a frowning stare. Devon touched her cheek. "Go to your father. We'll talk later."

She hurried down the corridor to the plane. Devon's tense face, a reflection of the chaos raging within her, was painted on the inside of her eyelids.

"I didn't know you were going to be on my flight."

Brittany turned from the window slowly at the familiar voice. She felt distinct surprise but was too immersed in her own worries to care that Grant Broderick was on her flight.

"It was a last-minute change of plans," she said in a strained voice.

He looked concerned. "Something I can help with?"

She shook her head.

Grant took his cue and moved back to his seat, saying encouragingly, "I heard about your diamond purchase. Congratulations. A wise move."

Brittany gave him a wan smile and turned back to the window. She watched the moving shadow of the plane on the bright pavement as the pilot lined it up for departure. Grant was remarkably well-informed, Brittany thought detachedly. But then, so was Devon.

With a peculiar feeling of unreality, she let the present sink into oblivion, her mind wholly absorbed with the future. What would life be like without her father? She had to face the fact that the unthinkable would soon be a reality.

Devon went straight to the pay phone on the wall and put in a call to Jay. He chafed at the sound of his friend's answering machine, slamming down the receiver. Then he put in a call to Jay's beeper, leaving an urgent message. With a sigh he walked quickly back up the concourse, knowing Jay would keep calling Devon's home number until he answered.

"Gallagher."

Devon heard Stan Brinkley's surprised voice and stopped dead. Stan was the operative he'd hired to watch Broderick.

"Don't tell me he caught a flight tonight," Devon said harshly, as he walked past Stan into an airport shop.

Stan was a plain, slightly balding man with an unremarkable face. He stood a few feet away from Devon and picked up a white mug that said Hollywood Star! on it. "Hell, yes. He caught the flight that just left."

"To Acapulco?" Devon's every nerve went on alert.

"Mexico City's his destination. Jay's on the flight. He boarded before Broderick and went coach. There's no way Broderick could know him even if he does spy him."

Devon wasn't thinking about Jay. With long strides he sprinted to an observation window, seeing Brittany's plane taxi into flight position. He was filled with a fear so intense that he went ice-cold, his forehead breaking into a sweat.

Why had he listened to her? If anything happened to her now...if Broderick meshed her into his plans somehow...

The plane gathered momentum, hurtling toward the end of the runway with incredible force before lifting into the sky. Devon watched helplessly, his teeth clenched. Did Broderick suspect he was being investigated? Undoubtedly. Did he know Devon was behind it? Possibly. Would he use Brittany as a shield, knowing how special she was to him? Devon didn't know.

He walked back to the ticketing area with a pretended nonchalance that had his insides trembling. "I need the next flight to Acapulco," he told the agent with a smile. "And I don't give a damn how long the connecting time is anywhere. Just get me there as fast as you can."

Chapter Nine

The hospital was dim and silent as Brittany pushed through the double doors to reception. Her steps echoed strangely in the wide room. Against one wall was a circular reception station and a dour-faced matron who looked at her through eyes that had seen it all.

"Do you speak English?" Brittany asked, hanging on to the thin threads of her self-control. Her flight had been interminable—crowded, noisy and delayed in Mexico City. But at least Grant Broderick had departed there; she hadn't been able to handle even the few brief remarks he'd made to her. She'd needed to be alone.

"American, yes." The woman's speech was accented but entirely understandable.

"My father is here. A patient. His name is Calvin Daniels."

"Yes." Rather than brave directions in a foreign tongue, the receptionist pointed down an angled hall to the right, motioning that Brittany should turn at the end of the corridor. "One-one-two," she added, and Brittany thanked her.

Pain weighed heavily upon her bones as Brittany walked alone through the quiet hospital halls. The anticipation of what might await her had her nerves stretched to breaking.

She pressed her hand on the door of room 112, swinging it inward. Her mother, who was sitting in a chair by the bed, looked up when she entered. Brittany gave her a tiny encouraging smile, her eyes drifting to the bed.

She needed no professional opinion to know that her father wouldn't make it through the night. He was dozing, his breathing fitful, sporadic. His face had a gray pallor and his lips were slack. He seemed shrunken beneath his skin.

Her throat filled with unwept tears. Brittany walked slowly to the bed and clasped his dry hand. In a daze she leaned down and brushed a kiss across his forehead, not waking him. Her heart was weighted with stones.

Goodbye, daddy.

Ellen Daniels turned a handkerchief around and around in her hands. She came to stand beside Brittany. "He seemed just fine last night," she said in an uncertain voice. "Then today..."

Brittany placed an arm around her mother's trembling shoulders and hugged her fiercely.

Her mother had always been a pillar of strength. To feel her body quake now in sorrow tore Brittany apart. She fought back her own grief, locking her feelings for her father away in a secret place deep inside herself. She would deal with them later, when she was alone.

She squeezed his limp hand and wished she'd had a chance to tell him just once more how much she loved him. She'd hadn't even had time to tell him about Devon.

Ellen Daniels looked nearly as drawn and gray as her husband. "I'll bring you a cup of coffee," Brittany told her huskily. Her mother nodded wearily more to please her daughter than from any need of her own.

Once outside the hospital room Brittany leaned against the wall, emotions storming through her, racking the strong muscles of her body and leaving her weak and dizzy. She closed her eyes in tight despair and drew a shuddering breath. It wouldn't be fair for her to fall apart now; she had to be strong for her mother.

With a squaring of her shoulders that was more mental than physical, Brittany pushed herself away from the wall. She walked slowly down the halls in search of the hospital cafeteria and vending machines. She would make it through this night—for her father.

The hospital looked as ugly and functional as any Devon had seen in the United States or abroad. It was squat and sprawling and made of gray stucco but it radiated efficiency.

Devon took the front steps two at a time, unmindful of his tired muscles that were screaming for sleep. Late-morning sunshine hurt his eyes, and a quick look at his clothes assured him that he looked as rumpled and bleary as he felt.

Devon swept through the door, passing a regal, expensively dressed Mexican woman aiding an elderly matriarch toward the desk. He didn't notice. His mind was on Brittany. He'd spent the night waiting in airports, first in Los Angeles, then Mexico City, for a through flight to Acapulco.

He'd had a lot of time to think and worry. He'd called the station that aired "Perspective" and explained his next taping would be delayed. Other than heaving a weary sigh, the station manager hadn't argued with him; he'd worked with Devon far too long to argue once Devon made up his mind.

"Things are coming together on the Broderick exposé," Devon had offered as an olive branch before he'd hung up. "I'll call in when things settle down in Acapulco."

Devon purposely hadn't brought up Brittany's name.

Brittany. His jaw clenched. If Grant Broderick was trying to involve her...

"Which room is Calvin Daniels in?" Devon asked the woman at reception, carefully unclenching his fist.

The woman's expression never altered. "Mr. Daniels is no longer here," she said in careful English. "He died last night."

The muscles in Devon's face slackened. "His family?" he asked hoarsely.

"They have gone."

With a feeling of unreality Devon walked back outside, into the subtropical heat and away from the cold reality of the hospital. There was nothing like death to make you feel your own mortality, he thought grimly.

He inhaled deeply, closing his eyes against the unbelievable brightness. He pulled the slip of paper with Brittany's parents' address from his wallet. Then, feeling a great deal older, he got into his rented car and turned south.

His desire to comfort and protect Brittany was fast becoming a burning urgency. He had to be with her, whether she wanted him or not. He'd respected her need to be alone with her father, but even that paled with the specter of Grant Broderick hanging over her. Devon wasn't going to leave Brittany alone for one minute until he was satisfied Broderick wasn't after her in some way.

The road swept away from Acapulco proper, up the dizzying face of the cliff that formed a sheer drop to the glittering aqua bay below. As Devon's car crested the top he glanced back. A billowing scarlet parachute caught his attention. It hung below him and above the bay, seemingly suspended in midair. In its center was a gold-and-black phoenix rising toward the heavens.

Devon watched the parasailer and the tiny boat that was pulling it to shore. Then he drove on, turning onto the small switch back road to the Danielses' residence.

He parked his car behind a silver-blue Lincoln Continental and got out. He shoved his hands in his pockets, feeling a twinge of guilt. For years he'd fed his hostility toward Brittany by reminding himself of her mercenary streak. But he suspected now that she'd supported her parents for some time as well as herself. Brittany's father's illness hadn't come on suddenly and he knew that Ellen Daniels had never worked.

The house, too, reinforced Devon's opinion of Brittany's altruism. It was beautiful and by sheer location—the view across the cliffs and bay was soul shaking—had to cost a small fortune to rent. It was like something straight out of a travel brochure: white stucco walls with a blue-tiled roof, white pebbled walkway tumbling with carmine, pink and lavender flowers, broad deck with a royal-blue umbrella table facing the bay and blue-and-white-striped awnings capping each paned window.

It was a kaleidoscope of color and sunshine. Devon felt the sun burn into his scalp as he walked to the front door, feet crunching on tiny white gravel.

Brittany opened the door. She was as pale as the sunlight was bright, her eyes dark and shadowed, her mouth lined with grief. No makeup adorned her face and she looked so young and vulnerable that instinctively he reached for her.

"Devon," she said, burrowing into his shoulder. For a long time the only sounds were the rustling breeze and their own heartbeats.

"I went to the hospital first," he said quietly. "I know."

Her tears dampened his collar and she sobbed once, brokenly. Devon pressed his cheek into her crown and offered silent support. He wished he could absorb her pain.

Brittany rubbed a hand across her eyes and attempted a trembling smile that disintegrated before it truly formed. She looked at him and whispered, "It's just so hard to say goodbye."

"I know, I know," Devon soothed, gathering her close.

"My mother isn't doing very well."

And are you? Devon looked into her beautiful, ravaged face. He smoothed away the wetness on her cheeks. "Will my being here cause problems?"

"No." Brittany shook her head. "Mother might even be glad."

"I won't leave you," he said hoarsely. "Not again."

Brittany's eyes welled with fresh tears. "I couldn't tell you about my father before."

"It doesn't matter." Devon sighed and rocked her gently in his arms.

Ellen Daniels walked slowly into the room. She looked far older than Devon remembered. "Devon?" she asked blankly as she caught sight of them on the porch.

Devon met her worried gaze over the top of Brittany's head. "I wanted to come and offer my support. I hope you don't mind."

"No. Brittany needs you."

Her matter-of-factness surprised Devon but stress made people forget to be careful. A new crisis was the best catharsis for a past one. Devon had been forgiven before he could even apologize. And now no apologies were needed.

Brittany left Devon's arms reluctantly and went to sit beside her mother on the sofa. She clasped her mother's hand tightly. Ellen's breaths were little more than controlled sobs. Brittany turned helpless eyes to Devon, her fragile composure threatening to crack again.

How strong had Brittany had to be, Devon wondered. Her mother was too undone herself to realize how tough Calvin Daniels's death had been on her daughter. They both needed someone stronger than themselves to help get them through.

Devon bent on one knee in front of Ellen. "Tea or coffee or a drink?" he asked. "You need something. Let me get it for you."

Her still lovely, lined face crumpled. "What would you suggest?"

"A drink. You need to unwind. You, too," he said softly, turning to Brittany.

Ellen Daniels tried to pull herself together. Devon could see the visible tightening of her will. "Okay," she said. "Yes, please." Then she grabbed Devon's strong hand as if it were a lifeline. At the feel of his masculine strength she gave up all pretense and let the tears come unstopped, her soft sobs filled with desolation.

Brittany, too, let go. She folded her hands in her lap, staring at them unseeingly as crystal tears dropped one after another. She barely noticed when Devon's arm circled her waist, but she heard the soft words of love and consolation and she closed her eyes and gave herself up wholeheartedly to the shelter and comfort he offered her.

The breeze sweeping up from the bay was swift and darting, wisping Brittany's hair around her head like a fragrant dark cloud. She turned her face to the sun and let the solemnity of the memorial service sink to the back regions of her memory. Two days of mourning hadn't eased her pain but she was closer to accepting her father's death.

Her mother, too, was coming to terms with it, although her life was going to change drastically. Brittany had been gently urging her to come back to Los Angeles, and Ellen was beginning to consider it.

Brittany swung her arms wide and stretched. Devon had done so much for them. She regretted not letting him come with her in the beginning. His presence would have made that first night so much easier. But she hadn't known what he would be like in a crisis like this one, and she'd needed her independence, or so she'd thought. She hadn't realized how tender and empathetic he could be: never leaving her side, selflessly attending to both her and her mother's needs, making arrangements and offering silent unyielding support.

She picked up a glass of iced lemonade from the deck table and let out a deep sigh, enjoying the peace of the azure skies and the beautiful sunshine glittering on the water. She leaned into the canvas deck chair and stretched her bare feet, wiggling her toes. White shorts and a pink halter top were all that separated her from the blazing heat, but the breeze made lounging on the back deck bearable.

Devon was making phone calls. He'd been making them all afternoon, ever since the three of them had returned from the memorial service. Brittany's mother was lying down and Brittany had planted herself in the sunshine.

She was a little curious about Devon's calls but had heard enough to realize that he was making excuses to his boss for his surprise vacation. Brittany was secretly pleased that she mattered enough to him for him to interrupt his work schedule.

She closed her eyes, listening to the distant murmur of Devon's deep voice on the phone, hearing the tone, not the words. She was becoming familiar with his soft murmurs and gentle words and touches. These past few days had convinced her that Devon was capable of far more love than he gave himself credit for. He'd shown it to Brittany in the tender way he'd treated her and looked at her. Admitting it to himself was just a matter of time....

The charge in the air alerted her to his presence, although his soft-soled shoes had made no sound. "Done?" she asked, opening one eye.

Devon was leaning on the deck rail, his back to her, his palms supporting his weight. His white cotton shirt billowed in the capricious breeze. Devon had had to make an emergency shopping trip, as he'd arrived with only the clothes on his back, and though he'd balked at first, Brittany had talked him into a white peasant shirt with gathered sleeves and a pair of khaki bush pants. From the back he looked like a native, but when he turned, the sapphire depths of his eyes gave away his heritage.

"Yeah, I'm done." He loked pensive. "How're you doing?"

Brittany inhaled and gave him a brave smile. "I'm glad the service is over."

"Hmm. Would you feel like going for a drive? Maybe a walk along the bay?"

Brittany sensed a tenseness in him that had been missing the past few days. Or maybe she'd just been too numb to notice, she reminded herself. "Sure."

They looked at each other. Brittany thought he wanted to tell her something, but he merely crossed his arms over his chest and said, "I don't have much time left. I've interrupted my schedule as it is, and the station manager—"

"It's okay. I understand about work." Brittany thought gloomily about how she'd run out on the Toujours session. She'd managed to explain to Jessica but that didn't mean Marjorie Vandoren would understand.

Still, being at her father's side before his death had been more important. And it had brought Devon to her side, renewing her faith in his ability to make commitments. She wouldn't trade that for all the Toujours and Marjorie Vandorens in the world.

His shirt was stretched taut across his chest and Brittany could see dark hair curling above the open collar. She'd been far too upset to think about him sexually, yet now a ripple of awareness passed over her. He looked magnificent. Bold and unconquerable.

Brittany felt her nipples tighten beneath her cotton top. She shifted her weight, and the canvas chair gave a protesting squeak.

Devon's eyes missed nothing. He narrowed his gaze on her in a truly fascinating way, the sensual line of his mouth accelerating her pulse. A slow flush turned her recently tanned skin a delicate shade of pink. He knew what she was feeling!

"We could forget the ride..." he drawled, letting his gaze skim over her in a way that brought fresh heat to her face.

"With my mother here?"

Devon pondered that. "Let's go make out in the Lincoln."

Brittany laughed, the sound clear and surprising after the solemnness of the past few days. She didn't need to tell him she loved him; it shone from her eyes.

Devon groaned and kneeled beside the deck chair, running his palm over the warm skin at her belly. Brittany sighed and sank into a kind of suspended ecstasy, a beautiful haze she never wanted to be awakened from.

His fingers wriggled beneath the band of her shorts. Brittany inhaled at his touch, then shoved him away, smiling. "The last thing I need is to give my mother something else to worry about."

"No problem. She's out for the afternoon. She took a tranquilizer."

Brittany frowned. "Did she?"

"She needed it, Britt. She was a bundle of nerves. But I think after this she'll be over the worst of it."

Brittany put her arms around his back, feeling the heat of the sun on his shirt. He kissed her slowly, deeply, his wayward hand moving down her bare thigh. Her skin trembled as she felt him smile against her lips.

"Don't be so self-satisfied," she scolded.

"Why not? You love it."

She tried to protest but he made a low growling sound in his throat that had her silently laughing instead. His hand was creating liquid fire against the soft, sensitive skin of her inner thigh. Her laughter died, lips slackening as she melted. His mouth moved slowly over hers, testing and tasting, the tip of his tongue teasing hers.

She didn't realize she was pulling on him, trying to cover her aching body with his, until he said in amusement, "What about mom?"

"I thought you said she was asleep." Brittany opened her eyes, blinking against the glare. She shadowed them with her hand and focused on the glinting humor in Devon's.

"Want to risk it?"

Brittany thought about what would happen if her mother awoke and accidentally caught sight of them. "No," she said positively, trying to sit up.

"I thought not." Devon's palm slid over her smooth skin once more before reluctantly lifting. "I've got another plan," he admitted.

"What?" Brittany's flesh felt cool without his fevered touch.

"Las Brisas."

"What?"

Las Brisas was a famed resort not far from the Danielses' rented house. Perched on the cliff top, its bungalows—known as *casitas*—were lavish and private, some with their own private swimming pool. Las Brisas was world renowned, not only for its exceptional accommodations, but also for the pink jeeps provided for the use of the guests during their stay. The jeeps could be seen all over Acapulco, a prestigious and tell-tale clue to the vacationer's hotel.

"We'll get a room for the night. We don't have to stay all night. We can come back here sometime this evening and I'll go back to the hotel in the morning and check out."

"It's nearly Thanksgiving. The place will be booked solid."

"Thanksgiving is only an American holiday," Devon pointed out.

"Yes, and Las Brisas will be full of Americans."

"Not completely full."

Brittany narrowed her eyes on his face. "You've already made a reservation, haven't you?" she accused with dawning comprehension. At his "I-cannot-tell-a-lie" look she chuckled softly. "I think I've just been had."

"Not yet, sweetheart," he said, his grin just short of a leer. "But I won't make any promises about later."

"I feel like a naughty kid," Brittany said as Devon's dark head bent over the troublesome lock on their door.

He slashed her a look full of humor. "So do I. And I'm enjoying the hell out of it."

Devon pushed open the door and Brittany stepped inside the room, her attention caught equally by the lovely appointments of the room and the outstanding view beyond the sliding glass door. She made a sound of delight at the vision of the private pool, its pale turquoise waters topped with hundreds of lazily floating red petals.

"How in the world did you get this room?" she asked in wonder.

"Last-minute cancellation, bribery and—" Devon shrugged and gave her a self-effacing grin "—I paid for three nights."

Brittany turned swiftly. "But we're not even staying one!"

"It's the quality of the time, not the quantity. Come here."

Devon pulled her against his chest, the beat of his heart fast and hard. He molded her softness to his hardness, his mouth hungry on hers. With each stroke of his hand down her back she felt the tensions of the past few days fade and a small part of her grief ease. "I love you," she whispered, unable to keep her feelings from pouring out.

"Oh, Britt..." Devon was overwhelmed. "I'd rather cut off my right arm than see you suffer anymore."

Brittany gently took his hand, sliding her fingers between his, and tugged him toward the bed.

She sat on the edge of the bed and pulled his mouth down to meet the soft invitation of hers. "We'll check out the pool later," she said huskily, then her hands restlessly stroked the crisp fabric of his shirt, feeling his muscles shift as he moved over her, pressing her back into the quilted satin spread.

His gaze was hot as it raked her from head to toe, his fingers trembling as they undid her buttons. The evidence of his passion was wildly exciting. Brittany rained kisses across his neck and face as he pulled the pink top over her tanned shoulders.

She hadn't worn a bra and the dusky tips of her nipples beckoned unashamedly.

Devon closed his eyes for a moment. "I had this picture of slow seduction in my head but it looks as though I'm not going to make it."

Brittany nipped gently on his ear. "No control?" she asked innocently.

"Very little," he rasped.

"Good."

He kissed her breast, his tongue flicking her nipple lightly until she was dying from wanting him to capture it in his mouth. She moved restlessly and Devon trapped her by placing his hips between hers. He wiggled the lower half of his body with obvious intent.

Brittany exhaled on a sigh, then she glimpsed the trace of amusement lurking in his eyes.

"You're going to be begging for me before I'm done," he said in a low voice, his rough tone sending a thrill up her nerves even as she recognized his teasing.

"Oh, brother," she groaned.

"You've been forewarned. I'm not responsible for my actions from this point on."

She was divided between laughter and desire, but his sinuous movements took her breath away. "Is that a challenge?"

His palms slid under the soft curve of her hips, lifting them. He kissed her gently, his blue eyes glinting with daring.

It was impossible to ignore his tender assault. She knew she would lose and didn't care. "You certainly know how to make the game hard," she said on a sigh.

Devon's laugh was soft. For a moment Brittany hadn't realized what she'd said, until Devon's grave voice answered, "It's you who've made it hard."

Brittany smiled, her dimples deep. "I never knew you were such a dirty old man."

"Well, now you do."

She would have kept up the banter, but his lips suddenly encircled one nipple, tugging impatiently. Brittany's thoughts splintered, his tongue tasting and wetting her flesh until she wanted to cry out.

"Devon, I..."

His hands slid to the waistband of her shorts, soft touches feathering her skin. "Come on, Britt, beg me."

Beneath the teasing was an element of need. Humor slid away beneath the tide of passion. She wrapped her legs around him, both she and Devon still fully clothed. "I want..."

Devon was moving so persuasively that her mind jumbled up the words. She felt her clothes being stripped off piece by piece. She watched as Devon ripped the shirt off his back. She ran her fingers over his chest, scraping his nipples lightly, feeling his skin ripple.

"I want you," she whispered, her eyes wide and luminous.

Devon slowly lay down, the hair on his chest tickling her breasts, tension in the hard feel of his body, his desire bold and evident, pushing against her hips.

He sank against her. "And, oh, love," he groaned hoarsely, "I want you."

Brittany wasn't really asleep. They'd made love, gone skinny-dipping under billions of pinprick stars, then made love again and now she drifted in a love-induced haze. So, when the telephone jangled suddenly in her ear, she jumped with instant anxiety. Devon stirred, too, but less sharply, and he raised his head slowly, looking around the room with vague distraction.

He made a protesting sound and buried his face in the pillow, his arms wrapped possessively around Brittany.

The phone buzzed a second time.

"Damn," he said softly, "I left a message where I'd be in case something should happen at work."

He tried to disentangle himself but she gripped him with her legs and arms. "Pretty sure of yourself, weren't you?"

One lean arm was reaching for the phone, but he turned to regard her quizzically. "Not really," he said cryptically, picking up the receiver.

"Devon?" she heard a faint male voice ask, then the receiver was placed against his ear and she could hear only noises.

Devon's conversation, however, was plain if somewhat guarded.

"No...I was waiting to hear from you...." A long pause ensued while the voice on the other end ran on and on. Devon suddenly yanked himself upright with such force that he practically ripped himself from her arms. Brittany leaned on her elbows, dazed.

"What do you mean?" Devon demanded. Brittany saw the horror on his face a split second before he pulled the familiar mask over his expression, glancing at her with the controlled countenance she'd feared most.

Brittany's heart was pounding. The color drained from Devon's face.

"I can't...." He glanced at his watch. "The earliest would be tomorrow night. Damn it, Jay," he said through his teeth. She saw a muscle in his jaw jump to life.

"Make sure of it! And, God, don't be wrong!" were his final words before he slammed the receiver into the cradle.

She didn't ask what had happened. She waited with extreme patience. Did it have something to do with her? How could it? What would it be?

Brittany realized that Devon's shoulders were trembling. Afraid, she touched him gently. "Devon?"

It wasn't anger that consumed him. It was something else. Fear.

Devon wasn't the type of man to fall apart over nothing; he'd handled the Melina Sanders shooting of Paul Geller Glade with steel nerves. Wild suppositions dashed through Brittany's mind and she opened her mouth to ask frightened questions. With a muscular twist Devon turned around, pinning her shoulders against the bed.

"Britt, listen to me."

She couldn't have said a word in any case, even if she'd wanted to. She lay docile and anxious, her heart pounding like a raging surf in her ears.

"I've got to leave for Los Angeles tonight."

She'd never really believed a person could break into a cold sweat, but her forehead and back felt damp and frigid at something in his tone. "Why, Devon?"

"Business. New developments that I hadn't planned on. I want you to come with me."

Brittany felt his urgency; the grip on her shoulders almost hurt. "The Broderick case?" she whispered.

"Yes."

His clipped tone invited no more questions. "I can't go, Devon. My mother..."

"She'll come, too."

Brittany's brain started to clear. Her fear subsided as she began to recognize the implications. "No. She needs to stay and get herself together. Surely you can see that."

Devon knew he was acting irrationally but he couldn't help himself. That irrationality was a barometer of the volatile emotions he felt where Brittany was concerned and he simply couldn't convince himself she would be safe without him.

"I'll come back in a few days. We both will," Brittany said reasonably. "If you have to go, then go. It's okay. We'll meet in L.A."

Devon shook his head fiercely. She saw his struggle. "I don't want to leave you alone," he said in a penetrating voice.

"You're afraid...for me?"

Devon suddenly cradled her close, holding her in a way that both alarmed and delighted her. "You're the most important thing in my life," he said passionately.

"I'll be okay, Devon," she assured him, touching his lips with her fingers. "I wish I could convince you that I have no connection with Grant Broderick. He's an acquaintance. I don't even really want to know him."

Devon gritted his teeth. "I know," he agreed reluctantly, thinking fast. As if he'd come to a decision, he nodded, then added tersely, "But if Broderick should try to contact you, make up an excuse. Say you can't meet or talk with him. It's important, Britt."

Brittany was a little surprised by Devon's obsession with Broderick, but she agreed. "That should be easy. I doubt he knows where I am, anyway."

"He was on the plane with you."

Brittany stared into Devon's clear blue eyes. It bothered her a little that he was so involved with this case. She couldn't help but wonder if his motivation to come to Acapulco had had something to do with Broderick.

"I'm not kidding, Britt," he said to the frown that creased her fine brow. "Don't have anything to do with that man." He released her slowly, dropping a kiss on her forehead. "I'll explain everything when I can."

"When will that be?"

"Soon, I hope. When you get back to L.A."

"Devon..."

He was already pulling away from her, mentally as well as physically. She could already see the change, the intense concentration that crossed his face. "Hmm?" he asked absently.

"You'll be all right, won't you?"

He was yanking on his clothes and Brittany reached for hers, feeling suddenly cold and bereft. She didn't like this feeling of being used and forgotten. With an angry mental shake she pulled herself together and started to dress hurriedly, echoing Devon's urgency.

The last thing Devon needed now was for her to go paranoid on him. He had other things on his mind. More important things. Far more important than herself.

"Of course I'll be all right." Devon deliberated a minute. "The only thing is that I might not be able to go to Seattle for Thanksgiving."

"That's okay." Brittany watched him stuff in the tails of his shirt, her teeth digging into her lower lip. She was depressed that she wouldn't get to meet Shannon, wouldn't be able to be with Devon, but she had no intention of letting him see. She hated feeling shut out like this. But it was as much a part of Devon as his passion. He was a newsman first and he always would be.

You're the most important thing in my life.

Brittany buttoned her blouse, head bent. She begged to differ on that point. The most important person, maybe, but certainly not the most important thing. His job would always come first.

It was ironic, really. He'd accused her of putting her career above all else, when in reality it was Devon who was—and had always been—devoted solely to his career.

Chapter Ten

Brittany tried to ignore her bone-deep weariness as she unlocked the door to her house. It was good to be home alone. She wasn't opposed to having her mother stay with her until she was resettled, but she was grateful anyway that some friends from Ellen's old neighborhood had insisted that she move in with them. Her mother had demurred but it had been obvious to Brittany that she wanted to be around people her own age. With a final kiss and an understanding hug, Brittany had left her mother at the Stantons', promising to help find her a place of her own as soon as she could manage the time.

The time. Brittany lifted one shoulder, trying to ease her tense muscles as she walked down the hallway to the bathroom. The trouble was, she thought tiredly, turning on the taps to the bathtub, she didn't have any time. Since she'd arrived in Los Angeles two nights earlier all she'd managed to do was settle her mother and make one or two calls.

She'd called Devon first and left her name on his answering machine. Afterward she'd felt lonely and strange. It seemed a poor welcome home to have to leave her name and number. She couldn't think of anything clever to say, either, and after whispering a shy "Can't wait to see you again," she'd hung up. So far, Devon hadn't returned her call.

Brittany stripped off her clothes, trying to rid herself of the uncanny sensation that everything was falling apart between them. The past few days in Acapulco she'd thought of Devon constantly, torn between fear and jubilation every time the phone rang. Would it be Devon? Her nerves could barely stand the suspense.

But he hadn't called. It was with a feeling of anticlimax that Brittany had straightened out her mother's affairs and helped her move back to Los Angeles.

Brittany pinned up her hair, resolutely pushing her doubts aside. It was a cinch that whatever Devon was working on wouldn't be resolved overnight, and though it had been over a week since he'd left Acapulco, chances were that he was still embroiled in the Broderick case. There was absolutely no reason for her to be alarmed that he hadn't returned her call.

She wrinkled her nose and tested the water with her toe. It was still difficult for Brittany to believe Broderick was the criminal Devon thought he was. He hadn't bothered Brittany in Acapulco; Devon's fears had been greatly exaggerated there! Broderick struck her as extremely ambitious but it just didn't seem possible that he was a smuggler. The man had a lucrative career and prestigious clientele. He was trying to get a foot in the door politically. Why would he take such incredibly stupid risks?

The phone rang just as Brittany was about to get in the water.

Devon! Quickly she wrapped a lavender bath sheet around herself and scurried to the phone.

"Hello?"

"Have I got great news for you," Jessica Barlowe said with a smile in her voice. "Marjorie Vandoren hasn't given up on you. They want to reschedule the Toujours session for next week."

"Wonderful." Brittany tried to inject some enthusiasm into her words to hide her disappointment. "That is great news."

"You don't sound particularly elated."

Brittany searched her mind for an excuse. "It's been a really trying week, Jessica."

"Oh, yes. Sorry." Jessica's embarrassment made Brittany feel like a fraud. "How's your mother doing?"

"Really quite well. She's got together with some of her old friends again. I'm relieved."

Brittany could hear the sound of a television in the background as Jessica said, "That's good. Is she there now?"

"No, she's staying with some friends. We're all pitching in to find the right house for her to buy. She won't hear of an apartment."

"Hmm. My father was the same way after my mother died. We tried to live together for a while but we both went crazy. He's a Felix Unger." Jessica paused, then turned the conversation back to business.

"I've also rescheduled your interview with *In Touch* magazine."

"Will wonders never cease?" Brittany murmured. "I'm amazed they still want to interview me."

"It's their business. Without people like you, they're out of a job. I've slotted them in the day after Toujours."

"Jessica, don't arrange anything else for me after *In Touch* for at least a week, okay?"

Jessica hesitated. "Sure. Any special reason?"

For some reason Brittany didn't want to tell her that she hoped she and Devon could still steal away to Seattle, even though Thanksgiving had come and gone. She had it in the back of her mind that Devon might still take a minivacation and she wanted to make sure she didn't foul up his plans.

"I've just felt a lot of pressure lately," Brittany said at length. "I want some time set aside just for me."

"Done. I hear you."

The tinny sound of music issuing from Jessica's television sounded familiar. A split second before Brittany recognized the theme music for *Perspective*, Jessica gasped. "Turn on your television," she urged. "Quick. Good Lord, it's Grant Broderick. Devon Gallagher's got him on *Perspective*!"

Brittany hung up without saying goodbye. Heart pounding, she switched on the TV, counting the seconds before the picture and sound crackled to life.

The first audible noise was Devon's deep voice in the middle of a monologue.

"...the young man who was killed last week in an automobile crash in Mexico City. Eric Cordell was suspected of being involved with Broderick's gemsmuggling operation. Cordell's death triggered an investigation by Mexican police. The discovery of over a half million dollars' worth of cut diamonds in the wreckage of the car brought the incident to the attention of international authorities.''

Brittany gasped. It was all true! All Devon's suspicions were true!

"Because of Cordell's suspected link with Broderick, no report was made at the time of the discovery of the diamonds. Last Friday, Broderick's business records were searched by the FBI and the IRS independently. It's been suggested that Grant Broderick is sole owner of Marcel and Kingston, a gem-brokerage firm in Los Angeles. It is suspected at this time that he has been selling stolen gems to unwitting buyers for the past three years...."

The blood drained from Brittany's face. Marcel and Kingston? Her diamonds? With a feeling of unreality, she remembered Devon's reaction when she'd admitted to buying fifty thousand dollars' worth of diamonds. She was dazed. He'd known. He'd known even then!

"The investigation is continuing. It's been suggested that Broderick and Cordell smuggled the gems in via regularly scheduled flights between Los Angeles and Mexico City, following the example of Christopher Boyce, the young American who sold military secrets to the Russians. Boyce's partner, Daulton Lee, stowed small packets of drugs and money on the planes, passed through customs, then caught the flights again later so he could pick up his parcels."

Brittany's palms were clammy. She thought of Broderick on the plane next to her, the way he'd grabbed for her luggage. Had she been so close to discovering his secret?

Her knees felt too weak to support her. She sank onto a leather ottoman inches from the screen. She was in shock. Devon had known so much. He'd prodded and questioned and coerced her into telling him all she knew about Grant Broderick. She'd answered because she loved Devon but he'd only wanted to use her. He'd wanted a blockbuster story. And he'd got one. At her expense.

The scene switched to Broderick, hands cuffed, walking between two policemen. Reporters were barraging him with questions but he kept a thin-lipped silence. Devon's voice was dubbed over.

"Employees at Marcel and Kingston and people hired personally by Broderick are being questioned by the authorities."

A shot of the twisted wreckage of Eric Cordell's car was followed by a brief report on why the accident had occurred. Apparently Cordell had been seen dealing with one of the same individuals Grant Broderick visited in Mexico City. Cordell suspected he was being followed and had accidentally driven his car out of control.

"Anyone who has purchased gems at Marcel and Kingston should report their purchase to the police." Devon listed off the names of several other gem-brokerage houses, as well, but Marcel and Kingston was at the top of the list.

Brittany was numb. She watched as Devon's report got into the finer details of Broderick's operation, then decided she'd seen enough. More than enough to convince her that she owned fifty thousand dollars' worth of stolen diamonds.

She hadn't even received them yet.

Brittany felt stiff and disjointed as she retraced her steps to the bathroom. She refilled the bathtub with warm water and slid into the steamy liquid in a daze, wishing hopelessly that the heat could reach the coldness in her soul.

Devon had known.

Brittany wanted to cry at the bitter agony of it. Why hadn't he told her? Why had he fed her illusions of love? Why had he let her think she meant something to him? It was painfully obvious now that she'd been a source for him, nothing more. Otherwise he would have told her, sheltered her, warned her that he was going to spring the trap on Broderick.

Instead she'd become a casualty.

Brittany scrubbed her face with slow, careful strokes, desperately trying to contain the turbulence inside her. It wasn't losing the money. It was losing Devon...again. Or more accurately, never having had him. How could he have used her so cold-bloodedly, her heart cried. And this time it was worse. This time he'd pretended to be falling in love with her.

When the phone began ringing Brittany ignored it. She knew who was calling. She soaped down her skin until it was covered with lather. The phone rang on and on.

Brittany drained the tub and turned on the shower, lifting her face to the hot spray. She didn't know how long she stood there, letting the hard jets of water batter her skin, but suddenly she realized it was ice-cold. She turned it off. The phone had stopped ringing.

She couldn't talk to Devon now. She was shredding inside, ripped apart by his incredible selfishness. She laid her forehead against the cool shower tiles and fought back a tide of hot tears.

How could she have been so blind?

When Brittany finally stepped from the tub it was in a much cooler state of mind. She had her most treach-

erous emotions under control. Devon had been interested in her for the sake of a story, she thought with
dreadful logic. So what? It had happened before. She'd
lived through it then, she would live through it now.

The phone began its insistent peal again. Brittany
tossed on her robe and tried to block it from her mind.
Eventually her guilty conscience warned her that the
caller might not be Devon. It could be her mother.
Knowing she had to face the inevitable sometime, Brittany picked up the receiver, hesitating only briefly before she spoke.

"Hello." Her voice sounded odd and tight in her own
ears.

"Brittany?" Devon was shouting. Pandemonium
reigned in the background.

"Yes." Her voice was a thready whisper and she
cleared her throat and said more distinctly, "Yes."

"I'm sorry, I can hardly hear you. Some of the *Perspective* crew are having a celebration."

It sounded like all that and more. "Because of your
report?" she guessed.

Brittany's voice was cold and withdrawn but Devon
couldn't hear the nuances. He had to cup a hand over
his other ear to hear at all. "Brittany, are you still there?
Did you see the show? That's what all the noise is
about. The station manager thinks we blasted the competition out of the ratings. Brittany?"

"I'm here, Devon. Congratulations. It was a hell of
a report."

"What?" Devon shifted the receiver, lines drawing
between his dark brows.

"I said you deserve everything you get!"

She hung up quickly, trying to achieve a calm she
didn't feel. Bitterness washed over her. It welled within

her, choking her. Before the phone could start ringing again she unhooked the receiver, letting it hang in a twisting coil from the wall phone.

"Oh, God..." she whispered tremulously.

She covered her eyes with one hand and drew in a shuddering breath. She was sick. Sick with herself. And Devon's shattering success over the whole Broderick fiasco was more than she could stand.

Rationally, she knew she was the one who had misconstrued everything. Devon had been patently clear. He'd wanted her, pure and simple. She'd been the one using terms like "love," "respect" and "commitment."

You're the most important thing in my life.

In her newfound cynicism, Brittany wondered if that was because she'd been a link to Broderick. Because of her own stupid, naive involvement, Devon had clung to her.

Brittany was too upset to remember Devon's personal reluctance about being around her at all. She didn't know about the real fear for her safety, a fear that had consumed him when Jay Lundgren had placed his midnight call to Acapulco.

She crawled into bed and brought the covers up to her chin. She had to build a shell around herself—a tough barrier that even Devon couldn't break down. It was the only way for her to get through this in one piece.

He hadn't even had the decency to warn her first!

She closed her eyes and rolled into a ball, concentrating on willing her pain away. The hurt inside was like a fire burning her up. It was a painful reminder of how she'd felt after she'd lost her child, after Devon had abandoned her.

Bang! Bang! Bang!

Brittany's breath stopped at the savage beating her front door was taking. The noise echoed down the hallway. Someone was slamming his fist against the door.

"Brittany!" Though faint, Devon's voice carried the unmistakable ring of fury. "For God's sake, open the door!"

She wanted him to just leave her alone. She toyed with the idea of sticking her head beneath the pillow and waiting for the storm to pass.

But Devon's persistence was renowned and he made the most of it. When coercion failed he simply leaned on the bell. It buzzed with malevolent fury until Brittany leaped from the bed, her own anger finding its way out of the pain in her soul.

She yanked open the front door.

"What the hell, Brittany?" Devon demanded furiously, straightening. "What's the idea of hanging up on me? I didn't even get a chance—" He broke off and raked her with angry eyes. "You were in *bed*?" he finished incredulously.

Twilight was painting lavender shadows across the sweep of her lawn and the shimmering sea. Devon looked at her pale face, shadowed eyes, rumpled hair and robe and got his first real clue that something was drastically wrong.

"Are you sick?" he asked swiftly.

"No." She looked at his handsome face and something broke inside, her misery pouring out to every pore. "Yes."

His brows blunted. "Now what the hell does that mean?" A moment later his gaze softened and something like regret slid across his dark features. "Look, I know how you must feel."

Oh, do you? Brittany clenched her teeth together.

"I'd like to come in and explain."

"I'm not sure I want to hear it."

Devon tried to touch her face but she drew away. "Brittany..." He was baffled.

"You can come in," she said, wrapping her arms around herself, shivering a little in the breeze.

"And then?" Devon's instincts warned him he was treading on slippery ground.

Brittany pursed her lips against the angry remarks that were forming inside and threatening to spill out at the least provocation. She could feel Devon's narrowed stare knife between her shoulder blades as she led him into the kitchen. She chose that room deliberately because of its gleaming utility, thinking she would be less likely to be swept away by romance.

She regarded him with impassive eyes. "Okay. Go ahead, you've got the floor."

Devon was taken aback by her coolness. Brittany was determined not to let him wound her again. She'd lie down and die before he got one more programmed response from his "source."

"You have a right to be furious about the diamonds," he said. "That is what this is about, isn't it? You did see the show."

"I saw the show."

Devon nodded, his eyes watchful. "It's over. The whole damned thing is over. Broderick hasn't confessed yet, but the evidence speaks for itself."

"You mean the stolen gems?"

He inclined his head. "Among other things." He sighed. "I would have given anything to have prevented you from buying diamonds from that man,

Britt. I nearly passed out when I learned you'd invested."

Brittany looked away, concentrating on the cool appointments of the room: the blue tile floor, the shining white countertops. "Yes, that's right. I saw your reaction. You closed up with suspicion."

Devon frowned at her, shifting his weight in unconscious readiness. He sensed trouble on the horizon but didn't have time to figure out what had gone awry.

"I was after Broderick anyway," Devon said grimly, "but when he started involving you, I couldn't wait to bring him down."

Brittany closed her eyes. "You can stop with the noble act, Devon. I know what you wanted. And you got it. Now live with it."

"I don't know what the hell you're—"

"Figure it out," Brittany snapped back. "You're good at that."

Devon's gaze narrowed, seeing the bright spots of color on her lovely cheeks. Her haughty anger was as beautiful as it was baffling. A niggling suspicion began to haunt the back of his mind. After a long moment he asked in a deadly voice, "Are you that torn up about losing your money?"

Brittany made a sound of disbelief. "Shouldn't I be? Fifty thousand dollars is worth worrying about, wouldn't you say?"

Devon turned to stone. Only his eyes were alive, glittering with a fury that would have made Brittany shrink in other circumstances. "I see, it's a choice between the money or me," he snarled. "And I'm the loser."

"Wrong, Devon!" Brittany lanced him with a shaking finger. "Fundamentally wrong! There is no choice. If you've lost, you've done it to yourself. For years you've made me feel guilty over my career, but no more. You're the one with the career problem. You take and take and take!" Her hand balled into a fist and she unclenched it with an effort.

"That's what all this hysteria is about?" Devon asked, his voice wavering between suspicion and incredulity. "My career?"

Brittany took a quick breath. "I've been used," she told him flatly. "And it cost me fifty thousand dollars." *And what was left of my battered heart,* she added silently.

Devon's mouth hardened. "I'll try to get your money back for you," he said, his lip curling cynically.

"You're not listening, Devon. I don't give a damn about the money. I don't care if I ever see one cent of it!" Brittany's voice quavered. "I won't wait in the wings for the crumbs you can spare, either. I thought I could, but I can't," she added on a whisper.

"Just what the hell are you talking about?" Devon exploded.

"You should have told me!"

Brittany wheeled around, giving him her back. Her eyes squeezed shut on tears she couldn't let escape. Though she knew the questions had no place, they came unbidden to her mind, turning her anger to desolation: *Why can't you tell me the whole mess is a mistake? Why won't you cradle me close to your heart and tell me you love me? Is it so impossible for you to really love me?*

Devon sighed heavily. "You're probably right. I just didn't want to..."

He didn't have to finish. She knew what he was about to say. The words would only add flame to the fire of her accusations.

"You didn't want to risk sabotaging the investigation," Brittany answered in a flat voice, turning back to face him.

Devon's face was dark and tormented. "I never wanted to sacrifice you, Britt."

"No." Her smile was tight. "I don't think you did."

"I'll do whatever it takes to put things right," Devon said, crossing the room in a few lithe strides. He dropped his hands on Brittany's shoulders. "Now that the Broderick story's out, I'll have some time to myself. Maybe we could pick up where we left off in Acapulco."

Brittany didn't want to think about Acapulco. She didn't want to remember her willingness to believe Devon was capable of loving her. He wasn't capable of loving anyone. He was interested only in idealism and success.

She shrugged off his hands. "And how long would we be together? Until your next assignment? Don't con me, Devon. I'm a convenience for you."

Her cold words angered him. "You're a helluva lot more than that," he growled.

"I wish I could let myself believe that, Devon. I really do."

He swore violently. "You don't let yourself, you just believe."

Brittany turned soulful eyes to the blue storm of his. "Then that's the problem," she said in a painful whisper. "I don't believe you."

Minutes seemed to creep by while his eyes bored into hers, as if his will could force her to see feelings that didn't exist. At length even Devon was defeated. He looked away, his face tight.

"I'm going to Seattle to see Shannon," he said tautly. "I missed Thanksgiving so I'm taking a few days off." He waited, as if expecting some response from her. "Do you want to come?"

"I..." Brittany lifted her shoulders and tried not to feel so utterly miserable. "I'm doing a photo session for Marjorie Vandoren. Toujours cosmetics."

She couldn't have said anything to make Devon recoil faster. He looked as if she'd slapped him. "Did you ever want to go?" he asked harshly.

"Of course I did!"

Devon looked untamed. He actually forced her chin up, raking her face with bitter eyes. "Damn you, Brittany," he said in a low voice. "I don't understand you at all."

"That's right." Her throat was hot and hurting. "You don't."

"What makes you tick? Money? Fame? God, you almost had me believing you were above all that!"

He had the power to wound her in a way no one else could. His contempt burned through her, bringing a misery that made her want to cry out. "The trouble with you, Devon, is that you believe what you want to believe. You never gave me a chance."

His head jerked back. "A chance? Lady, I'd have walked through fire for you."

Brittany shuddered. Every fiber within her strained to embrace the emotion in his tone. But she couldn't, wouldn't. She needed to shield herself from the pain that would be lying in wait at the end of that road.

"Words," she said flatly. "Just words, Devon. No meaning."

"You've got it all worked out, haven't you?" His lips thinned in disgust.

Brittany could scarcely breathe. His fingers on her chin were brutal. "I know when I've been used. Grant Broderick isn't the only one who wanted something from me. Next time you go after a man like him, you'd better look in the mirror."

"Damn you," he swore through his teeth.

There was nothing left to say. Brittany gave him her bravest front, regarding him with a cool, dispassionate elegance that took every ounce of willpower she possessed. If Devon found anything left in her that he desired, it didn't show on his face. He looked grim and lethal. She bled inside at the antipathy radiating from him, but that was nothing compared to how she felt after his parting remark.

"I was beginning to think I was wrong about love," Devon flung at her, his hand on the door. "But, sister, you just proved me right."

"Turn your head. No, not that way. To the right, *the right!*"

Brittany's mind registered the frustration in the photographer's voice and she realized belatedly that she was looking over her left shoulder. Meekly, she turned the other way.

"Get a line on that lipstick," the Toujours photographer complained. "Sara! *Sara!* Get out here and fix her lips."

Brittany sighed, letting her shoulders fall. She didn't blame the man for being upset. In her agitated state of mind she'd accidentally smeared the lipstick at the corner of her mouth.

"Don't move," he ordered harshly, and Brittany began to long for Ramon's edgy sarcasm. This man, Peter Somebody-or-other-who-was-important-and-she-

would-be-well-advised-to-remember-that-fact, was totally without a sense of humor. At least Ramon had an
interesting style that added diversion to the monotony
of her work. She promised herself she would never
complain about him again.

Sara came and worked on Toujours's Bloomin' Rose
lipstick, giving Brittany a sympathetic look. "The man
needs caffeine to relax," she whispered, her blond head
turning in Peter's direction. "He gave it up for his
health but it's ruining all of ours."

"I thought caffeine had the opposite effect."

Sara smiled serenely. "Not with Peter. But don't get
me wrong, he can be wonderful when he's in a room all
by himself."

Brittany watched her leave, her misery lifting for a
shining moment as she shared Sara's amusement. Peter
gave the petite makeup artist a scowl but Sara just raised
a blithe hand of acknowledgment. Then his attention
swiveled back to Brittany and she tried hard not to an-
tagonize him further.

Lights were arranged, Brittany's white hat was adjusted to keep the shadows from her face, Sara was
called back in to touch up Toujours's Love is Blue eye
shadow, then Peter finally got to work. The shutter
clicked steadily while Peter made motions with one
hand for Brittany to turn and turn again. She managed, with limited success, to push thoughts of Devon
to the back of her mind and act exotic, a little coquet-
tish and even a bit seductive for the surly photographer.

"All right, that's enough," he said with some reluctance, as if her performance was somehow inadequate
but would have to do.

Brittany walked to the closet-sized dressing room, glad the grueling morning was over. Every muscle ached; her feet were killing her. She shed the white backless sun dress and stepped out of the navy heels, tearing with controlled viciousness at the pins that held her hat in place.

"Ouch." She inhaled sharply at the pain in her scalp, taking more care to remove the last pins.

With moody eyes she looked around the dressing room. Her work, the one part of her life she could always count on, had lost its appeal. She didn't want to stand in front of cameras anymore and show off her beauty. That beauty had been nature's gift; it had nothing to do with Brittany Daniels, the person. It had given her a career that now seemed as hollow and pointless as Devon had once said it was. It hadn't helped her personal life at all.

She scrubbed the makeup off with her own brand of cleanser and slid the complimentary jar of Toujours Epidermal Cleanser and Skin Replenisher into the side pocket of her purse. The face reflected in the mirror drooped with misery and Brittany tried on a smile, seeing the muscles perform but no light lift the gloominess from her eyes.

"You're the girl who has everything," she reminded herself in a whisper.

She stared at herself. Without warning tears filled her eyes, blurring her vision. Embarrassed, she wiped them away with trembling fingers.

Feeling sorry for herself wasn't about to change anything. Even Devon couldn't change things now.

Brittany left the Toujours photography studio in a blue mood, not willing to stand around and wait for the results of her session. Let them call her. She really didn't care either way. She knew she was suffering from bad-attitude-itis but even that realization couldn't penetrate her all-over depression.

When she got home, a small gilded note embossed with Marcel and Kingston's address stated that her package was ready to be picked up. It recommended that she make appropriate security arrangements.

She crumpled it in her fist.

Later, when she'd had time to think things through, she smoothed out the paper and stared at the customer-invoice number. Recriminations weighing heavily on her mind, she phoned the local authorities, explained her plight to the voice on the other end, was patched through to another voice, then another, and was finally connected with the man appointed to the Broderick investigation.

"Mr. Gallagher explained that you would be calling in," the man said in the even voice of a professional. "We'll look into your particular gems and see what their status is."

Brittany had never worked with the police before but she was enough of a realist to know his words meant: *Your gems were probably stolen and therefore you're out your money. Tough luck, but that's the way these con men work.*

"Thank you," Brittany said quietly.

And thank you, Devon, for looking out for me.

Brittany hunched her shoulders dismally. She was being unfair. Though Devon hadn't told her the gems were stolen, he had warned her not to have anything to do with Grant Broderick. No one had forced her to invest. She'd done that all by herself.

Cara McPhee, the reporter from *In Touch* magazine, wanted to interview Brittany in the "relaxed surroundings" of her own home.

"It's more natural," she'd told Brittany over the phone. "It'll be easier for you to unwind. You'll feel more comfortable and that's what it takes to get a good interview."

In Touch not only published a monthly magazine but twice a week produced a syndicated program that was shown on one of the regular television channels. Cara wanted to get a preliminary interview before she could promise that Brittany's segment would be used on television. Brittany couldn't have cared less one way or the other.

It was a strange malady that had come over Brittany since she'd realized the truth about Devon. All her life Brittany had been a scrupulous saver. Now she felt the urge to spend wildly. Only the fact that she had so few hours free from work saved her small fortune. That and an enervating apathy that made even pouring herself a cup of coffee a real task.

Cara McPhee picked up Brittany's vibrations early in the interview. "You seem dissatisfied with your life...almost jaded. Can you explain that?"

Brittany smiled a trifle wistfully. Cara had been right to set the interview in her own home. There was something about the woman that inspired confidence, and as they sat on Brittany's back patio, sheltered from view by high but neatly trimmed shrubbery with a loquat tree casting shadows over their table, Brittany had to fight the urge to pour out some of her misery.

She sighed. "No. I can't explain it. I've lived through some personal tragedy lately. It's possible I'm suffering from after shocks."

"You mean your father's death."

"Yes. But I'd rather not talk about it."

Cara's gray eyes were sympathetic. She was a striking woman with an air of determination, her brown hair swept upward in a chic, nouveau style. She looked around Brittany's terraced patio admiringly. "You have a beautiful home. Would it be too personal a question to ask if you'd purchased it yourself, with your income?"

Brittany shook her head. "Not too personal. Yes, I did buy it myself."

"And the rest of your money...how have you invested it?"

"Lots of ways." Brittany shifted uncomfortably.

"I understand from speaking to some of L.A.'s top modeling photographers that a person as successful as yourself could be in the six-figure income range. Are you?"

Cara was flipping through a small notebook but Brittany heard the interest behind her casual tone. "It depends on the job," she answered reservedly. "I freelance. Each job is a new contract. My income has a lot to do with how much I'm willing to work."

Cara smiled broadly. "And you're a workaholic, from what I understand."

"Not really."

Cara closed her notebook and regarded Brittany through intent gray eyes. "This is fascinating. We've barely touched the tip of the iceberg. I think we could put you on our evening show."

Brittany wasn't entirely certain that was what she wanted. "I'll have to think about it," she demurred.

Cara's brows raised. "Well, don't take too long," she said meaningfully before she left.

When Jessica heard about Cara's offer she didn't hesitate to state her opinion. "The exposure's worth its weight in gold," she pointed out. "You may get more job offers from that one spot than you would through three years of word of mouth."

Brittany didn't have the energy to explain to Jessica how little job offers meant to her at this point. Reluctantly, she agreed to do the taped interview, and Cara lost no time arranging for the camera equipment to be set up in Brittany's home.

Brittany hadn't heard a word from Devon in over a week. While the *In Touch* people argued and kibitzed about which room they should tape in, Brittany checked the paper to see when, and if, Devon was going to be on *Perspective* that evening. The show had a revolving cast, with Devon as their prime investigative reporter. When she didn't see his name she folded the paper on the table, wondering if he was truly in Seattle with Shannon. An ache throbbed at her heart, threatening to break down some of her carefully constructed walls.

"Ready?"

The shaggy-haired cameraman gave Brittany a friendly smile. She followed him into the living room, marveling at the amount of equipment and bodies they'd squeezed around the furniture.

Cara sat next to Brittany on the plum-colored couch. She asked a few impersonal questions to ease Brittany's mind and set the mood, then she nodded to the cameraman. The camera swung Brittany's way and adjusted for a close-up.

"As many of you are aware," Cara said into the microphone, "the lovely face you see belongs to top model Brittany Daniels. Brittany lives in southern Los Angeles, and when she isn't working on free-lance assignments she's relaxing in her spacious home."

Cara made a cut sign with her hand and the taping stopped. "We'll fill in with interior shots here and I'll dub over later. Let's get right to the questions."

A line formed between Brittany's brows. Cara's incisive tone was new and a little disturbing.

"Miss Daniels...Brittany..." Cara continued with a huge smile, as the cameras refocused. "May I call you Brittany?"

"Please do."

"You used to work for the Nora Castle Modeling Agency, didn't you?"

Brittany nodded and smiled in return. "Yes."

"How long were you there?"

"Just a few years."

"And you've been on your own about the same length of time?"

"A little bit longer, I think."

Cara cocked her head to one side, her expression thoughtful. "What were your reasons for going out on your own?"

Brittany inhaled slowly, feeling tension knot between her shoulder blades. It was highly possible her relationship with Devon could be scraped up, and she wanted to make certain it wasn't. Carefully avoiding any mention of his name, she listed a few reasons why she'd split off from Nora's agency.

"What about Devon Gallagher?" Cara suddenly interjected.

Brittany blinked. "Pardon?"

"I notice you've scrupulously avoided mentioning his name. Weren't you romantically involved with him? Isn't he one of the reasons you quit?"

"No!" Brittany was appalled.

"Marjorie Vandoren of Vandoren Cosmetics admitted to seeing you with him at a party recently. Be honest, Brittany. Aren't you two getting back together?"

Brittany felt wild. She had absolutely no response. The last thing she or Devon needed was to have their affair splashed across the newsstands and TV screens.

While Brittany tried to recover, the cameras switched to Cara. She gave a frightening detailed account of who Devon Gallagher was, what his accomplishments were, then, as if Brittany weren't seated right next to her, she freely speculated on Devon's relationship to her.

"Cara," Brittany said feebly. "Ms. McPhee..."

"Devon Gallagher has just added another notch to his impressive reputation. He's the man who spearheaded the investigation into investment genius Grant Broderick's affairs, exposing his gem swindle. You were helping Mr. Gallagher, weren't you?"

The camera turned slightly, capturing Brittany's stunned expression. "No."

"You weren't? Then was the money you invested your own?"

Brittany was trying to stand up, trying to get out of the line of fire, when Cara battered her with a succession of questions that made her cringe.

"Do you think all the notoriety will affect Marjorie Vandoren's decision to make you her new 'face'? What would losing Toujours mean to you? Could your association with Devon Gallagher hurt your career?"

Chapter Eleven

I can't do this anymore!"

Brittany was on her feet, shaking. Cara looked surprised, then slid a knowing look to the cameraman.

"All right," she said with a pained sigh. "We'll go on to other material."

"No."

Cara was obviously used to the kind of reaction she'd elicited in Brittany. "You'd be better off to talk to us and set the record straight," she said reasonably. "This Broderick investigation is sending shock waves through the whole community. Since you had firsthand knowledge, we wanted to interview you first."

"You could have warned me," Brittany said accusingly, and Cara McPhee had the grace to look discomfited. "Firsthand knowledge," Brittany repeated with a shake of her head. "Your information's all wrong."

"You were with Gallagher in Mexico when the Cordell kid was in his accident," Cara pointed out.

Brittany looked at her helplessly. She realized belatedly how much the media knew about her own involvement.

"You made a hefty diamond purchase with Marcel and Kingston just a few days before the whole investigation came crashing down. Was that your money, or did Gallagher stake you?"

In the corners of her mind Brittany realized the tape was running again. She looked at the camera, looked back at Cara, then thought about the damage she had already done to herself and Devon.

Swallowing, she sat back down. She had two choices: to run or to weather Cara's insinuative questions and try to salvage the remains of her self-respect and Devon's.

There was really only one choice, she decided as she sat down.

"It was my money," she said distinctly, turning a calm face to a delighted Cara McPhee. "Like most of the people Grant Broderick swindled, I was seduced by the man's popularity and apparent investment genius. Devon Gallagher had nothing to do with it. He was merely the man who turned up the first investigative stone...."

Shannon Williams crossed her arms and gave her brother a half-impatient stare. Devon glanced up from the report Jay had sent him, then dropped his eyes again, glowering.

"You're supposed to be on vacation," Shannon reminded him, leaning down to stroke a fat yellow tabby. The cat lifted its head and closed its eyes.

"I am on vacation."

Shannon snorted. "No, you're not. You're at work. Like always. Devon..." There was a pleading note in her voice and Devon's mouth tightened.

"All right." Shannon threw up her hands. "Be that way. But for God's sake, try to be a little more sociable in front of the kids. Jenny asked me why you always look so mean."

Devon's head jerked up. "Mean?"

"Yes, mean. Since you got here you've had a hard look on your face as if you want to murder someone. But then every once in a while you look so terribly unhappy," Shannon added, seating herself beside him. "Like now." She touched the drooping corner of his mouth.

Devon looked into his sister's concerned face, loving her for her wild red hair, her expressive green eyes and her big heart. "Stop worrying about me," he said softly. "You've got more than enough to keep your mind occupied."

Shannon shook her head. "Nothing more important than you."

"Shannon, I'm fine. Save your energy for your family."

"You're my family, too!" Shannon's eyes sparked with fire. "Damn it, Devon, stop shutting me out. You get worse every time I see you. More cynical, more miserable. I'm afraid that one day I'm going to look at you and you won't even be there." To Devon's distress her eyes filled with huge tears. "Everything I have today is because you sacrificed for me. Please, Devon, let me do something for you. Talk to me."

Devon's chest ached with a spreading pain that infected every tissue. He swallowed hard. "I can't," he said softly.

"Yes, you can. Try."

He sighed wearily. "It's not that cut-and-dried."

"Is it your work?"

"No."

Shannon's forehead creased at Devon's positive tone. "Then it's a woman," she guessed. At her brother's barely perceptible flinch, she said in amazement, "The *same* woman? Dear God, Devon, don't tell me she's hurt you again."

"No one's hurt me." Devon got up from the couch, but Shannon yanked him back down with surprising strength.

He glared at her but she wasn't the least bit intimidated. "What's her name? Oh, no, you don't," she warned as Devon shifted away. "You're going to tell me this time. I won't let you up until you do."

Devon laughed harshly. "You'll lose that fight."

"Do you love her?"

"No." Devon's lips flattened.

"Are you sure?"

"Shannon..." he began in exasperation.

"No, wait, Devon. This is important. Do you love me?"

Devon stared at her in disbelief.

"Well, do you?" she demanded impatiently. "Why in God's name is that so hard for you to say?"

Devon opened his mouth, then closed it. He hated to admit it but Shannon was right. He couldn't express his feelings. They just wouldn't come.

"You're making too much of this," he muttered. "The truth of the matter is I just got through a bad relationship. It's over, and I'm lucky to be rid of her."

"This same woman."

Devon's jaw tightened but he couldn't lie to his sister. He nodded curtly.

"Well, then, I'd say you probably do love her. Otherwise you wouldn't have gone back for more abuse."

"You don't know what you're talking about," Devon growled.

"She's crazy to let you get away." Shannon went on with her own line of thought. "What's wrong with her, anyway? Is she stupid?"

"Give up, Shannon," Devon said wearily.

"I'd like to give her a piece of my mind. She can't do this to you."

Devon slanted her a look. He did love Shannon. She was so staunch, so loyal. "You better hang on to every piece you've got. You need them all."

"Laugh if you will," Shannon said, her eyes serious, "but you're dying inside over this woman. And it hurts me to watch."

There was a heavy silence between them. Devon did his best to shrug off what Shannon had said, but too many of her comments had cut too close to the bone. *Love*. It was an unfamiliar word to him in so many ways.

"Tell me about her, Devon," Shannon urged gently. "What's she like?"

Devon sighed. He dropped his head back, closing his eyes. It was no use. Once Shannon got her teeth into something, she never gave up, and while he was in her home there was no escape. "She's beautiful," he said after a moment. Shannon waited quietly. "And she's a model. I met her when I was working on that anorexia exposé. You know, at the Castle modeling agency."

"Uh-huh." Shannon settled in comfortably beside the brother she loved so much, relieved that he was finally going to unburden himself.

Brittany tried to ignore the dreadful pounding in her head. She fiercely pinched the bridge of her nose and emitted a weary sigh as Jessica ran on and on about the *In Touch* interview.

"You should have got up and left," she fumed, incensed. "What did that woman think she was trying to prove? You didn't deserve that treatment. It was tacky and unprofessional."

Brittany shifted the receiver. She didn't remind Jessica that the interview had been her idea. "It goes on the air tomorrow night," Brittany said. "I don't think I'll come off so badly. I'll look more like a victim."

"You *are* a victim!" Jessica inhaled through her teeth. "She actually brought up Marjorie Vandoren's name?"

"And Devon Gallagher's." Brittany shot a glance at her mother, who was sitting at the kitchen table drinking a cup of tea. But if Ellen was listening she gave no sign of it.

"Devon Gallagher's?"

"Because of the Broderick investigation." Brittany made a face and decided to bite the bullet. "Among other things."

"What other things?" Jessica became all business.

"It's too long to go into now, but Devon and I...we've known each other for years. But I managed to keep his name out of the interview as much as possible."

"But Cara did bring up Broderick, hmm?"

"Yes." Brittany motioned her mother to help herself to another cup of tea, but Ellen shook her head.

"Do you think this interview could affect the Toujours assignment?" Jessica asked tentatively.

"I have no idea."

And she didn't care. She didn't seem to care about much of anything these days. Thank God she'd asked Jessica to give her a week off; she needed time to work out her problems, and this time she couldn't rely on modeling to help her through.

"Well, all we can do is watch and keep our fingers crossed," Jessica said before she rang off.

Ellen Daniels looked at her daughter thoughtfully. "The interview was that bad, huh?"

Brittany heaved a sigh and poured herself a cup of tea. She settled into an adjacent chair. "It started out that way, but once I began answering her questions, it got better. She didn't ask me about dad," Brittany added swiftly, blinking back the tears that threatened. "I don't think I could have talked about him."

Ellen spooned a teaspoon of sugar into her tea. "But she did ask you about Devon."

Brittany's throat was tight and hot. Knowing what was coming, she placed an imploring hand on her mother's forearm. "Please. I don't want to talk about Devon."

"Oh, honey. I didn't mean to pry."

Ellen was distressed and Brittany sought to change the subject. "Have you thought about the houses we looked at?"

Her mother nodded, carefully stirring her tea. "Did you have a particular favorite?"

"No. I liked them all. But it's what pleases you that counts. You're the one who's going to live there, not me."

A long pause ensued, then Ellen asked, "Why did you put earnest money down on all three, Brittany? I'm only going to buy one, if that. You'll lose all that money."

Brittany took a deep swallow from her cup, the hot tea burning her throat. "I just didn't want someone else buying one before you were ready."

"Honey, that's not the reason."

"Sure it is."

Ellen took a deep breath. "I'm not letting you buy me a home, Brittany. I've got enough money to live happily as a renter."

"Mother—"

"Don't." Her voice was harsh. "I didn't get you into modeling to live off you. You're independent from me, Brittany. I want that clear."

Brittany looked at her with mingled love and exasperation. "But I want to buy you a house."

"No." Ellen was stern. "You want to throw your money away."

Brittany was staggered. "That's not true."

"I don't know what happened between you and Devon," she swept on, ignoring her daughter's white face, "but you've decided to give up everything you've worked for because of him! I can't let you do it, Brittany. I love you too much."

"It's not quite that way...."

"I have eyes." Ellen's lips were quivering. "Now stop behaving so foolishly. If you want Devon back, admit it. But stop punishing yourself. Tell him how you feel."

This conversation was almost more than Brittany could bear. She wanted to throw her head and arms on the table and weep. "It's not how I feel," she choked, "it's how he feels. He doesn't love me. He can't."

Ellen's heart ached for her daughter. "Oh, I don't think that's entirely true," she said, rubbing the back of Brittany's hand.

"It's true." Brittany tried to fight back the tears that were burning her eyes but they spilled down her cheeks. "And the worst part of all is that I can't stop loving him."

Ellen Daniels put her arms around her daughter and hugged her tightly. She hurt from a mixture of her own pain and Brittany's. As Brittany heaved silent sobs, Ellen offered warm comfort—the kind of comfort Brittany had given to her when Calvin died.

"Things will work out," she said softly. "You'll see."

California's reputation for mild weather took a beating when the warm autumn winds turned to cold blustery gales seemingly overnight. Brittany's one week off lapsed into two, and she would gladly have gone for three if Jessica hadn't called her with the good news.

"Congratulations. You're the Toujours woman. They want your first commercial done and out by Christmas."

"Christmas! Impossible."

"They're going to use what's already been filmed. I hear you're smashing. They're just going to tack on to the end a picture of blue foil-wrapped boxes tied with gold ribbons—something about blue love and Christmas."

"Love is Blue," Brittany corrected. "It's their eyeshadow."

"That's it. Anyway, it's terrific. The contract's being drawn up. I'll let you know when I have some more news."

"Great. Thanks, Jessica."

Brittany hung up, feeling odd. She searched her feelings as she prepared herself an omelet. Nothing there. No elation, no anticipation. Nothing. But at least she'd got over her self-destructive urge to throw money away. Her mother had helped her there.

The phone rang just as Brittany sat down to eat. For some reason the sound raised the hair on her arms. She crushed the notion that Devon might be calling, angry with herself for the sudden rush of adrenaline, the hot streak of excitement that flooded through her.

"Hello?"

"Is this Brittany Daniels?" a sharp female voice demanded.

Brittany could hear the fuzz of a long-distance connection. Her hopes sank. "Speaking."

"My name's Shannon Williams. You don't know me, but I've just learned a lot about you."

Brittany blinked. "Shannon?"

"Devon Gallagher's sister," she added, as if there was any room for doubt. She sounded as aggressive and headstrong as her brother. "Devon just spent a week with me and he told me some very interesting things."

"Devon...talked about...me?" Brittany asked faintly.

"Yes. After I pried it out of him," Shannon admitted with terse honesty. "I don't know exactly what happened between the two of you, but I do know he's miserable. And it's your fault."

Brittany was struck dumb, amazed at the woman's audacity. "*My* fault?"

"Devon's feelings run deep," Shannon swept on. "Don't you know that by now? Or don't you care?"

Brittany had no way of answering Shannon. She wasn't used to such direct inquisition. When it didn't appear that she would go on unless Brittany responded in some way, Brittany managed to choke out, "Yes, I care."

"Then can't you see how much he loves you?" Shannon threw out angrily.

Brittany coughed lightly. "I...no, not really."

"Well, for God's sake, open your eyes!" Brittany heard the sound of a child wailing in the background and the sudden and incessant barking of a dog. "Just a moment." Shannon covered the receiver with her hand and yelled, "Leave Renfro alone. He doesn't want to play. I'll be off in a minute. Just hang on till then."

For some reason the endearing sounds of home and family brought tears to Brittany's eyes. Her dashed hopes climbed upward again, responding to Shannon Williams's incredible matter-of-factness.

"Are you still there?" Shannon asked over the din.

Brittany felt her lips curve into the first real smile she'd had in weeks. "Yes, I'm still here." Was it possible? Could Shannon be right? Did Devon love her?

"Then stop playing with Devon's mind. He's a wreck. Just tell him how you feel and I'm sure you two can work out your problems."

"I'll try," Brittany promised, gratitude swelling inside her for Devon's wonderful sister.

"Do it," Shannon urged. "I want my brother back. And I don't think he'll be the same unless you help."

"Thank you, Shannon."

Shannon heaved a heartfelt sigh. "No problem. One of these days maybe we'll meet. I understand you were supposed to come here for Thanksgiving."

Brittany would have done anything to reach out and hug this woman. "There's always Christmas," she said softly.

Shannon let out a breath of relief. "Thank God. You do hear me." A splintering crash brought on a new spate of barking. "Uh...I've gotta go. It was...enlightening...talking to you."

"Goodbye."

Brittany pressed her hands to her mouth, hardly daring to believe what she'd just heard. Devon had talked to Shannon about her. Whatever he'd said, whatever state he'd been in, had convinced Shannon that he was in love with Brittany.

Wishful thinking.

Brittany sat down, trying to cool her heated emotions. She knew Devon pretty well, too, probably as well as his sister.

Or did she?

Devon still had difficulty trusting her, whereas he could feel completely at ease around Shannon. Would he confess his feelings to his sister, even though he couldn't to Brittany?

Dazedly, Brittany picked up the phone, her heart pounding. Then she hung it up again, pinching her bottom lip between her thumb and forefinger.

Several moments later, a moan of indecision issuing from her lips, she grabbed her jacket and purse. She would meet Devon face-to-face. If she'd been wrong to doubt him, if he truly did love her, she would be able to see it on his face. And if she'd been right...well, she certainly couldn't make the situation any worse than it was.

Brittany cranked the sunroof open on her car, letting the cold December wind play havoc with her hair. Her eyes were alive for the first time in weeks, sparkling lavender gems amid a flushed, hopeful face.

She was pulling into Devon's winding driveway when she felt the first twinges of anxiety. What if she were making a mistake? What if Shannon had been wrong?

She almost hoped he wouldn't be home but he was; his familiar BMW was parked in the carport adjoining his condominium. Brittany swallowed. She'd never been to his home. He'd promised to bring her but everything had fallen apart before he'd had the chance.

Hanging clematis brushed against her blouse as she walked underneath a wide trellis to his front door. Brittany rang the bell, dry mouthed.

She heard the sound of his footsteps, then suddenly the door opened and Devon was standing directly in front of her.

Her first impression was of how different he looked. He was dressed in the khaki pants she'd encouraged him to buy and a navy T-shirt. His face was drawn and tired, reflecting a new haggardness that made him look older. Deeply etched grooves beside his mouth made her heart ache but at the same time gave her new hope. Was it possible he was suffering because of her?

The door was still swinging inward, bumping lightly as it hit the wall. Apart from a brief flash of some emotion she was too afraid to name, Devon didn't seem particularly glad or even surprised to see her. He just looked at her in his uncompromising way, making her stomach flutter with insecurity.

"Hello, Devon," Brittany said.

He moved back from the door and reluctantly gestured for her to come inside. "Hello, Britt."

Brittany's heart sank. She didn't know what to think. On the one hand he didn't seem to want her there, yet he made no move to throw her out, either. She walked to the center of the room, drying moist palms on the legs of her white cotton pants.

"Would you like a drink first?" he asked, squinting his eyes on the horizon outside his huge living-room window. His view, like Brittany's, was of the Pacific, but Devon's condominium provided a breathtaking, light-bejeweled view of the Palos Verdes Peninsula while Brittany's looked straight over the sea.

"First?" she echoed.

Devon walked to the bar. "Before you pick up your diamonds," he said impatiently.

"Before I *what*?"

Devon's face was carved in stone. "Didn't Inspector Gravis call you?"

Brittany shook her head in bewilderment. "The man in charge of the Broderick investigation?" she asked.

"You spoke to him about your diamonds, remember?"

Devon's tone was laced with sarcasm. Brittany straightened her shoulders and said, "I'd forgotten his name, but yes, I talked to him when I got the note from Marcel and Kingston."

Devon paused, an ice cube hovering from silver tongs over her drink. "You haven't talked to him since?" he asked, brows drawing together.

She didn't want this conversation. She had too many other things on her mind. She wanted to tell Devon she was sorry for not believing he cared; she wanted to assure herself that Shannon had been right. She needed to know.

Brittany reined in her impatience. "Well, no. Should I have?"

"You haven't talked to him today?"

"Devon..." Brittany made a sound of exasperation.

"Then why are you here?"

Brittany hesitated, realizing she must be missing some vital piece of information. Devon walked toward her and handed her a glass of Scotch and soda, his eyes never leaving her face.

She looked into the amber liquid. "Not really my drink," she murmured.

"There's always a first time, and I'm fresh out of white wine."

Brittany took a sip. It tasted as bad as it looked good. "What did you mean...before I pick up my diamonds?" she asked.

Devon's blue eyes moved over her face, as if he were memorizing her features, feasting on them. "You really don't know?"

"No. Tell me."

"Your diamonds are legitimate. Either you made a favorable impression on your broker friend, or else he was one of the Marcel and Kingston employees who worked within the law." Devon shrugged. "Whatever the case, the investigation turned up an invoice from a reputed European diamond-distributing firm. Your gems match it exactly."

"And you've got them?" Brittany asked in a daze. "Here?"

"In a vault at my bank." Devon's mouth twisted with faint humor. "Inspector Gravis wouldn't let me just walk off with your gems."

"But why did you involve yourself at all?" Brittany wondered, eyes wide with hope.

Devon traced her chin with his thumb, then dropped his hand as if realizing how betraying that movement was. "Why did you come here today?" he countered.

Brittany looked into the face of the man she loved. It was time for her to set the record straight, time for her to make the first move. "I wanted to see you again," she said simply. "I never gave a damn about the diamonds." Her eyes searched the blue depths of his. "I've got pearls."

"Oh, Britt..." Devon swept the drink from her hand and placed both glasses on the bar. He hesitated only briefly, his eyes darkening, before gathering her to him in a bone-crushing hug. "Does this mean what I think it means?"

Brittany's spirits soared. She laughed up into his handsome face. "You're squeezing me to death."

"Good." He buried his face into the richness of her ebony hair. "You deserve it, for all you've put me through."

"Moi?" she asked with feigned innocence. "You did a lot of damage yourself, pal."

"And I've paid for it." A shudder went through his tall frame. "I don't know which was worse, these past few weeks or that moment on the phone when Jay told me Eric Cordell was dead. I was so afraid Broderick had had something to do with it and might come after you."

Brittany reveled in the feel of his strong arms around her once more. She made a solemn vow that this would be the last time they had to make up. "That was in the hotel room in Acapulco," she whispered, remembering his fear.

"Mmm-hmm." Devon's breath was warm against her ear, flavored with the sweet, musky smell of Scotch.

Brittany leaned back, her arms loosely tossed around his neck. "Well, you certainly got over that fast enough. You couldn't wait to make tracks to L.A. And you didn't even call," she scolded lightly.

"Yes, but I had you watched."

A ripple of shock went through Brittany. "No." She didn't believe he was serious.

"Yes." Devon's fingers pushed through her hair, his palms tilting up her face, holding her captive. "As soon as I got back to L.A. I sent someone down in my place, a surveillance man. I couldn't leave you alone down there, Britt. I couldn't."

He kissed her lightly on the mouth.

She could hardly take it all in. "But you didn't call when I got back."

"That was a mistake," Devon admitted on a sigh. "I was so busy. Everything was cracking wide open. And then I got your message and knew you were all right. I just figured that when I had more time I'd—"

He cut himself off on a sharp intake of breath, hearing the sound of his feeble excuse.

"It's okay," Brittany said, and it really was. She'd minded his passion for his career only when she'd viewed it as her rival. But with Shannon's revelations still fresh in her mind, Brittany had more insight into the man she loved.

"I don't know what I can do to convince you. What I can say, if anything—" Devon's jaw worked "—except that my career, everything...it's all meaningless without you."

His urgency told her more than his words. "I love you, Devon," she said softly. "I always have."

He sighed, his fingers relearning the textures and curves of her face. "Even though I've been a bastard?" he said with a slight smile. "Even though I've treated you abominably over your career?" At the dimpled smile that accompanied her nod, he groaned, "I don't deserve you."

"I haven't exactly been fair, Devon. I've been so paranoid fearing you wanted to use me. I felt so used in the past and it wasn't even true then," she said quickly, before he could interrupt. "I couldn't accept you at face value, and I thought loving you would be enough for the both of us." She smiled sadly. "But it wasn't."

Devon went completely still. "What are you saying?"

Brittany laughed. "Now who's paranoid? What I'm saying," she enunciated clearly, "is that loving someone doesn't have to mean repeating those three little words. You can love a person in lots of ways."

Devon gave her a long look. "Meaning?"

"That you love me, whether you can actually admit it or not."

Devon was astounded and Brittany was more afraid of her bold statement than she let on. They looked at each other, man to woman, friend to friend, lover to lover.

In thoughtful silence Devon directed Brittany to the couch, his lean thigh brushing hers as he sat down beside her. He linked his fingers through hers and studied them meditatively. "What I feel for you is as strong as any emotion I've ever known. Stronger. I ache for you. Not just physically but in every way. I missed you so much these past few weeks I spent half the time drinking, the rest sleeping. The only person I spoke to was my sister."

Brittany was thrilled by his honesty. She thought about Shannon but was too transfixed by the enormity of what Devon was saying. There would be time for that later. For now, she could only watch him and wait, wondering what she'd done to deserve such a perfect man.

He looked straight at her, his blue eyes direct, the dark lashes incredibly sexy. "If that's not love, I don't know what is. I've been in love with you since the beginning."

Brittany's breath came out in a rush. She hadn't even realized she'd been holding it. "You do have your moments," she said shakily.

The incredible tension broke and Devon smiled, kissing her lightly. "I take it that was all right. I didn't screw it up the first time or anything."

She grinned. "You really do go for the applause, don't you?" she accused, and Devon laughed, pulling her down atop him on the couch.

"Since I'm batting a thousand, I'll take another chance. Would marriage fit into your scheme of things?"

Brittany's eyes widened. She struggled to see if he was serious.

Devon regarded her through lazy eyes. "Well?"

Brittany had been ready to say yes for years. But, as much as it might cost her, she had to lay one last fear to rest. "What about my job?" she asked, swallowing. "I know you think..."

"Whatever you want, love. It'll be easier seeing your luscious face on magazines knowing you're mine to come home to."

"I've been offered Toujours," she said quietly.

"I know."

She blinked in confusion and Devon said, "It was on the news, Britt."

"And you don't mind? I haven't really said yes. I could still back out. All I'll have to do is call Jessica and—"

"Shh." He placed a finger over her lips, then followed up with his mouth. "I'm feeling magnanimous. Better seize the opportunity while you can."

She realized he was teasing her. He really had no more qualms about her career. "Then the answer's yes. Unequivocally yes! Oh, my God..."

"What?" Devon frowned at the stricken look on her face.

"I forgot to tell you about *In Touch* magazine. They nailed me, Devon, and your name came up. I tried to...what's so funny?" she demanded.

"How could you possibly think I don't know about that?" he demanded. "Cara McPhee has been telephoning me regularly. She wanted me to do the show with you, for God's sake!"

"She didn't tell me that!"

"Would you have considered it?" Devon asked curiously.

"Not on your life."

"That woman is brighter than I gave her credit for. No, no." Devon shook his head vehemently as Brittany tried to speak again. "No more talk. We'll watch the damage you did on *In Touch* later but right now..."

His fingers slid to the first button of her blouse and Brittany gave a small sigh of pleasure. She had a sense of peace she'd never had before. She loved Devon, heart and soul, and the incredible beauty of it was that he loved her, too.

RIGHT BEHIND THE RAIN
Elaine Camp #301—April 1986
The difficulty of coping with her brother's
death brought reporter Raleigh Torrence
to the office of Evan Younger, a police
psychologist. He helped her to deal with
her feelings and emotions, including love.

CHEROKEE FIRE
Gena Dalton #307—May 1986
It was Sabrina Dante's silver spoon that
Cherokee cowboy Jarod Redfeather couldn't
trust. The two lovers came from opposite
worlds, but Jarod's Indian heritage taught
them to overcome their differences.

NOBODY'S FOOL
Renee Roszel #313—June 1986
Everyone bet that Martin Dante and Cara
Torrence would get together. But Martin
wasn't putting any money down, and Cara
was out to prove that she was nobody's fool.

MISTY MORNINGS, MAGIC NIGHTS
Ada Steward #319—July 1986
The last thing Carole Stockton wanted was to
fall in love with another politician, especially
Donnelly Wakefield. But under a blanket of
secrecy, far from the campaign spotlights,
their love became a powerful force.

Silhouette Special Edition

COMING NEXT MONTH

RETURN TO PARADISE—Jennifer West
Reeve Ferris was swiftly rising to stardom, yet he couldn't forget
Jamie Quinn, the small-town girl who had captured his heart along
the way.

REFLECTIONS OF YESTERDAY—Debbie Macomber
Angie knew the minute she saw Simon that twelve years had
changed nothing; she was still destined to love him, and they still
seemed destined to be kept apart.

VEIN OF GOLD—Elaine Camp
Houston had the land, and Faith had the skill. They were an unlikely
team, but side by side they drilled the Texas soil for oil and found
riches within each other.

SUMMER WINE—Freda Vasilos
The romance of Greece drew Sara into Nick's arms, but when the
spell was broken she knew she could never leave her life in Boston
for this alluring man . . . or could she?

DREAM GIRL—Tracy Sinclair
For an internationally known model like Angelique Archer, having a
secret admirer was not that unusual, but finding out he was royalty
was definitely not an everyday occurrence!

SECOND NATURE—Nora Roberts
Lenore was the first reporter to get the opportunity to interview best-
selling author Hunter Brown. On a camping trip in Arizona she
learned more about Hunter and herself than she'd bargained for.

AVAILABLE NOW:

STATE SECRETS
Linda Lael Miller

DATELINE: WASHINGTON
Patti Beckman

ASHES OF THE PAST
Monica Barrie

STRING OF PEARLS
Natalie Bishop

LOVE'S PERFECT ISLAND
Rebecca Swan

DEVIL'S GAMBIT
Lisa Jackson